Inspector Ghote's First Case

a&b

Inspector Ghote's First Case

HRF KEATING

First published in Great Britain in 2008 by
Allison & Busby Limited
13 Charlotte Mews
London W1T 4EJ
www.allisonandbusby.com

Copyright © 2008 by HRF KEATING

The moral right of the author has been asserted.

A CIP catalogue record for this book is available from
the British Library.

10 9 8 7 6 5 4 3 2 1

13-ISBN 978-0-7490-7970-3

Typeset in 11/16 pt Sabon by
Terry Shannon

Printed and bound in Great Britain by
MPG Books Ltd, Bodmin, Cornwall

HRF KEATING is well versed in the worlds of crime, both fiction and non-fiction. He was the reviewer for *The Times* for fifteen years, as well as serving as chairman of the Crime Writers' Association and the Society of Authors, and, next only to Agatha Christie, he has been the longest-serving president of the Detection Club. Best known as the creator of Inspector Ghote, he has twice won the CWA Gold Dagger and in 1996 was awarded the CWA Cartier Diamond Dagger. He lives in London with his wife, the actor Sheila Mitchell, who regularly reads his titles as audio books.

ABOUT INSPECTOR GHOTE

Inspector Ghote came into being in 1964 when HRF Keating, disappointed his novels were seen in America as 'too British' to appeal, set *The Perfect Murder* in Bombay. It not only broke into the US market, widely reviewed and hailed by Anthony Boucher (forever commemorated in the annual Bouchercon meetings) as 'the best crime novel of 1964 (all comers)', but in Britain it won the CWA Gold Dagger.

Ghote went on to gain enthusiastic reviews, and readers, until in 2000 with *Breaking and Entering* Harry Keating brought the 22-volume series to an end, critics still 'charmed by all his questioning-pestioning' calling the final book 'as fresh, lively and entertaining as the first'. Over the years, Ghote appeared in the Merchant-Ivory film of *The Perfect Murder* and in a number of BBC radio plays. PD James called him 'enchanting and engaging', Len Deighton begged 'may Ghote go on for ever' and the *New York Times* proclaimed him 'one of the great characters of the contemporary mystery novel' while Edmund Crispin in the *Sunday Times* called him 'the most engaging of all fictional detectives', a tribute indeed from the creator of Professor Gervase Fen.

Ghote has also found a place in not one, but two collections entitled *Great Detectives*. In a 1978 American volume the editor, Otto Penzler, remarks it would be a mistake to think of Ghote as a weakling. 'He is intelligent and, just as important, wily.' In the 1991 British volume, edited by Maxim Jakubowski, James Melville, a fellow crime writer, said, 'It's hard to account for [his] huge and continuing success beyond limply asserting that Ghote is above all marvellously credible, not only to those acquainted with India but also those who aren't (and are diverted by the fact that Keating himself did not go there until a good many years after Ghote sprang into life).' He adds, 'Ghote is Everyman with whom each of us can identify in some way... He is as flawed, perplexed and occasionally irritable as we know ourselves to be; as amiable, determined and honourable as we would like to be.'

CHAPTER ONE

Let us find Inspector Ghote in the days when he was simply an Assistant Inspector in the crowded and confused area of Bombay called Dadar. He is holding a letter that has just come through the door of his flat. A long official-looking envelope, the surplus glue sealing its flap – the work of an over-enthusiastic peon – plain to see. So he is careful to tap the letter inside right down to one end of the envelope and then at the opposite end, between twisting thumb and steady finger, he carefully tears off a thin strip. At last he is able to fish out the folded enclosure. A notably stiff sheet. He opens it up, wondering what it can be, and reads.

From the Commissioner of Police, Bombay March 15th, 1960
1 Chaitra, 2017

I am informing you herewith that w.e.f. today's date you are appointed to the rank of Inspector and posted to the Detection of Crime Branch, Bombay Police. You will take up your duties beginning April 1st next, and should regard yourself as on casual leave during the intervening period.

* * *

There was a good deal more of properly bureaucratic information in the letter. But do not imagine that newly created Inspector Ghote is able to read any of it. Tears have come into his eyes. Tears of irrepressible joy. This is the moment he has been hoping for ever since he was old enough to understand what a police officer was and what it was that *a detective* did. His father, then schoolmaster to the many, many sons, both legitimate and illegitimate, of the Maharajah of Bhopore, had recounted to him, almost before he could understand the words, how once he had watched one Detective Superintendent of Police Howard discover almost magically who had contrived to murder the Maharajah, even aiding him a little in his investigation.

He had recounted, too, many a time, how at their parting from that British deity he had said that, should to his tally of daughters there would ever be added a son, 'that boy, please God, shall become a police officer.' The often repeated words had implanted in Ghote's young mind a determination to one day become one of those demi-gods possessed of an iron resolution to bring to light the perpetrators of crimes of all kinds, and especially the crime of murder.

Now it seemed, at last, the possibility was solidly in his grasp, though the father who had held it up to him and had brought him to Bombay and to college there had long departed this life to await another.

Yes, now, he found himself thinking, my dream has burst into the light of day. And, yes, yes, look at the Hindi version of the date on this letter. The first of Chaitra, Gudi Padva day, the very start of the Hindu calendar. What a fine moment for my new life to begin.

Thoughts pouring on, he said to himself I am no more an

officer caught up all day in the petty crimes happening in Dadar. I am at last a member of the Detection of Crime Branch. I am one among the set-apart band of officers who handle only important murder cases or affairs concerning people of the highest influence. I, not all that long out of Nasik Police Training School, son of a lowly schoolmaster, am to be a detective of detectives.

'Protima,' he managed at last to call out. 'Wife, wife. The letter that is just only being pushed through the door. Come and hear what it is telling.'

Protima, the folds of her sari spread wide by the baby she was soon to give birth to, hurried out from the kitchen of the sun-broiled flat right at the top of the barracks block in Dadar police station compound. A home Ghote had sometimes feared he was destined never to leave.

In a moment now he read out to Protima the whole of the Commissioner's letter, down to the final masterfully scrawled signature.

'Think, think only, how proud my father would be today,' he exclaimed, voice rising word by word to a chanted climax. 'I am at the beginning of the career *Pitajee* was always hoping would be mine.'

'If he would be proud,' Protima answered, her eyes bright with delight, 'how much more of proud am I. Husband, husband, if... If what is here—' She patted the rounded shape under her sari. 'If what is here is a boy, then perhaps he too will one day be following your footsteps.'

'But-but even so,' Ghote went on, heart pounding, 'even so my son should not be born in this hundred per cent too small junior officer's flat.'

He came to a sudden, perhaps a too sudden, decision.

'No. We must *ek dum* be finding somewhere altogether more right for a full inspector to have. Yes, a flat where I can be having a phone. A phone. An officer of Detection of Crime Branch must be in constant touch. Yes, a flat where we can at least get, before long, a priority phone. Definitely. We must begin this evening itself to look for something, and it must be not too far from Crawford Market HQ also.'

But unexpectedly now Protima failed to throw herself into the plan. She stood there altogether silent.

Looking at her face, a picture of doubt now, Ghote frowned.

'But what for are you all at once unhappy?' he asked.

'Oh, well... But-but—'

'What it is? You are feeling not so good, is it?'

'No, no. Not at all. Baby is altogether happy.'

'You are sure? You are not hiding from me something?'

'No. No, I am saying it. All is well-well. But-but it is something else.'

'What of else? What can there be?'

She looked down to the concrete floor at her feet.

'But what it is?'

'I-I cannot say.'

'No, come, you can be saying whatsoever you are wanting to your husband, just only now full Inspector Ghote.'

'But it is that.'

'That? That? What *that* is this?'

'It is because you are now Inspector Ghote and must be shifting straight away to a better flat. And I had so hoped...'

'Hoped? I am not at all understanding.'

Then, in a burst of words, Protima brought it out.

'It is *Hamlet*. Tonight, when you were still an Assistant

Inspector here at Dadar PS, we were going – you had promised and promised – to see that film they are at last again showing. One week only at Eros in Queen's Road. I have been longing and longing to see since I was at college only.'

'*Hamlet*. My news was driving it altogether out of my mind. Your favourite play of all, the one you are reading aloud so often. But we must go. We can go. Why did you not remind at once?'

'You were deciding, deciding so firmly. We had to go to look for a flat. One with a phone, and not too far from Crawford Market. All of a sudden you were deciding. It was so unlike you.'

'But—' He took a deep breath. 'But I can undecide also, isn't it?'

A delighted smile swept over Protima's face.

'Oh, Husbandjee, in one moment deciding. Next undeciding. You, who are always and always taking so long to make one only decision.'

For an instant Ghote wanted to deny he ever did that. But, deep down, he knew it was true. Or not too far from the truth. The news he had learnt, bubbling and bubbling inside him, had made him for once ready to jump to a decision. Without a moment's thought. Or without a much longer period of struggling to hit on whatever might seem to be the right answer.

'No,' he said. 'No. Today I have learnt the news I have been wanting and wanting to hear all the years of my life. So that must be celebrated. And what better way to do that than to go and see the greatest work – you have so often said it – of the great William Shakespeare? No, tonight we will go to *Hamlet*.'

Protima gave a little giggle.

'Yes,' she said, 'we will go to the film its star is announcing as – everybody at college was always quoting same – *the story of a man who cannot make up his mind.*'

But they were not to see *Hamlet* that night.

CHAPTER TWO

There had come a knock at the door of the flat. A thumping knock.

'What? What?' Ghote all but shouted.

Somehow he felt on this day of all days, at this hour of all hours, a knock should not come banging on the door of the flat that he was about to leave for ever. I am right, too, he thought. No one should be knocking. I am not on duty here. Even if the order for my posting has not yet come through to the duty-room below, I am not available. No one should be knocking at the door at this time. With thumpings also.

'Well,' Protima said sharply, 'you are going to answer, yes? Or is it you must be having one quarter-hour to decide to do it?'

'No, no. I am answering. I am answering. It was just only…'

One of the jawans from the duty-room was there, stiffly at attention, brass belt-buckle shining – Number 23900 – brass whistle-chain bright across his chest.

Ghote looked at him, with the small stir of anger Protima's jibe had roused in him still hot in his eyes.

'Yes, yes? What it is? What for are you knocking and knocking at this hour only?'

'AI, Sahib. It is just only afternoon.'

With a little jolt of surprise, Ghote realised that out in the compound down below it was plainly full daylight. Somehow the rush of expectations aroused by the letter the postwallah had brought scarcely a quarter of an hour ago had made him think he had read those astonishing words *w.e.f. today's date you are appointed*…at a time already long past.

The jawan's name had totally escaped him, though, now he came to think, he had as short a time ago as when he had inspected the ranks that morning looked at him standing to attention, crowd-control bamboo *lathi* held rigidly at his side. Now he was holding out a thin sheet of paper.

He took it from his hand.

'Very good. Dismiss.'

Looking down, he saw the sheet was one torn from an official pad of memo forms.

To: Inspector Ghote. Message per telephone from Assistant Commissioner Divekar, Crime Branch.

Yes. Yes, my dream has come fully into open day. That is my boss now, the head of Crime Branch at Police Headquarters in the very heart of Bombay, and he has sent me a message, per telephone.

To Inspector Ghote, at Dadar PS. Yes, I am now Inspector Ghote. And, yes also, it is true I am, if just only now, *at* Dadar PS. Soon, soon I will be at Crawford Market, at Crime Branch itself.

He dropped his eyes to the short message beneath.

You are to visit asap Sir Rustom Engineer at his home, 20 Marzban Apartments.

And that was all.

Of course, the name of Sir Rustom Engineer is well known to me. The first Indian to hold the post of Commissioner of the Bombay Police. Appointed by the British two years before Independence. Now, naturally, retired. Given, almost as the last act of the departing British, the title of *Sir*. But why am I to see him, Sir Engineer? And *asap*. As soon as possible? And how soon is that?

Protima was standing just behind him, her face bright with impatient curiosity.

He thrust the message out to her.

She seemed to have read it all almost before she had flipped the thin sheet open.

'No,' she said. 'First you must put on your Number One uniform.'

For a moment, disconcerted by the way Protima's thought processes had leapt to this decision over half a dozen intervening obstacles, he could only reply, 'But this uniform I am having on was clean this morning only.'

'And you have been wearing all day.'

'And have I put even one mark?' He stopped himself. 'But I have not at all decided why it is I am to see Sir Engineer *asap*. You are knowing that is *as soon as possible*?'

'Of course, of course. And I am knowing also what that is saying. It is saying *Now*.'

'Well, I suppose I had better perhaps go. But—'

An idea came to him. One that would at least give him a little more time to consider what the implications of the message might be, time to prepare himself.

'But what about *Hamlet*?' he said. 'That film is on at Eros *One Week Only*. If we are missing it tonight, who can say when another opportunity will ever be arising?'

And now Protima did seem to be halted in her tracks.

But not for long, though it was on an unexpected note that she began again.

'No, this is just like you, my good husband. It is just like your thoughtfulness only to remember I am so much wanting to see what Mr Olivier is meaning by *the story of a man who cannot make up his mind*. But, no. No, you have been asked by Head of Crime Branch itself to visit this Sir Something Engineer, and—'

'But it is Sir Rustom. He is one famous man. First Indian – though of course he must be a Parsi – to be heading Bombay Police. After so many English sirs before him.'

'Yes, yes. I am knowing all that. And that is why you must go, in best uniform also, to see him now. This evening. As soon as possible. No, I am sorry if I am not to see *Hamlet* tonight, but there may be another chance before end of week. So, no, you must go at once, my good husband, the good father of this child who will be here in six-eight weeks only.'

'But Marzban Apartments, where is that? I am not at all knowing.'

'Oh, must be one of those big new blocks they are putting up everywhere now at last Independence has come. You can easily find out. It would be somewhere up on Malabar Hill.'

Marzban Apartments was there on Malabar Hill, that coolest of places in always humid and sometimes unbearably hot Bombay. It stood there, a sky-reaching, shiningly new building, blessed, high above the stewing city, by whatever whisks of breeze might come.

Ghote, scarcely an hour later, stiff in the Number One best

uniform Protima had insisted on, stood for a moment looking upwards at it.

Yes, this is right. It is right that here such a man as Sir Rustom Engineer should stay. Perhaps the finest new building in entire Bombay. No doubt built, with that name Marzban, by and for Parsis, Sir Engineer among the most outstanding of them.

And I am to visit Sir Engineer. As soon as possible. Well, here I am, and almost as soon as I could possibly come. After all, it would have been altogether wrong to have set out before Protima had hurried to iron my Number One uniform. But why am I here? That is altogether a different matter. Why has Sir Engineer requested me to come? How did he ever get to know of me, when until just now I was no more than a simple Assistant Inspector at Dadar PS? And all I know about him is what I was reading in the newspapers when he was made head of the Bombay Police and then also again when he was retiring.

So, how is it I am here myself? Now?

One only way to find out.

Ghote braced his too bony shoulders, strode up to the glass entrance doors, pushed at them – are they resisting me? No, it is their heavy weight only – marched past the massively uniformed *chowkidar*, saw ahead a lift and its smartly white-clothed liftman, and made straight towards him along the length of the gleaming foyer, head held high.

'Flat Number 20,' he said. 'I am wishing to see Sir Engineer.'

'Sir Rustom,' the man answered. 'It is top floor itself.'

Ghote stepped into the smooth-walled softly shining box. The liftman pressed the button for *Flats 20* and *21*. They began their ascent. Nothing here of the anxiety-causing jerkiness of every other Bombay lift he had ever stood inside. Here it was difficult even to realise they were moving at all, save for the changing numbers on the small electric panel above the doors.

But then as the numbers reached nearer and nearer to 20-21 a terrible thought came. The liftman, what had he answered when I was saying *Sir Engineer*? Yes, it was *Sir Rustom*. And had there been on his unmoving face just a hint of mocking? So ought I to have said *Sir Rustom,* if I was not saying full-out *Sir Rustom Engineer*? Was I trying then to show I am knowing that distinguished man? What a mistake. And to be corrected by a liftman only.

The lift came quietly to the end of its upward journey. Its doors, as the liftman touched a button, slid quietly open.

Ghote stepped out.

And rapidly stepped back in again.

He slid his fingers into the right-hand stiffly tight trouser pocket of his fiercely ironed uniform, and found the small handful of coins he had put there. He gripped one, held it for a moment, decided to let it go, managed to grip two others together, hauled them out, thrust them into the hand somehow there waiting to receive them.

The right thing. I was doing it now. So I must be calling Sir Engineer as Sir Rustom. Good. Right. And, yes, Sir Rustom has said he is wanting me to see him.

Two separate large dark teak doors stood on the far wall of the narrow lobby in which he had found himself. In bright brass figures they proclaimed *20* and *21*. Unhesitatingly now he went over and put a firm finger on the shining white bell button beside the number *20*.

Almost at once the door was drawn back.

Ghote saw a servant in white jacket and white half-pant, neatly checked blue and white dusting-cloth across his right shoulder.

'I have been asked to come to see Sir Rustom Engineer. I am' – the most minimal of secretly triumphal pauses – 'Inspector Ghote.'

The man looked at him steadily.

'Regret, Inspector, Sir Rustom is not available.'

Of all the possibilities Ghote had entertained, this was one that had never for a moment entered his head.

'Not-not—' he stammered.

Then, recovering, he succeeded in asking, 'But, Sir Rustom, he is out of station? Or-or will he be soon returning back? If that would not be too long, perhaps I can be waiting. It is important that I am seeing Sir Rustom as soon as possible.'

The man assumed a look of muted sadness, echoing whatever his master would have offered had he been there.

'No, Inspector,' he said. 'Sir Rustom would not be available at all this evening. He has just only gone to see film *Hamlet*.'

CHAPTER THREE

'Oh, what a pity. We also could have been down at Eros, Cinema. At last I could have seen the *Hamlet* I was having to miss when everybody in Senior English was discussing and discussing about it.'

That had been Protima's reaction when Ghote had arrived back at their cramped flat perched at the top of the block in the Dadar PS compound and had told her, almost shame-facedly, of his unsuccess. For an instant a flare of anger rose up in him at the reception Protima was giving his bad news. She should, he thought, be asking and asking why Sir Rustom had gone to see *Hamlet* when, it seemed, he had requested Crime Branch to have himself visit as soon as possible.

But, at once, the mere sight of her sari – she had put on her sun-yellow one – billowing out like the sail of a yacht racing across Back Bay quenched that hardly risen flare.

No, the mother of my son – or of my daughter, my daughter – must be allowed to think whatever has entered her mind. She is needing calm, utmost calm. Thank goodness, I was succeeding to tell her this without anything of quarrel.

His holding back appeared to have earned him a reward. Protima gave him a long, silent look.

'Food is waiting,' she said. 'I was keeping hot till you would be coming back, as much at least as the rotten stove here would let me.'

'But soon, soon that stove will be one bad memory only, the cupboard also where we are having to keep food fresh by putting in a piece of tamarind,' he replied. 'Before too long we will be finding that flat where I can be near Crawford Market HQ and have at last telephone.'

'Yes, you are right. Before too much of time has passed Inspector Ghote will be having his new flat, And-and in it will be a cradle, a nice, nice wooden cradle that is swinging from side to side. And in that cradle will be Inspector Ghote's son.'

Ghote lightly laughed.

'Not Inspector Ghote's daughter?' he asked. 'Every mother is wanting a daughter, yes?'

'Yes and no also. For me, it is first a son, a son for you, and then it is as many daughters as I am liking.'

'Well, we will be seeing. And tomorrow I also would be seeing why Sir Rustom is wanting to be visited by Inspector Ghote. I was telling his servant *Ten ack emma, sharp.*'

Ghote had been standing in the lobby on the top floor of Marzban Apartments peering at his watch till the minute-hand pointed exactly to ten. At once he stepped across and gave the bell-push of Number 20 one sharp jab, quick but long enough to make sure the sound beyond would be heard throughout the flat.

At once Sir Rustom's servant – Was he also waiting just inside? Ghote asked himself – drew back the tall door.

'It is Inspector Ghote? Sir Rustom says you may see him *ek dum.*'

He led the way, almost at a trot, through into the big apartment. Ghote was aware only of walls lined with a sombre green paper decorated with darkly framed photographs of Sir Rustom's ancestors, mostly in the sepia shade which placed them firmly in the dim historical past, bleakly impressive men in tall backwards-curving, black-lacquered Parsi hats wearing the traditional white, loose-fitting *dugla*. And then the servant had tapped at a tall, polish-gleaming door and a voice from inside said 'Come.'

Sir Rustom, when Ghote found himself face to face with him, looked, although tall and very upright, by no means as forbidding as his ancestors, dark-framed along the corridor walls. Dressed in a plain grey suit rather than the *duglas* of his forebears with their hints of the mysteries of a little-known religion, and wearing a tie in the subdued colours of some club, the large-lens glasses on his long nose betraying the weak eyes afflicting many Parsis, he rose from his tall-backed, ornately carved chair and offered a fine, lightly wrinkled, long-fingered hand.

'Inspector Ghote?' he said. 'DSP Divekar told me that it was you he had found to do this small service for me. You are at present on casual leave, I understand?'

'Yes, sir. Yes, Sir Rustom. And I am sorry I did not get to see you sooner, when I was told to come asap.'

'Oh, my dear chap, there wasn't all that much hurry. I dare say Dinesh Divekar gilded the lily a little. But I hope you will find what I am asking you to do, though really only a very minor matter, will prove to be rewarding. At least in terms of experience.'

'Sir?'

'Ah, but I am forgetting myself. Will you take something? Rather a late riser myself nowadays, I have only just finished my breakfast. One finds oneself, you know, when one reaches my age, more and more pleased to lie comfortably in bed in the mornings. And last night, as a matter of fact, I got to bed a good deal later than my customary hour. I had been, you understand, to see that interminably long film *Hamlet*. But you? You must have breakfasted long ago. Won't you take something now? Coffee? Tea?'

Ghote, who had been up for a good many hours, was tempted. But he was much keener to know what the *minor matter...that will prove to be rewarding* would turn out to be.

And a little, too, he had wondered whether he could possibly ask what Sir Rustom had thought of *Hamlet*. And why he had found it *interminably* long.

'No, sir, thank you,' he said, 'I am not at all needing anything. I also was somewhat of a late riser. On account,' he improvised, 'of my wife being, sir, with child. I am liking to give her maximum of sleep.'

Sir Rustom sank into his tall chair, gripping its ornately carved arms.

'Good, good. Then let me – do sit down, old chap – put you in the picture. It is rather an odd story, but it would be of considerable help to me if you could make a few inquiries and set my mind at rest.'

Set Sir Rustom Engineer's mind at rest? What can it be that has caused him in his retirement this amount of worry? And how fine it might be if I myself am able to be of help to him.

'Yes, sir?'

'It's like this, Ghote. A good many years ago, while I was

still in the rank that you now hold, I was serving as an instructor at the Police Training School in Nasik, where, incidentally, I am told you did particularly well yourself. I happened there to make the acquaintance of an Englishman, a civil engineer engaged in that most useful of tasks, road-building. In the end we used to go regularly for shikar together, though I admit I am by no means a good shot. And neither was he, incidentally.'

A short indulgent laugh.

'No, our shikar expeditions were intended, I thought then and think now, to put that chance acquaintanceship on a firmer footing. You see, I gathered that my friend intended, when Independence arrived as it was to do just a few years later, to stay on in India. I had got the impression he came from a rather humbler background than the majority of the sort of English civil servants you find in the ICS.'

Ghote, about to put in another *Yes, sir*, bit his tongue. Best to appear somehow not to have taken in Sir Rustom's hinted criticism of his British friend.

Sir Rustom for an instant looked up.

'You will appreciate, being the sort of police officer I think you must be, that a man like my former friend would see himself as having a much pleasanter life here in India, servants always to hand et cetera, than he would have had – he was a bachelor in those days – in some wretched flat in a cheerless England hardly recovered from the effects of war.'

Yes, Ghote registered, Sir Rustom Engineer has praised me for seeming to understand even a man like his white sahib friend. That is something I hope I was learning from my treasured Hans Gross's *Criminal Investigation*, read and read again. That a good detective must *know men and be eternally vigilant*.

'You see,' Sir Rustom gave a little cough, 'at that time it wasn't every ICS man who was willing to go about with an Indian, and one was bound to wonder whether his purpose was to secure for himself in future days what you might call a friend at court.'

He fell silent, putting the long fingers of his hands together in five upwards pointing pairs, his elbows on the chair's carved arms.

'Poor fellow,' he said.

'Was he at last, then,' Ghote asked, 'having to go to UK, that – you were saying – so much one uncomfortable place?'

'No, no. I have misled you. No, my British friend, or perhaps I should say *friend of former years*, easily succeeded in remaining here under the Indian sun. And, indeed, for years I heard nothing of him. But then, quite recently, he wrote to me, claiming, as it were, the dues of that friendship he had cultivated in the days when he saw me – I can put it in no other way – as someone likely to become a senior figure in the New India, whenever that might come into existence.'

'He is then *poor* now in the way only that he is somehow needing your help?'

'Exactly so, Inspector. Yes, they have sent me the right man.'

A flush of pride all but caused in Ghote a give-away blush.

Yet more anxiously he asked himself what the retired English sahib must be hoping to get through the help of now distinguished Sir Rustom Engineer, once *by no means a good shot* in the ritual of Raj days shikar.

He was soon to learn.

'Yes, the poor chap writes to me in great distress to say that some weeks ago his much younger wife, of only two or three years I understand and in fact pregnant with their first child, had suddenly and inexplicably committed suicide. The act has left him, it seems, tormented day after day by a need to find out why. And, as I feel I do perhaps owe him something still, I think I should offer him what assistance I can. In fact, you, my dear fellow.'

Ghote sat there – He had perched himself on the edge of a sofa a yard or two away from Sir Rustom – filled in an instant with doubts and fears. Sir Rustom attempting to help this white sahib by sending me to him? Myself to go to this tormented Englishman and somehow discover why his wife has taken her own life? How possibly will I, a stranger and no countryman of his, be able to bring to light something that is altogether puzzling him? And then the lady is, no, was, pregnant. With their first child. Just only exactly like Protima. Will Protima...? No. No, that is impossible. But...but a first pregnancy, a time, isn't it, full of strange thoughts for the mother-to-be. Can that be...?

He pulled himself together.

'And-and you have sent for me, sir,' he managed to babble out, 'to-to solve this...this mystery?'

Sir Rustom looked at him, gravely intent eyes half-concealed by the thick-lenses of his spectacles.

'Yes, Inspector, I asked for some intelligent Crime Branch officer who could be spared for some days, and they have given me you. Let me say at once that I have few doubts, if any, that you will be able to give my former friend, Mr Robert Dawkins, out in Mahableshwar, such assistance as he may need. As I mentioned at the outset, his anxieties are in fact likely to be something that can quite easily be cleared up. I dare say, he's just been looking at the whole business somehow the wrong way round. Not the sharpest of the sharp, Robert Dawkins.'

'Sir, I am hoping if I am asking right questions… But, sir, at this moment I am knowing nothing about the lady who has committed suicide in this mysterious way. Sir, is she – was she – an English lady, or did he…?'

'No, no, my dear chap. Dawkins' letter made it quite clear. His wife's Christian name, as they say, was apparently Iris. Yes, Iris. Though I don't think I'll trouble you with some of the other things Robert says about her in his letter. Pretty incoherent stuff. Yes, best, I think, to let you find out the facts for yourself.'

'Very good, sir. I hope when I will have been there in Mahableshwar a few days—'

He came to a sudden halt.

A *few days*. But what if during those few days the baby is coming? Yes, yes, Dr Pramash has told Protima that it will be – she was saying – as much as *six-eight weeks* before birth is likely. But…but I have heard stories of a child arriving unexpectedly when the mother is no more than seven months into pregnancy. Less even. Calculations are not always based on proper facts.

But Sir Rustom was prompting him.

'A few days, you were saying…'

Oh God, how long have I been sitting here in silence? Keeping Sir Rustom waiting. And why? Because some ridiculous anxiety about the baby came into my mind.

'Sir…sir, I-I am sorry. Sir, it is just only, as I was telling, my wife is expecting our first child. And, sir, I am having at back of mind some worries about it.'

'My dear fellow, that's natural enough. But when is this

birth expected? Perhaps, if it's more or less imminent, we should find somone else to go to Mahableshwar. Though that may be a little difficult...'

'No, sir, no. No, birth may not be for six-eight weeks. Sir, I am hundred per cent ready to go.'

However likely it was that, away in the hill-station of Mahableshwar in the cool of the towering Western Ghats, Dawkins sahib's anxieties could quickly be laid to rest, in Bombay Inspector Ghote's troubles were by no means over.

'You may need some form of transport up there if your inquiries take you to any of old Dawkins' former haunts,' Sir Rustom had said, adding casually, 'You have a motor?'

A *gari*? How should I, till now no more than Assistant Inspector, have had money to buy a car?

Ghote looked, a little too wildly, all round the big drawing room seeking some answer to Sir Rustom's expectant query. Rosewood cabinets everywhere with on their shelves, just to be made out behind panes of glass, objects in brightly delicate china or gleaming in silver. On a table in the same dark wood there stood a big wireless set, its loudspeaker covered in a pattern of fretwork, equally dark. Two bookcases, again behind glass, were ranked with leather-bound volumes.

Will the plays of Shakespeare be among them? Certain to be. *Hamlet* with them, of course. What is it Protima is always saying to me: *Am not Prince Hamlet, nor was meant to be.* But now am I...?

'No, sir. No, Sir Rustom, I am not having any car.'

'No? Well, that may be a problem.'

For one hither and thither moment Ghote thought he

might not, after all, have to be away from Protima at perhaps the crucial time. Then that fleeting inadmissible hope vanished.

'But, no,' Sir Rustom said abruptly. 'No, no problem. Ever since, on retirement, I acquired for myself an Austin Princess, I have had in the garages here the old Ambassador I used on those occasions when a police vehicle was inappropriate. You can borrow that, Inspector. I imagine it still goes pretty well. And, as to petrol and that sort of thing, and the hotel you find up there, I can, of course, let you have here and now whatever you may need.'

'Thank you, sir,' was all Ghote could find to say, although his mind was racing with all the complications suddenly thrust upon him.

'Yes, and if whatever I have about me is not enough, Sir Rustom went on, 'I dare say Dawkins will let you have the necessary. He must be pretty well off. A decent pension no doubt, and— Well, not to put too fine a point on it, in his working days, here and there in India, he may not have been above accepting what they called a *token of appreciation*. No point, of course, in expecting a British officer to take a money bribe, but what if he's offered a basket of fruits? And what if underneath…? Mind you, when Robert and I were pals, of a sort, I took dashed good care not to inquire too deeply into things like that. Even to this day, I wouldn't like to assert anything.'

Ghote did not know which way to look. He had always been told the British were utterly above corruption, and now this business of baskets of fruits being thrust under noses. Baskets, no doubt, crowded with choice specimens, and hidden under them…

Mercifully, Sir Rustom was going on.

'Must give you Robert's address in Mahableshwar. Got it on his letter somewhere. Let you have it before you go. Never do to find yourself out there not knowing where the old fellow hangs out.'

CHAPTER FOUR

Newly made Inspector Ghote was soon to be afflicted by more, and worse, troubles than those that had come to him in Sir Rustom Engineer's spacious flat. Coming back to Dadar PS in Sir Rustom's little grey-coloured, and horribly noisy, Ambassador, he could do no more than thank his lucky stars that, by no means a practised driver and in a vehicle, it appeared, made without any rear-mirror, he had not come to grief amid the tangle of Bombay's traffic. Bullock-drawn carts and horse-drawn ones had appeared suddenly and mysteriously in front of him. Lumbering red double-decker buses, often with yet more lumbering and dangerous trailers behind them, had loomed and hooted behind him. Swaying victorias had trotted past at will, on both sides of the little car. Bicycles, it seemed by the thousand, had flocked together in his path. And, totally regardless of everything and everybody, pedestrians had rushed back and forth across roads seemingly so traffic-crowded as to be impassable.

But when, exhausted, he had mounted stone step by stone

step to the top of the familiar tall barracks block he was met by a whole set of new difficulties.

If Protima had taken it well the day before when he had told her they would have to miss seeing *Hamlet*, she did not take it at all well when, with considerable caution in expectation of one of her sudden explosions of anger, he now informed her that he was about to have to leave Bombay for he did not know how long.

'No,' she burst out. 'No. Think of me. Here in this horrible flat. All alone, and waiting, waiting for the first signs that Baby is coming. Who will be there to go down, down, down to a telephone to ask Dr Pramash to come *jaldi jaldi*?'

'But-but I may not be there in Mahableshwar for more than two-three days and Dr Pramash himself was telling it would be as much even as two whole months before-before anything is expected.'

'Two whole months. What does a doctor know about when the baby is going to come? A mother can tell. She is knowing what is happening inside. She is knowing that it will be two-three weeks at most before birth pangs are there.'

'But no. Very well, I am admitting that the mother-to-be must somehow know what is going on something of better, perhaps, than a doctor, but—'

'A doctor you are saying. But Dr Pramash is not a doctor only. He is a man. A man. How can he be knowing what the woman who is carrying that child must know?'

Ghote felt himself, not for the first time in their marriage, up against a wall, high as the sky above. The wall of Protima's knowing what she knew.

In a hundred different ways, some almost impossible to believe in, others clearly things to be reckoned with, he had come face to face time and again with these walls of not-to-be-questioned assertions. *But you must be knowing: no mango except only an alphonso is worth buying.* Or, looming as implacably, *Why must we be staying and staying in this flat inside a police compound?* No use whatsoever in replying that the rule is that Assistant Inspector accommodation in Dadar is laid down as being inside the compound.

'Very well,' he replied now, knowing it was useless, 'it may be that Dr Pramash himself is not a Number One expert in knowing what a mother-to-be is knowing. But in all the books about childbirth, from all the experiences of all the mothers in India, it is well known the time a child is in the womb is nine months. Nine months. And our son—'

'Why are you now saying *son*? My mother knew she was carrying a girl when she was carrying me, I tell you. Of course she knew. A girl is an altogether different feeling, and—'

'No. No, last night only you were saying and saying that the child there, inside you, would be my son. Our son. Yes, you were saying the time for daughters would be later.'

'And am I not to be allowed now to say what I am wanting? Yesterday was yesterday. Today is today.'

And it was then that it was Ghote's turn, for once, to explode.

'Yes. Today is today, and today I am going to Mahableshwar, and I must be there as long as my duty is calling for me to be.'

Not much more than ten minutes later he was once more at the wheel of Sir Rustom's little noisy Ambassador, pushing through Bombay's traffic, careless of every vehicle that came into his path. And conscious, too, that he had plunged out of the flat and run down and down the many stairs of the block without having said goodbye to his pregnant and waiting wife. And without having taken with him even the smallest suitcase of necessary clothes.

The galloping of a horse, the mind of a woman, whether the monsoon will be late or early, even the gods cannot predict these. The old Sanskrit saying beat and beat in Ghote's head all the length of the coast road from Bombay to the beginning of the long climb up to Mahableshwar. Then at last the rage he felt at what his wife had proclaimed as being the only possible truth about her pregnancy fizzled to an end.

As the steamingly hot Ambasssador twisted round hairpin bend after hairpin bend the slopes of the hills ahead grew steeper and steeper. The vegetation to either side became ever more rough and tangled, trees among it sprouting up here and there at their wild will.

At last, suddenly in the trackless waste feeling himself altogether abandoned, he began to think about where he was and why. And, with urgency, about what he would soon have to be doing.

I am on the way to Mahableshwar. I have never been there before, although I am well knowing it is one of the hill-stations where the rich of Bombay are staying when the weather is getting unbearable for them in, say, the scorching month of Jyestha while all are waiting and waiting for the rains to come. But there is this also. In the story of Krishna that my mother was telling me time and again in my childhood days, it is now the month when the blue god, at last united with his Radha, knows he must depart on his travels, even though his going will rend her heart.

Yes, it is in just this way that I also am departing, as is my bounden duty, on travels that – will they? – rend the heart of my Protima. Yes. Yes, as soon as I am getting there and finding some hotel, I must telephone and—

But, no. No, no, no. No telephone in our altogether miserable flat there at the top of that block in Dadar PS. No, the best I will be able to do now is just only to write to her. And how long will it be before the postwallah is again putting a letter through our door? Not a letter telling Assistant Inspector Ghote that he is to be a full inspector, and in Crime Branch, but a letter telling Inspector Ghote's pregnant wife that he is loving her still, and that, if he could, he would be with her at every minute.

A zoom-down of depression.

But my duty now is to be far away in Mahableshwar investigating. Investigating what? How to tell Protima, if I should at all reveal the secrets of an old, retired English sahib, that the sahib's young wife has, for no reason he is able to guess at, killed herself? How to tell her that this duty of mine will be to find out what that reason was? And how, myself, will I be able to find that out?

And, even, I cannot say to Protima that my duty will keep me in Mahableshwar itself only. I may have to go – Sir Rustom was hinting such – to other parts of India, parts where the lady who became Dawkins memsahib may have lived before she was married. And I am at this moment not even knowing where in Mahableshwar I will find Dawkins sahib.

Oh God, that address Sir Rustom was giving me. Where it is? Did I leave it behind when I took off my uniform jacket when I was coming into the flat?

But, no. No, I am wearing same at this moment. No wonder I have been so hot. And, yes, feel in the pocket. And, thank God, there is, yes, a sheet of stiff writing paper, and on it, the address, *Primrose Cottage*. One very English-sounding name, altogether right for Hawkins sahib. No. For Dawkins sahib. Must remember. Dawkins, Dawkins, Dawkins.

But something else. *Hawkins*. Like only a hawk, fierce bird of prey, carried for hunting by some rajah on his thoroughbred horse with the chained bird digging its claws into the leather gauntlet on his wrist. But in one of those English books my father was giving me to read as a boy was I seeing the name Hawkins? Yes. Yes, the brave sailor who fought some Armada with, yes, Sir Francis Drake. A sahib of sahibs in the days long before there was even one British sahib.

So will I be meeting a sahib like Sir Hawkins? A sahib not at all wanting, now he has had some time to think after writing that letter to Sir Engineer, to have some Indian police officer come poking his Indian nose into things he should never even have heard about. Is it that Sir Rustom, feeling a little of guilt at neglecting a one-time friendship, was going too far in sending myself to inquire about one altogether private matter?

And then, before he was at all ready for it, he found the tricky and laborious climb was over and he had arrived in Mahableshwar. For a long moment, sitting in the car wondering why it suddenly seemed so quiet – Oh, yes. I was just only one minute past switching off engine – he tried to decide what he ought now to do. Yes, of course. I must first of all be finding some hotel, as Sir Rustom was saying, not at all realising I was not someone used to going about here and there and just only booking into whatsoever hotel was best. How am I to know what is the most suitable hotel for a full Inspector of Police?

He looked up. And there on the far side of the wide road was a painted sign. *Hotel Restful*. Restful... Without another thought he thrust the car door open and stepped out. To find himself after the long days in sultry Bombay, after the hours and hours imprisoned in the ancient Ambassador, suddenly in the cool. The cool of the hills. Into his head came the words *'tis a nipping and an eager air*. Where had they come from? Of course, *Hamlet*. Often and often he had heard Protima say them when she had insisted on reading aloud the whole of the ghost scene, taking all the parts herself, full-out.

Yes, one good omen.

He went across, steps almost tottering after his six hours or more at the Ambassador's wheel, and stepped unhesitatingly into the hotel's welcome shade.

At the desk he saw, appropriately nodding in restful sleep, a bulbously fat man. His face, propped on a podgy hand, wore a contented smile as if the last thought drifting across his mind before sleep had descended had been an altogether pleasant one.

Wake him? Or look elsewhere for someone to make inquiries of? But there was no one in sight, no sound of voices from anywhere further inside.

He stepped forward and gave a gentle two-fingered tap to the podgy hand resting on the desk.

The moon-like face raised itself just an inch or two. And fell back.

Leave him? But, no. I am too much of exhausted not to need to find out if I can stay here.

A shake now of the uppermost fat-encased shoulder. Not a very gentle shake.

The fat man heaved himself upright.

'Hotel Restful. Proprietor speaking,' he intoned into space.

'I am sorry to have woken you, but I—'

'No, no. I am not sleeping. I am never sleeping when it is day.'

Ghote, on the point of telling him how untrue this was, decided in a flick to produce the tactful response.

'No, no, Proprietor sahib, I was not at all thinking you were asleep. Not at all.'

Satisfied with the denial, the flesh-mountain immediately fumbled under the desk and produced a large greasily stained black book.

'You are wanting to stay? Particulars, please.'

Very good, Ghote said to himself some ten minutes later, after arranging for Sir Rustom's Ambassador to be put safely out of harm's way behind the building and being promised a clean and comfortable room, I have made one swift decision in choosing this place. And it is seeming to be a good one. Altogether restful. What nonsense for Protima to be comparing and comparing me to Hamlet and *the story of a man who could not make up his mind*.

But, as he sat with a cup of tea, he found he could not altogether decide – it was still quite early in the evening – whether he should go straight away to see Dawkins sahib and tell him he was the officer Sir Rustom Engineer had arranged should come and discuss with him the suicide of his wife.

He sat for a long moment, teacup halfway up to his mouth, and tried to envisage how that interview might go.

Can I say straight out *Mr Dawkins, I am here to talk with you abou*—? About what? About how your wife was killing herself? No, it must be in some way that Dr Hans Gross would have managed to use. What is there in the very first words in his great book? *Tact is indispensable for many awkward situations will be circumvented by its use.* There must be some more tactful way of doing what I will have to do. *Mr Dawkins, I am here to discuss with you a certain matter, the matter I am here to-to ask about...?* No, equally impossible.

And, after all, would it now really be the best time for such a talk? When, no doubt, at the end of the day, Dawkins sahib will be altogether tired out and not wishing to hear about any sort of business, never mind such a delicate matter as this. Or when he would be – yes – expecting at any moment to have dinner, to sit at his table in the cool, with in front of him a glass of... Yes, of beer, of good British beer sent from England. He would be just only waiting for his bearer to come in with a deliciously smelling curry, hot-hot the way British sahibs are always liking it. An enemy to be daringly overcome, Hawkins, the raider.

No, I cannot go there to Primrose Cottage at such a time as this.

But...but is it really now the hour for a British sahib's dinner? Is it altogether too early for that?

He glanced at his watch.

Half past six. Yes, too early.

But perhaps my watch has stopped? It might have done. Sometimes I am altogether forgetting to wind. It cannot be as early as half past six. No, it is. I was hearing just only now the clock of that Christian church I saw sounding out the half-hour, a long humming boom. So, should I get up from this comfortable canechair, although it is sagging a little, and walk to Primrose Cottage? Proprietor was saying it is just a short distance after taking the road to the right at the church.

But what if in those few minutes only I will find myself standing face to face with one angry Englishman? A sahib who, perhaps, is no longer asking and asking himself why his wife was committing suicide.

No, it would really be better to face that man when, at the start of a new day, he is ready to deal with whatsoever may come his way.

Or, will it be best?

Very well. No, it would not. Not truly. But I am exhausted now. I have driven all the way from Bombay. I am hot, and—

Yes, this is it. I cannot be going to see an English sahib unless I am having one good long cool shower. What would Protima say if she was knowing I had at all thought of going to him, so sweaty as I am?

Yes, decided. Tomorrow morning, nine ack emma. At the door of Primrose Cottage.

CHAPTER FIVE

After a night of restless sleep on a bed that, despite Hotel Restful's proprietor's extravagant praise for it, had turned out to be no more than a simple charpoy, its criss-crossed ropes too slack to offer any proper support, Ghote, dressed still, for want of anything else, in his Assistant Inspector's best uniform, was at precisely nine a.m. examining a garden gate constructed ingeniously from rurally twisted tree branches with the board at its top bearing the words *Primrose Cottage* in appropriately old-fashioned lettering.

Some twenty yards beyond stood the big bungalow. But, though its roof was covered with a heaped layer of grass, still green, Ghote had to admit that it failed altogether to look like one of the thatched cottages of England he had seen in pictures.

Oh, yes, of course, he said to himself, that roof covering must be just only *kulum* grass. Although I have never before been in Mahableshwar, I was once somehow learning that, because of the violence of the monsoons here, many houses are protected by having *kulum* grass spread thickly on their roofs. Isn't it that sixteen-eighteen feet of rain is falling here in just only one monsoon month? That is almost the only thing I am knowing about Mahableshwar, except that nearby are the biggest strawberry fields in all India.

Yes, this bungalow, he thought now with a tinge of disappointment, is just like the others I was passing on my way here, built for coolness, though with at the back tall chimneys telling me there must be times of the year when a glowing wood fire is needed.

But now, in the joyous month of Chaitra, the grass in the garden here is green and delightfully fresh, and in that long flowerbed beside the path bright red cannas are just breaking into bloom, a single yellow one dancing among them. But what I cannot see are any primroses. No primroses at Primrose Cottage, how can that be? However, I am not at all certain what are primroses.

Wait. Away over there, under that tall deodar tree, its bluey-green branches sweeping downwards, isn't there, crouching at work, a small boy wearing nothing but a raggedy half-pant? Could I quietly go over and ask him where are the primroses? It would be good to know. I may need something to talk about to Dawkins sahib while I am trying not to bring out that word *suicide*.

But, no. I may be observed going over to where the boy is working, and in any case I am very much doubting whether I would get one bit of sense out of a *mali*'s boy like that.

No, go in. Go up to the door of the bungalow, and ring or knock. It must be done.

He gripped the top of the narrow gate and pushed.

The gate stayed firmly shut. He pushed at it again. And again. Sweat broke out all over his back and the narrow width of his shoulders, not long before rinsed clean under Hotel Restful's shower. Or rather under its reluctant trickle.

Then, stooping at last to see over to the gate's far side, he found a small black painted metal latch. It, too, resisted him – will I ever get to see Dawkins sahib himself? – until with a crooked tugging forefinger he managed to force it upwards.

Abruptly the gate, with a dreadful squeal, swung wide under the force of his weight. The path to the house, close-packed flat reddish stones a shade darker than the earth beside them, stretched before him.

Go. Quickly, quickly go.

The house door. And, yes, there is a bell, if one that you have to pull at rather than press.

The sound inside of a prolonged jangling.

Oh God, have I made too much of noise?

The door was suddenly drawn back.

A *khansamah* stood there. A pillar of a man. High above his head there rested an elaborately tied orange puggaree. A red waistcoat, gleaming with bright-polished buttons, encircled the broad chest. Narrow, brilliantly white trousers showed off long legs, with on the feet below, gleamingly polished black leather chappals.

Sweepingly across the steadily immobile face looking down at him there was a curled and oiled black moustache of massive proportions.

Ghote's immediate deduction, before he had time even to give out his name, was that Dawkins sahib, with such a fellow as this in charge of his household, must have a large staff indeed. Much larger than he had at all expected. How could the Englishman of the modest status Sir Rustom was mentioning run to such a household? But then to the surface of his mind floated Sir Rustom's words: *tokens of appreciation.*

Hastily he coughed and spoke.

'To see Dawkins sahib. It is Inspector Ghote.'

In a single jabbed shout the *khansamah* called out 'Bearer'.

And in seconds a bearer was there.

'Inspector Ghote to see Sahib,' the *khansamah* pronounced.

'This way, please. This way, Inspectorjee. Sahib was telling he had a telephone about yourself.'

A few paces into the interior. The bearer's tap on a door. A distant voice answering. The door gently pushed open. 'Sahib, it is Inspector Ghote wishing to see.'

And then Ghote was face to face with the white sahib he was here to question and being told by him to sit. He saw – it was his immediate reaction following his encounter with that towering pillar of a *khansamah* – a man who was short. Shorter by a good deal than somehow he ought to be, as he stood in front of a plump little sofa, its cushions so many blazes of bright unlikely flowers. And, yes, now I am taking one quick look, Dawkins sahib's heavy tan shoes have had their heels definitely heightened, by almost half an inch.

Now Dawkins sahib hopped back on the sofa and blurted out something like, 'Sit. Sit, man, for God's sake,' then pushed aside his book, something called *Wisden's Almanack* Ghote noted, together with his reading spectacles.

Already Ghote had taken in that the man he was here to help was a good deal more formally dressed than, up in the cool of the hills, a retired white sahib might be expected to be. The sharply white shirt, under his yet whiter drill suit, was buttoned to the neck and from it there poured down a broad silk tie, striped somewhat like Sir Rustom's one seen only yesterday but in altogether more clashing colours. And the collar of the shirt, unlike Sir Rustom's, was stiff with starch.

Does Dawkins sahib know, Ghote wondered for one disrespectful instant, that it is altogether likely the starch sprayed on it was squirted from the lips of the man who was ironing it?

He saw now, too, that Dawkins sahib was extraordinarily well-shaved, all but for a bristling little moustache of a fading ginger colour. Again, Ghote imagined a bearer leaning over him as he lay back at ease, shaving brush swiftly dabbing at sun-reddened plumpish cheeks, a fine-honed razor then expertly wielded till those cheeks were as gleaming as the *khansamah*'s chappals.

More reddish hair stood up in a sharp crest above a face that, with its set mouth and unmoving pale-washed blue eyes, made Dawkins sahib man look – the notion struck Ghote like a slap – firm as a rock. A jutting British rock.

How...? How shall I be able to say to this rock that I have been informed he is in great distress? You cannot be distressing a rock.

What to do? What to do?

From somewhere deep inside came an answer, Dr Gross's answer about tact. Yes, say something nice.

'Mr Dawkins,' he shot out. 'Sir, I was altogether delighted by the name I was seeing on the gate of this bunga...of this cottage. *Primrose Cottage*. It is so altogether English. Very-very one hundred per cent.'

And the rock softened. Just a little.

'Named the place myself, matter of fact, when I bought it from a man leaving with all the rest in '47. Damn bad show that, always thought. The place was called *The Deodars* then, garden full of 'em, bloody monstrous trees. Had all but one chopped down. Then thought I'd better find a name that suited. Hit on Primrose Cottage. *A primrose by the river's brim, a simple primrose was to him.* Never went to any damned university, or even to much of a school. Father couldn't rise to the damn fees. But I've read my Wordsworth all the same, and always liked that bit. No damned puffing up, eh? Straight to the point. Plain man's talk.'

'Yes, sir. But what exactly is a primrose looking like? I am not thinking I have ever seen same.'

Dawkins sahib grunted.

'Won't see any here,' he muttered. 'Never found any to plant. Be damned expensive to try to get some from Home.'

'Sir, that is one great pity.'

Ghote came to a halt. The *something nice* had been said. And exhausted, to last drop. Nothing for it now but...

At that moment Dawkins sahib suddenly jumped to his feet and started wildly looking all round the room.

Ghote looked at him in some puzzlement. But an explanation soon appeared.

'Specs? Specs?' the little rock shouted out. 'Where the devil did I put my specs? Always disappearing, damn things.'

Ghote could, in fact, see them quite clearly. They had slipped a little way down between the cushions of the flowers-bright sofa.

But...but should I? Should I point out to this indignant white sahib something as obvious as this?

'Damn servants,' Dawkins sahib shouted now, 'one of them must have put the damn things somewhere. Other day I had to come all the way up from the Club when I—'

He came to an abrupt halt.

But Ghote's nerve had broken.

He was already on his feet, stepping over to the sofa. Now, keeping his back between Dawkins and the gap between the sofa cushions, he rapidly extracted the gold-rimmed glasses.

'Sir, it is these you are looking for?' he asked.

Dawkins wheeled round.

'Ah, yes. Yes. Damn it all. So, Inspector Er... What's all this about, eh?'

Ghote let this slide over him.

'Sir. Dawkins sahib,' he said. 'Sir, I-I was sent here to you by your friend who is now called Sir Rustom Engineer, and, sir—'

Dawkins sahib broke in.

'Good old Rustom. Yes. Used to go on shikar with him. Know that, do you? Many a fat chital deer fell to our guns, those days.'

A grunted laugh.

'Well, more to my gun, if I say it. Old Rustom never much of a shot, matter of fact. Think he used to come along because I was an Englishman. Never myself went in for any of that stand-offish nonsense some people did. Chap's a chap, I used to say.'

'Yes, sir. Sir Rustom was recalling same.'

Never mind the blank lie, Ghote thought. What I must be doing is keeping on same side as-as this British rock.

'Yes, dare say he does remember. We were good friends, you know. Good friends. So... So, when I found I was in trouble, it was natural I should drop old Rustom a line. And... And he sorted you out for me, did he? Inspector, eh? Know your onions, I dare say. What did my fellow tell me your name was? Always mutter, damn servants. Can't cure 'em of it.'

'It is Ghote, sir. Ghote.'

'Right then, Inspector Ghote. Take it old Rustom's put you in the picture, and all that. So what are you going to do about it?'

Ghote swallowed.

Then hoped Dawkins sahib hadn't noticed.

'Sir…' he brought out at last. Then inspiration came. 'Sir, although Sir Rustom was telling what you had put in your letter, he was not able – sir, he is a busy man – to give as much of time as he would have liked to filling in each and every detail.'

Another lie. But only doing the needful.

'So, sir, perhaps, I am thinking, you could tell me full circumstances?'

There, I have asked. And without one mention of the word *suicide*.

Dawkins sahib, rock or no rock, looked abruptly disconcerted.

'Full circumstances, Inspector?' he said, making it totally plain that these were something he was very unwilling to discuss.

Ghote braced himself.

'Yes, sir, in every detail. If I am to find out anything, I must be put hundred per cent into picture.'

A long moment of blank silence.

Then a shrug of the substantial shoulders on that surprisingly short body.

'Very well, Inspector. Sit you down. Take a pew.'

Ghote hastened to plant himself back on his chair. He pulled out his notebook and extracted a pencil from the top pocket of his uniform jacket.

Dawkins sahib, sitting in the middle of the fat chintz-covered, flowers-patterned sofa, his short legs just clear of the floor below, gave a little cough.

'Right then. Here goes.'

But nothing went. Not for as much as a minute and a half, even two minutes, of painful silence. Ghote, sitting there fixedly looking, not at silent Dawkins sahib but to the side of him at the bright-patterned sofa, remembered abruptly something his schoolmaster father had once told him. *Chintz*, however British the word sounded, was in fact the Hindi word *chint*, 'bright with many colours'. For an instant he felt a tiny dash of superiority.

But at last Dawkins sahib, sahib of sahibs, began to produce his account.

'Like this, actually,' he said. 'I was over at the Club. There most mornings, get a look at *Times of India*. Damn people refuse to deliver it here, unless I pay extra. Heard the phone ringing, and then one of the Club servants brought me a message. I should go back home immediately. A nasty accident. I just thought then that there had been a fire in the kitchen or something and I was not going to get my tiffin. But, of course, when I got here – came across the golf course, quickest way, nobody about, too soon for the visitors – he showed me... He showed me Iris—'

He choked, looked down at the fine carpet at his feet.

'There she was. On the floor, dead. Up against the french windows here. Head wound, blood everywhere. Had to get rid of the old carpet. My twelve-bore beside her, trigger almost in her right hand. Gun's kick must have jerked it free. 'Spose she'd fetched it from my study, just next door here. In a locked cupboard, of course. Duty to keep guns safe. Imagine

Iris must have known where I kept the key, and she—'

But now Ghote felt impelled to look up from his scribbling and ask a question.

'And where was that, sir?'

'What? What?'

'Where it is you were keeping the key to that almirah where your gun was?'

Dawkins sahib blinked, looked all around as if he needed to see where it was he used to put the gun-cupboard key.

'Oh,' he said eventually. 'Of course, in the bedroom. Drawer where my socks go. Used to pop the key in underneath them. Yes, there.'

'So your wife could be well knowing where it was?'

'Well, could have known, yes. May have been in the room sometimes when I tucked it away. Made no secret of it.'

'Yes, sir, of course.'

A moment's pause.

'But, sir, tell me please. For your gun there must be cartridges. Was it loaded already?'

'Good God, what do you take me for, man? First rule when you're given your very first gun. Before putting it away check there's no round in the breech. Elementary.'

'Yes, sir. So your...so Mrs... Sir, she must have obtained ammunition.'

'From a drawer, small drawer, in the cupboard. She-she must have taken out just one cartridge. One.'

'So, sir, she – your wife, sir – must have known also where were the cartridges for your-your twelve-bore, sir.'

'Yes, dare say she did. Don't often use the gun, not nowadays. But she may have seen- Must have seen me looking in the cartridges drawer, some time. Yes, must have done. But does it matter how she knew that, the wife I'd have trusted with my life?'

So now, Ghote thought. Now I have got back, fully, to what it is I came here to find out. He is saying he would trust his wife, Iris memsahib, with his life. But, if Sir Rustom was right, he still is not able to understand why she could have killed herself in the way he himself was just only describing. And that is what I am here to be finding out. If it is at all possible to do same.

'Mr Dawkins,' he said, 'I am understanding from Sir Rustom that you have no idea, none whatsoever, why your... why your wife should have done that thing. Sir, had she given even one hint that she would do it?'

'Good God, no, man. She was pregnant, you know. Seven months gone, as they say.'

Seven months gone. The words instantly burnt themselves into Ghote's mind. Seven months pregnant, almost exactly the same as Protima. Or is that same? When Protima was so angry that I was leaving for Mahableshwar, she was saying and declaring our child, my son, would come sooner, much sooner, than the time Dr Pramash has said. In much, much less of time.

He longed at that instant not to be in Mahableshwar, inside Primrose Cottage trying to assess and weigh each smallest detail of that British rock's account of his wife's death. He wanted to be at home, even if that was the sun-broiled flat with its rotten stove at the top of the tall block in the Dadar PS compound. He wanted to be hearing, truly hearing, every detail of Protima's pregnancy.

But I cannot be there in Bombay. I have been given a task. By Sir Rustom Engineer. And here in Mahableshwar I must stay. And listen to whatever is said to me. Listen now to Dawkins sahib, with my each and every ear.

'Yes, sir,' he said, 'I am well understanding now why you were so-so distressed at what your wife was seeming to have done. Without any explanation whatsoever being there. You are certain of that, is it?'

'Good God, man, of course I'm certain. Why else do you think I would in sheer desperation write to an acquaintance from years back seeking some shred of help?'

At this revelation of weakness from the man he had begun to think of as rock-like in his stability, Ghote could not but feel an overriding desire somehow to accomplish the task he had been given.

'Sir,' he forced himself to say, 'please to look at every circumstance of your life in the past months. Sir, could there have been something you were saying to Iris memsahib that might, for no good reason, have made her feel some despair?'

What have I done now, he asked himself. I have put myself, it is seeming, into the mind, into the very heart, of this British rock. And-and have I made some terrible wound there? Some wound that may at any moment cause him to kick me with force out of his house?

But the rock stayed silent and immobile as-as a rock.

Then at last words issued from it.

'No. No, Inspector. You do well to ask me that. It seems, after the appalling thing that has happened in my life, I must put up with every sort of damned impertinence. So, I answer, once and for all, that nothing, not one shred of anything, passed my lips that could have given Ir—. That could have given my wife, damn it, any reason at all to...to do that appalling thing.'

'Very good, sir. I would not ask any such question again.'

'I should bloody well hope not. Do you think an officer like the chap who came up from the police station here was as bloody rude as that? As bloody insensitive? No, Inspector What-was-his-name...what the devil did he...? Darrani, that's it. First-class man, first-class, asked me no more than he saw was necessary, told me straight away there could be no question of me not being over at the Club, dozens of witnesses, when the sound of that shot brought *Khansamah* in here and he found...he found...found Iris dead, lying there as I described it to you.'

Ghote wished now he was anywhere, anywhere else than sitting perched on his chair facing this man who had returned to find his wife dead, his own shotgun from that locked almirah beside her. He no longer wanted even to be at home back in his flat high above Dadar PS. He just wanted not to be where he was.

But I am here, he acknowledged to himself. I am here, and it is my bounden duty to ask more questions, to poke and to pry, until I have found the answer that is baffling Dawkins sahib. And baffled also, it seems, that 'first-class officer', Inspector Darrani.

'Sir,' he said, suddenly seeing a way of getting a respite from the fearful situation he had become entangled in. 'Sir, I think it would be best if I am going now, *ek dum,* to see my colleague, Inspector – you were saying – Darrani, who was here almost as soon as tragedy was occurring.'

Dawkins sahib looked at him. Stared at him.

'See Inspector Darrani?' he said. 'No need for that. I've told you. Told you. That man's an absolutely first-class officer. He'll have done every single thing necessary. Got it all taped.'

'Yes, sir. Yes, I am sure what you have said about Inspector Darrani is hundred per cent correct. But that is the reason why I must be seeing. What he was learning may be of the utmost help to me.'

'Humph. Have it your own way, if you must. But don't you go running off this instant. I've a good deal more to say to you. And-and if I don't say it here and now, I probably never will. We are talking about my dead wife, you know. The way she-she damn well killed herself, and for no reason. No bloody reason at all.'

'Yes, sir. Of course, sir, if you have more to be telling I am here to hear.'

But, Ghote thought, I do not at all believe that what you may now say will be very useful. It is altogether easy to see you are still in one state of distress. But, if I am getting to see Inspector Darrani, I may be finding out ten times more.

But, no, I must stay here. Stay here and let this friend of Sir Rustom's, however much or little such he is, have his say.

Yet then, it seemed, Dawkins sahib had nothing to say. He sat there on the squabby sofa, its chintz cushions patterned in those unlikely flowers, and glowered into mid-air.

So how long must I also sit?

'She was born in India, you know.'

The words abruptly emerged as if from some deep well.

Ghote could almost hear the squeak of its bucket as it was being hauled up on its roller, almost felt himself leaning over the wide circle of the well wall trying to see if there might be anything more in the wooden bucket as it slowly rose up.

'Met her when I was visiting an old friend. Forest officer. Staying on like me, Government of India contract. Chap called Watson. Out in a dak bungalow, not far from Poona.

Poona. Can't be doing with calling it Pune, as they tell us now you have to. Somewhere near Poona. Married, of course. Then, drinks before dinner, and in came this girl. Very quiet – unobtrusive, might say – but dashed attractive. Liked that. Can't stand females who always make a dead set at you. No, but look, look, I'll show you. Photo I sent her down to Bombay to have taken, just after we were married.'

Abruptly he jumped up from the fat sofa, strode over to a heavy roll-top desk on the far wall, tugged out a keyring, selected one of the bunch, plunged it into the keyhole of its long drawer.

'Damn. Bloody thing jammed. Wrong bloody key.'

He twisted and pulled. To no avail.

'Half a mo'. I'll have to get *Khansamah*, if I can't... Always knows what to do.'

Cautiously, Ghote got up and went across.

'Can I be of help, sir?'

'No, blast you.'

Tug, twist, tug.

'Oh, all right, damn it, see what you can do.'

Ghote moved in front of the desk, put himself squarely at the middle of the long drawer, peered at it for a moment.

Then he reached for the jammed key – it was plainly just a little too large for the keyhole – took hold of it, got it gently to turn a little back to the left and—

Out it came.

Dawkins sahib pushed him aside, snatched the keyring from his hand, stuck in another key, turned it and jerked the drawer wide.

In a moment he had pulled out from it a photograph in a neatly painted frame.

But what Ghote had seen as Dawkins sahib tugged the drawer open was a thick scattering of what looked like old letters.

What if any of them are ones written to Iris memsahib, he thought. Letters from friends and family that might give one clue to her state of mind? Can I ask if I may see?

But Dawkins sahib was intent on something else.

'Look at this photo,' he jabbered out. 'Just take a look at it. Iris, as she was just after we were married. And, you know, I actually had to persuade her to go and have it taken. Shy as a violet, she was. Violet eyes, too. Like a violet herself, might say. Violet hidden in the woods. And, damn it, I fell for her, though always thought of myself as a bachelor born. Fell for her, and, no time at all, married.'

He thrust the frame – it was painted in two shades of pale blue – into Ghote's hands.

Ghote looked. The photograph did not appear to be a very good one. All right, I can see the colour of those eyes that Dawkins sahib called *violet*. They are striking, as he said. Very different from his own washed-out blue ones, though somehow not quite as I expected. And something is seeming also to be not altogether right about them. Perhaps some fault of the photographer. But I must not be staring too long.

He took a quick glance at the print at the bottom of the frame. *Photo By Too Good Clicks, Bombay. Tel: 4028*

Yes, perhaps Mr Too-Good-Clicks is not a too good photographer.

He handed the photo back. Dawkins sahib seized hold of it and shoved it into the drawer, slamming it shut.

For a moment Ghote wondered why it had not been hanging on the wall above the desk or perhaps displayed on some table in the room. But there was something else lodged in his mind.

'Sir,' he ventured. 'Sir, inside that drawer you were just only opening, sir, I was seeing what were looking like old letters kept there. Sir, if they were written to you by your wife, then there may be in them some clues. Or perhaps they are letters written to her. Sir, may I examine?'

'No, you may damn well not. Letters to my wife? Private letters? How dare—'

He stopped abruptly.

'In any case,' he said, 'those are not letters either from or to my wife. Do you think she put any letters she wanted to keep into the drawer of my desk? What sort of an idiot are you? Damn it, my wife has-my wife had a desk of her own. Wedding present from myself, actually. Pretty little bureau. In what she used to call her sewing room, sort of little place where she could be private, if she wanted to be, do a bit of mending or something. Just as I have what I call my study.'

Ghote for a moment contrasted this arrangement with that of his own wretchedly small flat, or even with what he might expect in the new larger, telephone-equipped flat he hoped soon to have. Would he and Protima want separate places to hide away in? Never.

But he also very much wanted to go and look over that sewing room, to open that new bureau. Were the bright sofa cushions here also happy Iris memsahib's three years ago choice? In the sewing room he could carry out one good, simple step in the task he had been given. To see if there were letters there to give some clue to Iris memsahib's state of mind. But he thought this was not at all the moment to make such a request.

And, in any case, Dawkins sahib was saying something, and in rather more of a mutter than in his usual giving-orders manner.

'...happy from that day on. Only once, once, did we have a bit of a row. Had the *mali*'s boy... Wretched brat never does what he's told. If I've said it once, I've said it a hundred times. I will not have any damn yellow canna flowers spoiling the look of that bed by the front path. Every plant in it has got to be red. Red. Must have order. Order. What we brought to India. Order. But does that boy uproot even one yellow- But never mind all that. What I was telling you was I had the boy pegged down as stealing my watch. And Iris, typical woman, had to say *Chintu's such a sweet little chap* couldn't have stolen anything.'

But, catching those words *bit of a row,* Ghote was suddenly elsewhere. Once more back in Bombay.

What if Protima and I are having one *bit of a* row, or, worse, one very bad quarrel? Like we were having just yesterday? And...and it is bringing on the birth? Much, much too soon? A miscarriage. What if...

I must have time to think. I must stop this English rock going on and on.

I must get away.

'Sir, yes, that is altogether most interesting. But, sir, as I was saying, I must be seeing Inspector Darrani. Sir, he may be investigating some case elsewhere at any moment. Sir, how do I get to Mahableshwar PS?'

CHAPTER SIX

Ghote, striving to remember what directions for finding the police station Robert Dawkins had eventually given him, heard, as he wrestled with the obstinately stiff latch of the garden gate, a small voice apparently emerging from the very depths of the massed ranks of red canna plants beside the path.

'I was seeing, Inspector sahib. Seeing all.'

Peering sharply down between the tall plants he found the words had come from the crouching brown-backed ribby form of the *mali*'s boy he had earlier spotted under the sweeping branches of the surviving deodar of all of them that had once given an Indian name to Primrose Cottage.

For a moment he stood looking down in silence at that bare back. What was puzzling him was how the boy – was he perhaps ten, or twelve? – could have known that it was a full inspector of police he had spied coming along the path rather than an officer wearing assistant inspector's uniform. Then it came to him. Of course. Servants. Once one servant knows something, every servant knows it.

'Seeing? Seeing all? What all were you seeing?' he

demanded in sharp Marathi. 'Stand up and look at me. What is this you were seeing?'

The boy got to his feet, scarcely taller than the brightly blooming red cannas all around him.

'Inspector, Iris memsahib I was seeing. Lying there just after sound of gun.'

'Lying there? Lying where? When did you see? When just?'

'Inspector, when I was hearing that sound I was thinking *What is that? There should not be shootings here.* At last I was hurry-hurrying down to bungalow itself. I had thought shooting came from inside.'

'Very well. You did right. But what exactly were you seeing when you were getting there? Did you go inside itself?'

'No, no, Inspector. I was first looking-looking through windows all round bungalow. In case one dacoit was there inside. But in end I was seeing Iris memsahib lying there. Inspector, where there are two big door-windows. I was a little lifting the *chik* that was hanging outside and looking in.'

Right, those french windows and the roll-down cane blinds hanging in front of them to keep out the sun, brilliant enough at this time of year.

'Looking in? And what did you see?'

'Inspector, Iris memsahib, with blood all over, and on gun also. Sahib's gun I was once seeing. There, close to me. And then...then, Inspector, *Khansamah* was coming into room, and I was jumping back where he could not see. Inspector, *Khansamah* is always ready to beat, if he is just only hearing me.'

'I dare say he is.'

A thought came to him then. This boy is almost certainly one damn liar.

'No wonder he is beating,' he snapped out. 'When you are stealing whatsoever you can lay hands on. Sahib's watch even. Do you think I do not know you stole that?'

The boy stood there, two canna flowers brushing each of his shoulders, a look of outrage plain on his face.

'Inspector, I was not stealing. I was not, Inspector. Dawkins memsahib herself was finding Sahib's watch when Sahib was saying I stole. Inspector, he had left it on top of *thunder-box* in bathroom. She had straight away thought it must be there. She said Sahib is always leaving his watch, his spec, there when he is having shower and forgetting after. She came when Sahib was saying I had taken and I should be handed to police. She was bringing watch itself.'

Ghote took a second or two to sort out the babble of justification. What was a *thunder-box*? Yes, of course, the comical name the British give to the commodes in their mofussil bathrooms. But then he realised that an account so detailed, with its mention of a *spec* also, was almost certain to be true.

Yes, Dawkins sahib had in fact left unfinished his story of the theft of his watch. He had said something about his wife stating the boy was *a sweet little chap* and so could not have been the thief. But he had left it at that, leaving me to believe he was the one who was in the right when he and his new wife had had their one and only quarrel. I was not thinking very much about what he had said then. I was too much remembering my quarrel with Protima, and how if I was angering her at any time it might bring on miscarriage. Any sudden shock, however small, might do that. Dropping something and breaking it. Or a door slamming in a gust of wind. Anything.

But, yes. Yes, what the boy has been saying has altogether ring of truth.

Then am I now to believe he did really go up close to those french windows, move aside the *chik* blind and see Iris memsahib lying there with the gun nearby, all covered in her blood?

But, wait. The boy was saying the gun was between her and the windows. Could he truly have seen it, tucked away just there?

He brought back to mind the shape of the big room as he had taken it in when Dawkins sahib, sitting on that squabby chintz-covered sofa, heavy shoes jutting out at the ends of his fat little legs, was telling him about coming back from the Club to find his wife's body. Yes, that sofa itself stands just next to the french windows. So, yes again, Iris memsahib's body could have been lying there. She would have been sent falling backwards by the force of the pellets from the twelve-bore as she had fired it close to her face.

For a moment he allowed himself to picture that terrible scene. Iris, on her back close up to those french windows, blood from her ruined face everywhere, staining the bare floor and the carpet that had had to be got rid of.

Yes, nothing at all wrong with the picture the boy himself has put before me.

So, yes, then the *khansamah*, hearing the shot, must have come in, if not very much hurrying. A fellow like that, pillar-tall and stately, did not hurry. And at once this boy here must have slipped out of his sight, and then quietly made his way back to where he had been working, perhaps under the big deodar.

Worth checking?

Yes.

'So, when you were seeing *Khansamah* coming into room, you were first hiding from him, and then going back to where you had been working? Where was that? Tell me exactly.'

'Inspector, it was under deodar, where it is out of sun. *Mali* had said I was all day long to break open canna seeds. You are knowing those seeds will not sprout, so hard they are, unless each one is broken open. Inspector, I was there hitting and hitting with my stone when I was hearing gun. And, after I was at bungalow, I was going back to do more in case *Mali* would be beating.'

Right, Ghote said to himself. It is all hanging together. So, now for Inspector Darrani. I must get to the police station as quickly as I can, or he might, as I was saying to Dawkins sahib, be going to investigate in some village miles away. Right, hurry. Hurry.

Despite Mahableshwar's relative cool, when Ghote arrived at the police *chauki* in the middle of the smaller bazaar he realised he was streaked with sweat. He glanced at his Number One uniform, worn now ever since he had seen Sir Rustom, and showing every sign of it. Must, must, must, soon as I can, buy somewhere one-two decent mufti shirts and one trouser also.

Then he took in the tall stately building that confronted him. What a British-looking place, he thought. All in that white-white stone, as firmly planted here as Buckingham Palace itself in London. Each and every window kept polished and sparkling like diamonds only, looking out at the whole of Mahableshwar as if alert for the smallest piece of wrongdoing.

But no time now to think about all that. Inspector Darrani may at any moment be leaving by some door at the rear.

He ran up the wide steps and entered. At the dazzlingly polished counter he stated, as authoritatively as he could bring himself to, that he was Inspector Ghote, Crime Branch, Bombay, wanting to speak to the officer in charge.

A jawan at once led him inside. But he was not to meet Inspector Darrani.

When in answer to the jawan's respectful knock on an office door there came a barked *Enter,* he saw the last man in the world he had expected. Not 'Inspector Darrani', as Dawkins sahib had repeatedly called that 'first-class man', but someone he had once known all too well, a fellow cadet at Nasik Police Training School, then Probationary Assistant Inspector Barrani.

And now it was Barrani, immediately recognising who his visitor was, who greeted him – 'Ghote *bhai*, sit, sit' – with the most patronising of welcoming smiles.

One may smile and smile and be a villain. Shakespeare, in Protima's voice, offered a warning.

Obedient to it, Ghote gave himself a quick internal shake.

'Barrani *bhai*,' he said, swiftly claiming equal brotherhood, 'what a piece of luck to find you are the in-charge here in Mahableshwar. You see, I have been asked, by in fact Sir Rustom Engineer' – if you have strings to pull, pull them now – 'to give Mr Robert Dawkins, in his state of distress you must be knowing about, some advices.'

'To give him advice,' Barrani promptly corrected him. 'That is how it is said in Englishman's English. You ought to remember such, in case you are ever becoming full inspector and have to deal with English sahibs as I do.'

But under this put-down, Ghote was able to feel himself unscathed.

'Yes, yes,' he said. 'I am, as one matter of fact, now full inspector myself. I am just joining Crime Branch in Bombay.'

He allowed himself a tiny pause in which to take note, at those words *Crime Branch*, of Barrani's instantly suppressed reaction, and was not disappointed.

'But unfortunately,' he went on, 'I was at once asked to come here top-speed, and had no time to be getting correct uniform.'

Barrrani now gave Ghote's creased and crumpled Assistant Inspector's Number One outfit a steady disparaging look. And into Ghote's mind there came a picture of the ever-decisive fellow changing into gym kit. He always used to do it with unhesitating efficiency. Never a moment spent choosing whether shirt came before shorts, whether removal of boots came – snap, snap, snap – before removal of uniform jacket.

And at Nasik, Ghote now remembered all too well, fiercely Pathan Barrani had first earned the name, well deserved, of *Bully Barrani,* soon improved to *Bullybhoy*. Both versions equally apt. Barrani had an unswerving belief that whatever he happened to think could not be other than right, and that everybody else should beyond doubt recognise this.

Especially, as it had turned out, Probationary Assistant Inspector Ghote who in his early days at the School had found, to his surprise, that the questions in the various tests they had been set were a great deal easier to answer than he had ever expected. His name quite often had headed the lists. But that was not for long. Soon, thanks to the way Bullybhoy appeared to have imposed his views, even on the examiners, of what was right and what wrong, *Barrani* began to supplant *Ghote*.

When Bullybhoy after each exam took to explaining at thunderous length how his answers had to be the only possible ones, Ghote had made up his mind to avoid henceforth getting any topmost marks and to keep above all out of Bullybhoy's way. With the simple result that Bullybhoy had made him his chief target for laying down the law among the whole body of cadets, first year or final.

But there had been worse. Much worse. During their last year at Nasik a notice had been posted one day saying there was to be a major Youth Police congress in Moscow. Every country in the world, bar of course any anti-Communist ones, had been invited to send one cadet delegate. It had been immediately somehow understood that, though in theory the choice was to be made by drawing lots, Probationary Assistant Inspector Barrani would be the one to go. Ghote had not even paid the fee to charity necessary for a name to go into the hat. But, when it was found he was the only cadet who had failed to put himself forward, he had been officially rebuked and told he was to enter.

Then, when the draw was made, the name that emerged proved to be not *Barrani*, but *Ghote*.

So, rather against his own wishes, he had found himself in icily cold Moscow endeavouring to bring honour to his native land. And to a decent extent succeeding. Until almost at the end of the congress he succumbed to the evident charms of a female Intourist officer. Or perhaps had fallen to her wiles, since she turned out to be a secret smuggler of books and other inadmissible objects from the dread United States. Almost immediately, too, he had been detected concealing a letter, to be posted in India, arranging for a supply of blue jeans. So he had found himself then inside the walls of the

Lubyanka. He had been lucky, however, to experience no worse a fate than to be flown home in immediate disgrace, by a stroke of luck just managing to keep the circumstances out of the public eye.

But Bullybhoy, of course, had discovered what had happened. And with one ferocious word had made Ghote understand that in the imminent final exams his name was not to come even near that of the destined star of the whole intake.

CHAPTER SEVEN

Now Ghote realised that before Bullybhoy took complete charge of their present encounter he had to jump in without a moment of hesitation.

'So, Barrani *bhai*,' he all but barked out, 'what can you tell me about your investigation at Primrose Cottage?'

'Nothing to tell,' Bullybhoy answered, with happy calm. 'All plain sailing, *bhai*. The woman shot herself, can't be any doubt about that. Examination of *corpus delicti* not even necessary.'

Ghote, despite a moment's difficulty over precisely what the Latin meant and recalling Bullybhoy had much flourished it in their Nasik days, came back with all the directness he could muster.

'Yes, the body. You are having it here? I would like myself to give it some examination.'

A gruff laugh.

'You are unlucky, Inspector. Altogether unlucky. I do not know how they manage in Bombay, but you must be knowing a *corpus*, whether *delicti* or not, begins to decompose inside hours in the heat. You must have been taught that at least at Nasik, for God's sake.'

Ghote forced himself to take that plainly insulting *for God's sake* on the chin. 'So what then has happened to Mrs Iris Dawkins' bod...to her *corpus*?' he asked, thinking that up in the relative cool of Mahableshwar there was surely no need for quite such immediate despatch to the burning ghats, or, since Iris Dawkins was no doubt a Christian, for rapid burial.

'Deep underground, my boy,' Bullybhoy replied. 'Deep underground in the European cemetery. Saw to that myself. Can't leave a white woman's body unburied, you know. Would not do at all.'

He sat there, behind his wide desk, bare but for a tall telephone, its receiver dangling from the hook at its side, and a bright-polished round bell, metal button ready at any moment for Bullybhoy's hand to slap down on it. Any order then issued, Ghote well remembered, never to be taken back. Once decided, decided for ever. That was Bullybhoy.

Ghote found himself now doubly determined not to be silenced in his quest for whatever knowledge of Iris memsahib's suicide Bullybhoy might have acquired.

'Very well,' he said. 'But now, please, could you be telling whatsoever you were learning when you went to investigate at Primrose Cottage.'

'Yes. Piece of luck there, say it myself. I happened to know Dawkins' *khansamah*. Had a word with the fellow once when I went there for drinks. Dawkins keen to have the police in his pocket. And, of course, myself keen to find out all I could about a prominent Mahableshwar resident. Never know what may come in handy, isn't it?'

Ghote had his thoughts about all that. But he was not going in any way to allow them to surface.

'The *khansamah* at Primrose Cottage?' he said. 'You were stating it was one piece of luck you were knowing him.'

'Yes. Yes, quite right. Always get to know the servants. May come in bloody useful. Must have told you that myself at Nasik.'

'Yes, yes, you did.'

With lip bitten.

'Right then. When I got up to that place – used to be called The Deodars, you know – responding to an urgent call on the phone...' Bullybhoy halted for a moment to give the tall instrument beside him a proprietary glance. 'Over there I found the *khansamah* was the chap who first saw the *corpus*. Heard the shot, and instantly investigated. That's what the fellow's like, quick as a leopard. So he was able to tell me every last thing. Trick is to sum up that sort of fellow well in advance, and then you can tell just how far to trust anything he says.'

He waited for approval.

'Yes,' Ghote said. 'I have done same myself in Bombay. Perhaps following your example, Barrani *bhai*, from old Nasik days.'

'Good man. Well then, he told me he had come hurrying into the room and had at once seen the woman's body lying in a pool of blood near some french windows they have there. You know what in English *french windows* means? No, you won't. Right, they are twin doors with glass-panes from top to bottom. Then straight away when he got there my friend, the *khansamah*, saw the gun where it had just fallen from her hand in her death spasm. Woman hadn't been holding it properly, of course. Women never can handle a gun.'

Ghote for an instant thought of producing some contrary evidence. He had known of Englishwomen whose shikar successes were on a par with that of their husbands.

But, instead, he asked 'Were you not somewhat astonished that Dawkins memsahib was able to shoot herself with that twelve-bore itself, with its trigger so far away from the muzzle? It has been something that has worried myself ever since I was hearing Dawkins sahib's account of the circumstances.'

'Yes. You might think that. But the *khansamah* knew all about the gun, of course. That twelve-bore's not much over two feet in length, one end to the other. Plus, knowing where it was kept, what cartridges there were for it. Both in the same locked cupboard. So I got him to explain to me how she might have done it. Would have been bit of a tricky business, of course. But a woman who has made up her mind to kill herself will do things a lot more extraordinary than you would think possible. No, you do not need to worry yourself over that.'

Ghote felt there was more he ought to ask, more about the twelve-bore. Had Bullybhoy actually confirmed those measurements? Or just taken the *khansamah*'s word for them? Had he – come to think about it – ever actually seen the gun, now, as Dawkins sahib had given him to understand, locked away back at Primrose Cottage.

But haven't I also failed to ask to look at it? A bad mistake to have made. And one Bullybhoy would seize on, if I was mentioning same.

No, when I am going back there, as I must do quite soon,

I can then be making careful inquiries. Exactly where the gun is. If it has been just only put back in that gun-cupboard. And if it was cleaned before it was replaced there.

And also – he felt a tightening of sudden anxiety – I must be asking Dawkins sahib if I can look through all the drawers in that little bureau he was mentioning, plus also the drawers in the bedroom that Iris memsahib had used. In either place there may be something still – old letters, a diary even – that will give me some hint as to why she did that appalling thing.

But that must be for later. Now it is what Bullybhoy himself may have found out.

He took a deep breath.

'The gun,' he asked with a touch of duplicity. 'Dawkins sahib was seeming to say it is now inside Primrose Cottage itself. But is that right? Should it actually be here, stored away in your *muddamal* room? I am supposing it would be needed in evidence at inquest.'

'Inquest?' Bullybhoy snapped back. 'Don't you know better than that? Inquest over and done with weeks ago. Gave my evidence, accepted, of course. Gun went back to Dawkins, naturally. And usual verdict *While of unsound mind.*'

'But was not that also very quick?'

'Of course it was. I was telling you, had to be. Word with the coroner. Case like that, soonest done soonest mended. Old British proverb. Don't want tongues wagging, you know. Enough scandal in a place like this without adding fuel to fire, bringing all sorts of trouble.'

Bullybhoy tilted back in his chair.

'Think that about sums it up,' he said.

'If you are saying...'

But how can I get more out of him?

'Yes, but let me tell you what has been causing me concern. And it was causing concern also to Sir Rustom Engineer in Bombay. It is—'

Bullybhoy broke in.

'You don't want to pay too much attention to old Engineer,' he said.

'But-but that man was the first Indian appointed to be Commissioner of Bombay Police.'

'Yes, yes, I know all that. But, don't forget, that was in times past. Dare say even then his posting was made just to quiet rising Indian demands. Fellow can't have been any sort of a tiger, even in his full prime. A damn Parsi. And nowadays he must be halfway to the Towers of Silence, ready for the vultures to make a dinner of his corpse.'

Ghote felt resentment rising fast.

Should I be telling this pig-head fellow he is wrong, wrong, wrong? That the day must be far off when Sir Rustom will be taken to those five Towers of Silence to have, under full Parsi rites, the useless flesh plucked by crows and vultures from his dead body?

But more advice from Prince Hamlet. *Break my heart, for I must hold my tongue.* No, there may be more to learn from Bullybhoy, if I am keeping open my ears.

He soon learnt better.

'Barrani *bhai*,' he had asked, 'why do you think after all that Dawkins memsahib was committing suicide? Why? That is what I must be finding out. Why did she do that terrible thing?'

Bullybhoy slapped his two hands down on the almost empty surface of his desk.

'She just did,' he said. 'That's all there is to it. She took that gun, thrust it up to her face and shot herself.'

He shook his head in weary rebuke.

'No, Ghote,' he said, 'you will just have to learn in police work not to ask questions that are having no answer.'

CHAPTER EIGHT

Ghote, dressed in one of the new shirts and the pair of cotton trousers he had hastily bought in the bazaar – not altogether happy about the shirt's overlong sleeves – fought once again with the obstinate latch on the Primrose Cottage gate. Why, why, why, he thought, must there always be difficulties? Even sending a letter to my poor, deserted Protima was altogether troublesome. Asking Hotel Restful's sleep-happy proprietor for a letter-form had produced complication after complication even before I was just able to write on that flimsy green sheet my few hurried and worried words. And then, eager to get the folded sheet into the post, could I easily find a postbox?

And now there is the prospect of having to ask Dawkins sahib for permission to investigate every drawer and pigeon-hole in the bureau that had been his wedding gift to his dead wife. No more now than a token of remembrance of those first happy newly-wed months. Just like the bright new sofa cushions that Iris memsahib must have bought for the house she had newly come to.

What would I be feeling myself if-if...

No, say it, if just only in my head. If Protima is somehow dying when the baby is coming and some poke-nose police officer is stating he must examine each and every letter she had received in past six months, her diaries also... But, no, she has never kept a diary. All the same, what would I be feeling then? I would feel the fellow was trampling on everything of her that was precious to me. I would want to kick him down all the stairs of the block, right to the stones of the compound itself.

And this damn latch is just one more compli—

Suddenly the wretched thing sprang out of its niche, painfully grazing two of his fingers.

But the gate had swung open. Nothing for it now.

He set off past the long bed of sun-seeking cannas. Then from Protima's much-quoted *Hamlet* there came fully into his head, hovering at the edge of his mind as such words often did, *when sorrows come they come not single spies but in battalions*. How true that was.

But, in front of him, there was the blankly closed front door. A last moment of hesitation. And one good strong pull at the bell.

The appallingly loud jangle of noise from inside. And, swiftly as before, the *khansamah* appeared, immaculate from the gleaming chappals on his feet to his dazzling emerald-green puggaree.

Green, Ghote thought. Green like emeralds. But-but yesterday wasn't it an orange puggaree he was wearing. No, must have got it wrong. The fellow can't have two such fine turbans. Ones like this might cost rupees fifty, even more.

Then, in no time at all – puggarees wiped from his mind – he found himself face to face once more with Robert Dawkins. Or rather, owing to Dawkins' lack of the height that the former British rulers seemed always to possess, he found he was looking downwards into two glinting bluish eyes above the pale red flick of a moustache. The face of the man whose dead wife's most personal correspondence he was about to request to examine.

'Please...' he began.

Then all the muscles of his throat tightened into one appalling rope-hard twist.

He made an immense effort to relax, and, as suddenly as the garden gate's latch had given way, a spate of words emerged.

'Please, Dawkins sahib, please, I must be examining your wife's papers, whatsoever old letters she may have somehow not thrown away, her diary even if she was keeping same. It is my bounden duty. If I am ever to be able to tell you why— Why she—'

The gush came to a sudden end.

'Spit it out, man,' Dawkins sahib barked. 'Spit it out. Damn it, I know, I've known for weeks, that Iris took her own life. With my gun. But I want to know why. I want to know what her reason was. If you have to stick your damn nose into all her affairs to find that out, well then, you do. Go ahead, damn you. Go ahead.'

He swung away. But he did not, as Ghote had almost hoped, march out of the room.

'All right,' he went barking on. 'Go into Iris's private room, search her damned bureau. Don't think about what that'll mean to me. Your nasty prying fingers. Your filthy eyes hoping to find something you shouldn't ever see. Go on then. Go on.'

No, I cannot do it, Ghote thought. I cannot go and poke through his wife's most private papers, even though he does not come to watch over me.

He stood stock-still, a thin stony pillar opposite the sturdy rock who had now plumped himself back down on the squabby brightly coloured sofa, short legs with their heels-heavy tan shoes not quite reaching the carpet below.

'No, sir,' he managed at last to say. 'Perhaps it would be more of logical to start with the chest of drawers in-in the bedroom.'

And mercifully back came a grunted, 'Just as you like.'

He hurried off.

So for almost all the rest of that day, Ghote poked away at Iris Dawkins' large stock of clothes.

How much a white memsahib is seeming to need, he could not help thinking. Yes, Protima has altogether a good number of saris, too many even. But compared to all this that I am having to go through they are nothing.

But systematically he pulled open drawer after drawer, slipping intrusive fingers between layers of cotton, layers of silk, daring only to take out and unfold the woollen cardigans so as to look into their pockets. But he found not a trace of any tucked-away letter he had hoped he might discover. On two occasions only did his seeking fingers encounter something stiff that at least promised written words. Both turned out at a quick glance to reveal shopkeeper's script on receipted bills for garments, mercifully of not too intimate a nature. On he went but for long found nothing at all that should not have been there. He dared once even to cast a look at the sombrely tall rosewood wardrobe belonging to the master of the house. But, no, leave that to the very last, he thought, and turned back to the remains of Iris memsahib's stock.

And hit on something. Something that from its folded bulk could be nothing other than a letter.

Swiftly he slid it free, held it between his fingers for one moment, straightened it with every care. And read.

Dak Bungalow, somewhere off Pune-Mahableshwar Road.

Altogether disappointing as an address. No date either. Just a sprawling female hand.

Dearest Iris,

Well, here we are at yet another temporary resting place. Why ever did I marry a Forest Officer? But not too bad, the place, actually. Wonderful jungle you can really go for proper walks in, super wide open clearings one after another all within easy reach and all awash with lantana bushes, masses of tiny flowers, orange, pink, white and yellow. And the birds! Those delightfully pretty little green bulbuls – Do you remember them as the Indian nightingale? – and the ones they call minivets, beautiful singers too, something like a cuckoo to look at, if at Home you ever saw rather than heard one, but bright yellow and scarlet. Such colour. Yesterday I actually spotted a Golden Oriole. God, how I'll miss it when we do have to go back Home – and Peter keeps saying he can't stick India much more. Heaven knows, I've tried to delay the dread departure as long as poss. But…

Still, enough of that. Why I am writing is to ask how it's all going with you. You liking married life as much as I did in those first wonderful months with Peter? Months rather far off in the mists of time now, must admit. But I often think of you, and Peter does too, I'm sure. But you know the male brute. Or perhaps after – what is it? Two years at least – you still haven't encountered much of the brute. It was almost that long before I discovered it there underneath the decidedly amorous...

Ghote momentarily held the letter away from himself. Then, stiffened his shoulders – duty is duty – and plunged back.

...newly-wed. But this is no time to recall the golden days of yore. What I want to have is news from you. It's been ages since I have, and I worry about you, you know. A long, long letter, usual forwarding address. And soon!
    Your ever-loving Pansy
    PS: And Happy Christmas, when it comes.

Was there anything, anything at all, among all those female gushings? Must be much the same, I suppose, in any woman-to-woman letter written in Hindi or, above all, in Protima's out-pouring Bengali. But nothing, admit it, that gives me the least clue about Iris Dawkins' life here in Mahableshwar.
    So, plunge on. Next drawer down.
    But no other drawer, no corner of the almirah here contained even the smallest scrap of paper. Nothing for it now but that little bureau in that sewing room.
    He looked at his watch.
    Past six o'clock. Where has the time gone? But I was, at least, doing my duty all those hours. It is my duty to seek out every piece of information I can find about Iris Dawkins. And I have been doing that. To my level best. Yes, I was so hard at work I was not even really hearing that church clock sound out its six humming booms.

Perhaps, if I am lucky, I will find that Dawkins sahib has gone to dining room for his dinner. But, no. No, six o'clock is too soon for an English sahib to be eating. Should I pretend to carry on here in the bedroom until I can smell that dinner in my very nostrils? But, no. No, I cannot stay where I am. At any moment I will be hearing the clunk-clunk of his heavy shoes when he is coming here to put on different clothes. English sahibs always 'change for dinner'.

No, that bureau. I must deal with same now. However much of poke-prying I am doing. Perhaps there I will find some hint of some sorrow in another letter, perhaps one Iris began, failed to finish and then could not bring herself to tear up.

He crept along and slid his head cautiously round the door of the drawing room.

And no one there. The bright-flowered cushions of the fat sofa as plump as they had been before rock-heavy little Dawkins sahib had put his weight on the one in the middle.

He hurried off to Iris's sewing room, and went straight over to the pretty wedding-present bureau.

He found it, a little to his surprise, unlocked.

Did Dawkins sahib unlock for me? he thought with a little leap of pleasure. Is that a sign he is truly wanting me to go through each and every drawer in it, each and every little pigeon-hole? In case I am finding some clue there that will end his torments?

But before very long it became plain there was nothing Dawkins sahib might have brought himself to expose to the intruder's eyes. There was almost nothing at all to be found. The pigeon-holes were all empty. It looked, in fact, as if the whole pretty object had hardly ever been made use of. True, in one of the drawers there was a box of rose-pink writing paper, with *Primrose Cottage, Mahableshwar* printed at the top of each sheet, and beside it a box of matching rose-pink envelopes. But there was no sign that even a single sheet had been taken out of the box. And in the slim top drawer, Ghote's last hope, he found only a discarded fountain-pen, its grey rubber ink-reservoir heat-shrunken and useless, as well as three iron-hard unusable erasers, an empty bottle of Quink ink, royal blue, and a couple of pencils with chewed ends. Iris's teeth? But nothing in the end to be learnt from those few human marks.

He stood up at last, easing his aching back.

Then something came to him. Surely the whole little, scarcely used bureau said something about the woman who had, two years or so earlier, been given it as a wedding present. Did she have nothing she wanted to keep? Did she never retain anything as a souvenir? Did she, so unlike Protima with that box she has full to brim with old Diwali cards and faded letters from distant family members, have no active inside life? No life enriched with the past?

Seemingly not, he thought. But this insight is nothing like enough to take back to Sir Rustom as the answer to the mystery he put before me. And, worse, it is just only a feeling I am getting. It cannot possibly be told to Dawkins sahib, the man who gifted his new wife with this pretty, feminine little bureau.

So is every possible way forward blocked to me now? Nothing learnt from when I was talking to Dawkins sahib. Less even from the battering I was getting from Bullybhoy. It is as if the tangled creepers and thorny bushes of the deepest jungle stretch across each path in front of me.

Black gloom descended.

My first task as a newly created inspector, as a member of best-of-bunch Crime Branch, however unofficially given to me, a complete failure?

He stood where he was, looking at the closed front of the bureau.

And then he thought of the letter he had found that seemed to have something more than desert aridity in it, the letter from a woman by the name of *Pansy*, written in some dak bungalow in the jungle not far from Pune. Yes, surely here was someone who had known Iris before she was married. And she may even have had an answering letter to the one she had written as long ago as just before that universal holiday, Christmas.

So should I go to Pune and track down this lady who loves the jungle so well? And, wait, Dawkins sahib told me it was as the guest of a man called Watson, who was, yes, a Forest Officer, that he had met his violet-eyed bride. Perhaps this letter was from Mrs Watson. If Pansy and Mrs Watson turn out to be one and the same person, I can be learning much, much more from her. Yes. Yes, I must go to Pune *ek dum*.

CHAPTER NINE

Almost at once Ghote realised his sudden decision to go to Pune – he hardly knew how he had made it – might not open some obstacle-free path in front of him. First of all, he would have to explain to Dawkins sahib why, after only two days of inquiries, he was deserting Primrose Cottage. Even before he asked to see him, he became prey to a feeling he had been absurdly hasty to pin his hopes on that single gushing letter.

'Good God, man,' the British rock shouted when he had hastily looked over the scrawled sheet signed *Pansy* which Ghote had handed to him. 'If paying any attention to this endless twaddle is your idea of a thorough investigation I don't like to think what'll happen to crime in Bombay when you get back there.'

Ghote forced himself to treat that as if it was no more than a single monsoon gust of rain-flicking wind.

'Sir,' he said, 'I was asked by your friend, Sir Rustom Engineer, to conduct this inquiry. He was altogether trusting me. So, sir, if, after full consideration, I am deciding that the best chance of finding what was in the mind of your wife when she was taking her terrible decision, is to speak to any of her friends from the past I am able to find, then, sir, I must do same.'

'Humph.'

Ghote decided to take that ambiguous sound for agreement.

'So, sir, can you be informing whether the lady who was signing herself just only *Pansy* is the Mrs Watson in whose house, you were telling, you were first meeting your future wife?'

'You expect a damn lot, Inspector.'

Ghote almost gave up in the face of this renewed blast of British contempt. But he brought himself to produce a reply.

'Sir, you must be knowing the first name of the lady there.'

'Must I? You've a pretty wrong-headed notion of how a British gentleman behaves, Inspector. That's all I can say. Do you really think one starts using a lady's Christian name the moment you're introduced to her? I dare say such things happen among Indians. But I can assure you they don't in any sort of civilised circles.'

Ghote let all that swirl past him.

'Nevertheless, sir,' he said, 'you were staying for some time with your friends, Mr and Mrs Watson, long enough, sir, for you to be deciding you were wanting to marry the lady with violet eyes you had met there. So, sir, you must be knowing whether Mrs Watson was called Pansy.'

"Spose she was, if it's any concern of yours.'

'Then, sir, can you tell me where exactly they are now living? That letter had as address only *Dak Bungalow, Pune-Mahableshwar Road*. But my chance of finding same would be very much better if you were able to tell me more.'

'Good God, man, you're a police officer. Don't you even know how a Forest Officer lives? Two or three months in one location, three or four in another. How the hell should I know which dak bungalow the Watsons live in now. You'll have to use a bit of initiative for a change. Buzz up to Poona and make inquiries off your own bat.'

But, even after Ghote had taken leave of Dawkins sahib, he was still prevented from setting off on his mission. He had got, in fact, only as far as the cannas bed beside the front path when a familiar voice came up to him from somewhere inside it.

'Inspector sahib. Is more.'

Chintu.

He peered downwards and spotted that ribby brown back just a few inches above the bed's baked and well-weeded earth.

'Stand up, stand up.'

Fuming over this new frustration, he heard himself sounding as commandingly sharp as Dawkins sahib. Or nearly so.

'What it is?' he managed to ask more calmly as Chintu rose up in front of him like a rapidly growing canna plant himself. 'You have more to tell?'

'*Jee*, Sahib.'

'Then speak.'

'Sahib, two things I was seeing that day.'

'That day? What day?'

'Inspector, on day I was hearing bang of gun and running to bungalow.'

'All right. The day Dawkins memsahib died. But if you saw

something more then, two things itself. Why did you not tell me about them before?'

'Sahib, I was thinking you would not believe.'

'Oh, were you? And why, if you were thinking that, do you hope I will believe whatsoever story you are now making up?'

'Inspector, no one is believing Chintu when he is telling something, and never, never when he is telling two things.'

Ghote thought for a moment or so.

Yes, the boy has something of right in what he said. One might believe him if he is producing one unlikely story. But to produce two, one after the other, would exhaust at once what small store of belief he had earned for himself.

He sighed.

'Then tell, if you must.'

'Inspector, on that day, the day I was seeing Dawkins memsahib lying there with gun by her side, and blood-blood also, before that-all was happening, while I was weeding in this bed, as *Mali* is saying I must do every day because of yellow cannas, I was seeing a man beside the gate there.'

'A man? What sort of a man? And what was he doing at the gate? Was he coming in?'

'No, Sahib. When he was seeing my face looking from between two cannas he was going a little away.'

'He went off? That is not much to be telling.'

'But-but, Inspector sahib, it was not all. Inspector, I am thinking that was one bad man. Very, very bad, Inspector.'

Oh, yes. Of course. Damn boy is thinking he did well telling me about seeing Iris memsahib's body there, and he is trying something more, however much of nonsense, in case it will gain him more credit. But it will not.

'And what are you going to tell me next? That this very,

very bad man was carrying one gun? Is that it?'

'No, no, Inspector. Why would I say such a thing? It would be a story only. Someone like that would not ever have gun.'

'So what would he have then?'

Damn. I should not have asked that. I should not have asked one solitary thing more. Encouragement is the last thing a tale-teller like this Chintu is needing.

But he had asked. And he was getting an answer.

'Inspector, he was wearing one many-colours coat.'

'And that makes him a very bad man?'

'No, no, Inspector, not that only. But I have not ever seen a man, even young-young as he was looking, with coat like that.'

'What kind of coat it was? Was it long? Was it short?'

'Oh, Inspector, short-short.'

'Coming to his waist only?'

'Yes, yes. Like that. Like that. And in all-colours stripes.'

Ah, now, I see what the boy means. He does not have the word for it, but he has good observation. Dr Hans Gross would approve. Yes, if this person, this young man as he is saying, must have been wearing what they are calling in English a *blazer*. When it is the season in Mahableshwar, when it is so hot-hot down in Bombay, you might quite likely see down in the town itself young men in blazers, students or boys from schools, even if little half-pant Chintu never has seen such. But at this time of year, the month of Chaitra, I would not expect-

'Inspector, there is more to say how he is bad.'

He looked down at Chintu.

'Very well, what it is?'

'His eyes, Inspector.'

Oh, we have come to that now, have we? I suppose he is going to tell me the fellow, whoever he was – if he was ever here at all – is having the evil eye, one heavy squint at very least.

'No, Inspector, it was hard to see. But…but, Inspector, I am thinking his two blue eyes were each different. No. No, I am wrong. One only was different. A little-little different. Not same colour as other.'

Again, Ghote found himself crediting what Chintu had said, despite the unlikeliness of it. That one eye being only by a little of a different colour rings true. If the boy was just trying to gain favour with me, he would have made those eyes one brown and the other blue or one green and the other grey, to make his picture of a *badmash* all the more striking. But, no, he is not trying that.

'All right. There was this young man at the gate, just there. And he was wearing an odd sort of coat. All right, again. And there was something wrong about his eyes. All right, if you are saying it. But why are you telling me?'

'But, Inspector, it was the day Dawkins memsahib was dying, and that man was looking and looking at bungalow. And, Inspector, I am thinking I had seen before, three-four days before. In road outside.'

Ghote accepted the implied rebuke, however juvenile the lips that had uttered it. It was true enough: if someone had been standing looking in at the garden on the day Iris Dawkins had killed herself it was perhaps significant.

Yet is Chintu still trying to get something of kudos by making up this story?

Who can tell? But give him what they are calling *benefit of doubt*.

He dug in his pocket. Found a small coin. Handed it over.

'All right, I will remember that man. Now I am going away. Perhaps for some days. But I will be back. So, keep your own two eyes open, yes?'

It took Ghote, when at last he felt free to drive to Pune, lying more or less halfway between Mahableshwar and Bombay, a good many troublesome hours searching for a dak bungalow somewhere off the Pune-Mahableshwar road, the sole hint of an address on Pansy Watson's undated letter. When he arrived in ancient, streets-jumbled Pune he visited as first priority the main post office. Even finding that was no easy task. Once there, however, he could not discover anyone to give him any real help. There were, he was told with sullen lack of interest, innumerable dak bungalows to be found in the jungle.

'Yes, Inspector,' his most informative reply came, 'I am well knowing *dak* is the word for the post. But that is dating from old, old days when messengers were running from one such bungalow to another. Then the English sahibs of the Forest Service were able to wait one whole week for what was sent to them, even for *Times* from London after it was coming by ship itself to Bombay. But now postal service is one hundred per cent well organised. We have full lists of all recognised addresses. Postmen are calling at them each and every day. We are priding ourselves on efficiency.'

'So why cannot you tell me where is the dak bungalow I am looking for?'

His informant, the best he had yet found, looked at him with patent pride.

'In our eyes, Inspector,' he said, 'it is very-very likely such a place is not at all existing.'

'Not—'

'Inspector, deliveries are not made to structures that have not been registered.'

But the check was not the end of his trail. One last dribble of inquiry taught him that the Maharashtra headquarters of the Forestry Department, also in Pune, now received for onward transmission all letters addressed to any dak bungalow. Final deliveries from there were made daily, 'except only Sundays and Public Holidays'.

Ah, he thought, this must be why Pansy Watson's letter had on it just only that sort of half-address. She must know that Iris would send her reply to, in the first instance, the Forestry Department's central office.

'But today is not a Sunday,' he said to his informant, 'and it is not even any of the too many public holidays we are having. So, tell please, where can I be finding Forestry Department?'

But merely locating the Forestry Department Pune headquarters – made much more difficult by the fact that the ancient city was divided into separate *peths,* each with its own system of house numbering – still did not produce an immediate answer.

'Yes, yes, Inspector, of course we are having full list of dak bungalows in which officers may from time to time serve.'

'Very good. Now, where exactly off the Pune-Mahableshwar road will I be able to find the one from which this letter itself was written?'

He pointed to the scrawled address at the head of the letter Iris Dawkins had kept for so long.

'Cannot say, Inspector.'

'Cannot say, cannot say. Why not? Why? The bungalow is

there, somewhere. One of the Service's officers by name of Watson was inhabiting same at some time before Christmas, and it is now March only. Why cannot you tell me exactly where I should go to speak with him, as is my bounden duty?'

'Because you are having no number for that bungalow, Inspector.'

'I know I have no number. I was not, until just now only, aware your bungalows are numbered—'

'Then, Inspector, I regret I am unable to help.'

However, it appeared, after some sharp words had been uttered, that a degree of help was to be had. Ghote was shown on a wall, somewhere deep inside the building, a map, yellowed and dimmed with layer upon layer of varnish. On it, just distinguishable, he saw a scattering of little red dots, each with a number beside it. Some, in the course of time, rubbed almost completely away.

But at last, armed with the list he had managed to make of the bungalows on either side of the Pune-Mahableshwar road, he was able to set out again, ready to visit each dot in turn, moving as necessary from one side of the road to the other. When, after more fruitless inquiries than he felt inclined to count up, he saw the fast-falling dusk beginning to turn the sky above to grey, he decided – it was one of those decisions that seem to be enforced by circumstances – to head back to Pune, find a hotel, get something to eat and, above all, go to bed.

So it was not until the next afternoon that, halting the little Ambassador outside yet another jungle-buried dak bungalow, looking little different from any of those he had already located during the day, he thought he might at last have come to the end of his quest.

Outside it he had seen an Englishwoman, a lady in perhaps her late thirties, sensibly dressed in wide-brimmed white sun hat, khaki skirt and pale blue blouse. She was bending over a raggedy small girl, burnt almost black by the sun, crying loudly and, it seemed, unstoppably. Could she possibly be Mrs Pansy Watson?

Somehow hopeful, he approached with caution. Neither the little girl nor the English lady seemed to have heard him. The loud end-of-everything howling rang on and on. As did, he realised now, the soothing murmur intended to quiet the weeping girl.

'There, there. There, there. It's only a cut on your leg. If you stop crying, I'll be able to get a better look. It's all right, it's all right. You calm down and then...then I think I can find some nice cool ointment for that leg, and perhaps, if you're a very brave girl, a piece of *gur*.'

It was the brief mention of that sticky rough sugar that at last did the trick.

Tears ceased. English lady straightened up. Ghote spoke.

'Excuse me, madam, but it is Mrs Watson?'

'It is,' she answered with a slight frown. 'And who are you, may I ask?'

What Ghote wanted urgently to say by way of final confirmation was *Madam, is your name Pansy?* But he did not think that he could.

'I am Inspector Ghote, Bombay Police,' he said instead.

'Bombay Police? Aren't you rather out of your territory, Inspector?'

But the question had been put in a tone of simple curiosity, and Ghote had no difficulty in entering on an explanation.

'Hundred per cent correct, madam. But nevertheless I am

here, as it were, on duty. Madam, I am assigned pro tem to Sir Rustom Engineer, the former Bombay Police Commissioner, in order to make certain inquiries. Of a somewhat delicate nature. Madam, it is concerning Mrs Iris Dawkins.'

'Iris. What about her?'

Ghote realised then that the news of Iris's suicide could not have reached the Watsons. Most probably Dawkins sahib, stunned as he was by her inexplicable act, had not been able to write any letters conveying the news except for his one cry of distress sent, just a week or so ago, to his 'old friend' Sir Rustom.

But now, he thought, plunged deep into a pit of embarrassment, it is up to me to be breaking worst of bad news.

He breathed deeply in.

'Madam, you have not heard? Then, madam, it is my duty, my sad duty, to tell you that Mrs Iris Dawkins was, just only some weeks ago, committing suicide.'

There. Said.

Pansy Watson, still with a hand on the tears-stained little girl's shoulder, lost in an instant all the roses-and-cream colour of her cheeks.

But, almost as quickly, she recovered herself.

'Inspector, are you sure? Sure that Iris committed suicide?'

'Madam, there can be no doubts. Madam, it is because of that I am here to inquire into what you are knowing of the state of Mrs Dawkins' mind, and also of what sort of a lady she was even in the days when she was living with you in whatsoever dak bungalow you then had.'

For a moment Pansy Watson said nothing.

Then, visibly making up her mind what was the best thing to do, she gave her head a little shake.

'No,' she said. 'No, Inspector, you mustn't expect me to be able to talk about Iris. Not just now. No, I think what you'd better do is to go and tell my husband the news. He'll be – a man, you know – he'll be better able to tell you what you want, I think. So, let me get this poor little thing some Germolene and – more important – her piece of *gur*. You'll find my husband – he's back from his day's tour now – inside the bungalow.'

'Very good, madam. Perhaps it will be best if you are able just only to carry on with your works of mercy.'

Watson sahib, Forest Officer staying on with a Government of India contract after the majority of his fellow Britons had sailed away, was a man strikingly different in appearance from Dawkins sahib, equally staying on, though not so as to collect one last good lump sum before leaving India for ever. Watson sahib was, to begin with, tall. Must be six foot, Ghote thought. Or more. Two inches more, at least. And he is lean also. Lean in body, lean in deeply tanned face. Yes, altogether the right sort of British sahib to have been going from one area of jungle to another calmly laying down the law, assessing and dismissing. While it was hard to imagine Dawkins sahib doing anything like that, or not at least with self-possessed calm. Think of how he has shouted and sworn at myself.

'Right,' came a sharp request now. 'Just tell me what a police inspector from Bombay is doing out here in the depths of the jungle.'

'Sir, it is simple matter. I have been seconded pro tem to Sir Rustom Engineer, who, as you must be knowing, was first Indian to hold post of Commissioner of Bombay Police, to—'

'Never heard of him,'

Ghote was a little shocked.

He swallowed and began again.

'Very well, sir. However, that is not altering fact that, although I am an officer of Bombay Police Crime Branch, it has become my duty to investigate the circumstances of the death in Mahableshwar of the late Mrs Robert Dawkins.'

'The death? What death? I've heard nothing about Iris Dawkins dying.'

Then, once again, Ghote found himself the breaker of bad news. In the face of this unyielding figure, it was something he managed less well than he had succeeded in doing when he had been telling the news to his wife. And got a very different reception.

'Suicide? Suicide? What the hell can you want to know about Iris's death? If indeed it was suicide.'

'Sir,' Ghote looked up, up into the tanned, broad-nosed, darting-eyed face above him. 'Sir, I have to inform you that just only some weeks ago Mrs Iris Dawkins took her husband's twelve-bore gun from its locked almirah in their cottage – Sir, Primrose Cottage, in Mahableshwar – and, without leaving anything of any last note, put it to her head and shot herself. Sir, her husband, whom you must be well knowing as a friend, has no idea whatsoever why she did same. And, sir, it has become my duty to try to find some reason.'

'Has it?' Watson sahib snapped out. 'Has it indeed? And who told you that I would know what my wife's friend, Iris Dawkins, might have been thinking when she took up that gun. If she did take hold of it? Seems damn unlikely to me, mouse of a thing like her.'

'But, sir, yes. It has been beyond doubt established that she was abstracting that weapon from where it was locked away, and shooting herself also.'

'Has it? Established by you, I suppose. Well, let me tell you, I would want a lot better confirmation of all this before I even began to credit it.'

Ghote found himself faced, out of the blue, with yet another difficult decision. There was really only one man he could bring forward as properly confirming what Watson sahib seemed so unwilling to believe. Bullybhoy Barrani. And to produce Bullybhoy as a more reliable officer than himself was something that, since he had so sharply revised his opinion of his former batch-mate's manner of investigating, hurt more than he could ever have expected.

But it must be done.

'Sir, if you are wishing, you have only to contact Mahableshwar police station and ask for the in-charge, one Inspector Barrani. He was making full on-the-spot investigation. He would confirm to one hundred per cent what I have told.'

It was not enough.

'Listen to me, Inspector-Inspector Whoever-you-are. I want to hear no more of all this.'

'But-but, sir, your friend Mr Robert Dawkins is seeking to know if his wife was saying anything, in far-off days before he was meeting her, to give one clue only to why she should have taken her own life.'

Watson sahib glared at him.

'Look here, I've told you already. I've had enough of this. More than enough. Damn policeman asking damn questions. Iris Petersham was trouble enough when she was here. People nodding and winking about what the Rajah of Gopur's brat, dead now no doubt, and good riddance, did all those years ago. If Rob Dawkins really wants to know anything more about Iris, he can damn well come and ask for himself.'

'Very well, Watson sahib. I will no longer be troubling you.'

Ghote turned to go. Just minimally he hoped that the tall Englishman would add something. Anything that would give a clue to why he had so abruptly flared up and refused to say another word.

Is it just because he is an English sahib who has spent many, many years here in India and has learnt to have one low opinion of all Indians, whether coolies or police officers? Or, is it just possible that he does know something more about Iris Dawkins. Good gracious, I am just only learning that she was called Petersham before she was marrying. And is what he is knowing something somehow not to be spoken about? Is he sticking together with all the British sahibs and memsahibs and keeping secret whatsoever he is knowing?

But not another word boomed out at him as, almost creeping, Ghote left the bungalow. Then, as he stepped out of the door, from somewhere in the jungle the song of a brain-fever bird, the incessantly repeated three plaintive notes, each higher than the last, assaulted him.

Was I hearing that singing when I was first arriving, he asked himself, bemused. If I was, it meant nothing to me. But now. Now when I had thought I was at last about to learn something about Iris Dawkins, now, defeated once more, I feel as if I am the one who is suffering brain fever.

What an impossible task I have been given. Nothing but one setback after another. Each more insurmountable than the last. First it is Dawkins sahib doubting and shouting. Then it was Bullybhoy sneering and jeering. And next it was all the troubles I was having to just only find this dak bungalow. And now here I am, at end of tether – whatever is that English *tether* – and that damn bird is sing-sing-singing at me. Unless that one-two-three up, up and up song over and over again is in my head itself only.

What am I to do? What can I do now? How can I go to Sir Rustom back at Marzban Apartments, be swept up, up in that silent-silent lift, ring at his door and state that I am reaching end of tether? And without any successes at all? What will he say then? *It is seeming you are not the officer I thought you were, Ghote.* One black mark against me, to be sent to Assistant Commissioner Divekar. To be on my record for ever.

CHAPTER TEN

About to get back into the Ambassador, Ghote's eye was caught by the sight of Pansy Watson's blue blouse some little way inside the open jungle surrounding the bungalow. With her little patient evidently quieted with gur and sent back to her mother, she was standing beside the thick trunk of a tree, a Flame of the Forest as far as he could make out though it was too early in this month of Chaitra for its fire-red blossoms. Pansy seemed to be straining upwards to reach a newly flowering branch of bougainvillea clinging to its bark.

Shall I go over and talk to her again, he asked himself. Perhaps now she knows I have informed her husband of Iris Memsahib's death, she would tell me what she is knowing about Iris Petersham, as she was.

But, no.

No, Watson sahib has turned me out of his house. He has refused to say one word about Iris. So, it would be wrong of me to try to get that word out of his wife. Altogether wrong.

He pulled the Ambassador's door wide open. A heavy waft

of overheated air – he had thoughtlessly left the little car in the full sun – came tumbling out to envelop him. He stepped sharply back.

But what it is I am here for?

The question presented itself in his mind. With its answer.

I am here, at Sir Rustom Engineer's personal request, to see if I can find what came into Iris Dawkins' head before she went to that almirah, took from it the twelve-bore and also from the small drawer inside a single coloured cardboard cartridge and, just a minute or two later, shot herself.

So I must make every possible inquiry. My bounden duty. And there, not fifty yards away from me, is the lady who most probably could tell me what Iris's life was like in the time before she did that unthinkable thing. I have, yes, some evidence in that letter she wrote. And especially of four words in it *I worry about you.*

They were there, written in that sprawling feminine hand. And they are proving that this lady over by the tree, which may or may not be a Flame of the Forest, was a good friend to Iris Dawkins. A good enough friend to be worrying about her. And why should she have been doing that? Answer must be: there was something to be worrying about.

So, go over and ask.

Or…or not.

Oh, decide, decide, you *man who could not make up his mind.*

No, I will go. It is my duty.

No, I will not go. After what Watson sahib was saying to me it would be wrong.

He thrust his head into the car's interior. Hot. Still stiflingly hot. He drew back and swung round.

In less than half a minute he had marched over, almost run, tripping once on a low-growing thorny shoot from a kika bush, to the towering tree and the woman in the blue blouse and pale khaki skirt.

A thought was exploding in his head.

'Madam. Madam, excuse me. Madam, there is something I must know from you. Madam, just at this moment I am realising why you would be sure to tell me. Madam, you are loving India. You are loving the beauty of the jungle. That branch of purple flowers you are holding now tells me that. Madam, more. You are loving each and every child of India. You were giving Germolene, and *gur* also.'

Pansy Watson looked towards him. She was smiling.

'Well, Inspector, you are right, of course. I do love India. I love everything about extraordinary India, all the beauty and, yes, all the horrors and the way they are somehow more colourful, more – what shall I say? – well, more beautiful than they would be back at Home, in steady everyday England. I'm not at all sure how I shall bear it when Peter... When my husband takes me there, to Home. I really don't know.'

'Then, madam, because you are a lady full of feeling. I would say almost an Indian lady, like my wife itself. Then...then, madam, please tell me why in a letter you wrote some time ago to your friend, Mrs Iris Dawkins, you were saying *I worry about you.*'

'A letter? I don't think...'

'But, madam, you were saying also *Happy Christmas when it is coming.*'

'*When it is coming*: doesn't sound quite my style. Oh, but wait. Yes. Yes, I remember. I did say, in a long letter I wrote to Iris, something like *Happy Christmas when it comes*. And

when it did come she did answer, though only with a card.
One with robins on it. God knows where she found that in
Mahableshwar. She didn't add much to the printed *Happy
Christmas* but she did underline that *Happy* and scrawled that
she'd write later. Though, in fact, she never did. But then, I
imagined, she just went on being happy, mindlessly happy,
forgetful of everything else. Because, you know, when she
accepted Robert she did, well, sort of step into happiness.
Poor thing.'

Ghote was struck then with a feeling of acute dismay. He
had heard things he was sure Pansy memsahib would regret
later having said to a stranger, and an Indian stranger at that.
But he could not help pressing further.

'Madam, *poor thing* you were saying. Madam, why did
you call her as such? Why were you all the time worried about
her?'

'Because Iris was a poor unhappy thing, if ever there was
one.'

She gave Ghote a steady look.

'I'm not sure I should tell you this. In fact, I'm sure I
shouldn't. But…but, well, I've already said more than I ought,
and you were careful to say when we met first that you were
making – I think you put it – *delicate inquiries*. Something like
that. So, I suppose, even though you are a police officer, you
must be a man of – What shall I say? – a man with some
sympathy for others. So, right, what the heck, I'll go on.'

'Madam, thank you.'

Which earned him another smile, though one not without
a last shade of indecision.

'All right, let me tell you the history of Iris Petersham's
unhappy life, her very unhappy life.'

Ghote stood there under the tall tree – Yes, it was a Flame of the Forest – and held his breath.

'Very well, the first thing you ought to know is that Iris Petersham was actually born Iris Mountford, the daughter, the only child, of Sir Ronald and Lady Mountford. Sir Ronald was an ICS high-up, Resident Advisor to the youngish Rajah of Gopur, a state, as you may know, that was, before Independence, small but wealthy and quite important. And something utterly appalling happened to both of them. They were out on tour together in a remote corner of Gopur. In camp. And one night—'

She came to a choked halt, bit her under lip and began again.

'One night an elephant in musth— You know what that is. You're an Indian, you should, though city-bred Indians often have no idea. It is the state an elephant gets into when it's in – I looked this up in the dictionary when I first heard of it, when I was about eleven – *a condition of frenzied sexual excitement occurring in male elephants and other species*. You can imagine the giggles and blushes that caused when I told my friends.'

She gave a laugh. And cut it short.

'Not a laughing matter, that frenzied elephant, for poor little Iris. God, no. You see, it trampled right over the Mountfords' tent and-and killed them both outright.'

'Madam, that is terrible. Terrible. And their daughter left, an only child you were saying. It is altogether horrible.'

Pansy Watson looked at him, the bougainvillea spray trailing in her hand.

'If that were only the worst of it,' she said.

'There is more? More, and more of worse?'

'There is. And it's what, I'm afraid, you ought to know if you're to report to – who did you say? Yes, Sir Rustom Somebody or other – with some sort of explanation of why poor Iris may have done what she did.'

She stood again in silence.

What it is, Ghote asked himself, that she is believing she must tell me? Something yet more shocking than Sir Ronald and Lady Mountford, sleeping in their tent worn out after one long day of shikar, in one moment altogether blotted out by that elephant in musth, leaving all alone their daughter, Iris?

Then Pansy Watson roused herself from her faraway thoughts.

'Yes. This, Inspector. Young Iris – she was twelve then, almost thirteen – was not in camp with her parents, as she well might have been. She was at the Residence in Gopur and was frequently invited to the palace, where she was friends with the Rajah's two children, a girl and a boy. But—'

Again a halt.

And it looked to Ghote that Pansy Watson might be about to change her mind, brush him aside and announce that what she had been about to tell him was something she could not bring herself to do.

Then abruptly she made a quarter turn so that the two of them came exactly eye-to-eye, blue to brown, just some eighteen inches apart.

And the bougainvillea branch, Ghote saw averting his gaze, had slipped from her hand and lay, ignored, beside her sensible tan shoes.

'Yes,' she said. 'Yes, what no one could have foreseen was that the Rajah's boy, a lad of much Iris's age, who was...'

She sought for words.

'Yes. Well, who was a lot more sexually aware than we, in England, think of boys of twelve as being. However wrong, probably, we are. Do you understand what I'm trying to tell you?'

Ghote did. He had got there in a single moment.

'Oh, yes,' he said. 'I am altogether realising what it must be.'

'You are, Inspector?'

Ghote felt he must do whatever he could to help this kind and friendly English lady to say what, perhaps, she had never said before, certainly not to an Indian inspector of police she had only just met.

'Yes,' he said, picking his way. 'This son of the Rajah of Gopur, aged, you were saying, twelve only, was having sexual intercourse with the daughter of the Resident in Gopur State, also twelve years of age. And-and, am I right, she had perhaps become pregnant by him?'

'Yes, you are right. I am one of the few people, the few English people, now that everyone more or less has left, who knows the full circumstances. Well, my husband does too, of course, though he never talks about it all. But I have managed, because I realise you really ought to know, to tell you. You're somehow...'

Her voice trailed off.

They stood there under the shade of the high Flame of the Forest, neither of them speaking.

At last Pansy stooped and picked up her purple bougainvillea.

'Well, there's more to tell,' she said. 'You had better know all there is to know now. Everybody who was aware of the situation at the time did their best to hush it up, of course.

Little Iris was ready to give birth. You know that, especially with the very young, such things hardly show at all, sometimes till the birth has actually begun? So it was possible to hurry Iris into St Agnes Convent in Poona, and for the child to be born – it was a boy – really in almost total secrecy. Then right away Iris was packed off Home, having actually seen her baby only once, not even long enough to take in the colour of his skin or his eyes, or anything about him.'

'This baby boy?' Ghote asked, almost breathlessly. 'What was happening to him?'

Protima. The thought had burst in on him like a rocket flare. Protima at this very moment carrying my child. My son? Or my daughter? But whichever it is, they, unlike that nameless, featureless boy born in St Agnes Convent in Pune, will be welcome, be loved, be cared for in every way.

Pansy paused, looked at him sharply.

'All right,' she said. 'The new-born child was simply sent off to Gopur as soon as it was possible. To the palace, I suppose, and later was lost to sight. No one there then would have wanted a half-and-half to be one day, possibly, heir-in-law to the *gaddi* and it was, of course, likely enough the Rajah would have other sons and would want to make the eldest of them his heir. But, in fact the Rajah's wife, in giving birth to her second child, became incapable of having other children, though not of living on and on herself. She's alive today indeed.'

A new wave of black thoughts swept over Ghote now. What if Protima, too, becomes incapable of having more children when our baby is born? And-and she may even die in giving birth.

Compressing his lips hard together he fought down the black ideas.

'But why,' he asked, voicing the only words that came to him, 'why was Iris's baby not sent – when he was old enough to travel – to England and his mother?'

'All right, I dare say you're thinking we memsahibs then were totally callous. It was, of course, the memsahibs who conducted the whole business. And that I was as callous as any of the others, but…but really I wasn't. It was just that I was much the youngest, only in fact some seven or eight years older than Iris herself, and I couldn't protest at what women much senior to me had decided was best.'

'Madam, I am understanding.'

It was the best he could do.

'Well, there's not much more to tell. And in any case at Home Iris had been semi-adopted by some fairly distant Mountford cousins, people called Petersham—'

'Ah, I see now how the name changed.'

'Yes. The name changed. And, I must tell you, Iris's circumstances changed too. For the worse. For much the worse. I suppose those people, the distant cousins, who frankly were no more than lower middle-class, resented being landed with a just thirteen-year-old they had till then, with the Mountfords being out here in India, hardly realised existed. But they treated her, as she told me eventually, as if she were a cross between a slave and pariah. Did nothing for her that they could avoid, never sent her to school, just kept totally quiet about her. So, as soon as she could, as soon in fact as she was of an age to act independently, she found herself some sort of a job, in London, I think, and then moved on from that to something a little better and, when eventually she had collected up enough savings, she came back here. To India, where she had once been happy. Came to us, as a matter of fact. She was hoping to find work, perhaps in Poona. And then she met Peter's rather stodgy friend, Robert.'

And now what, Ghote asked himself. Here am I, just only having been told what ought to be a great secret in the world of the white sahibs, and what shall I say? What shall I do?

Then it struck him that there was one thing he ought to do. One question he ought still to ask. An unaskable question.

He took in a deep breath. Do it. Do it now. Do it even before you have decided to.

'Madam,' he said, 'I must ask this. Madam, Iris Dawkins' husband? Could he... Was he... Madam, do you know this? Was he being unfaithful to her?'

It would be an answer, the answer to why she did what she did.

And Pansy Watson laughed. She actually laughed.

'Oh, Inspector, no. Not possibly. And not only because he was totally in love with Iris, comically in love with her. Though so restrained that I never once saw him actually kissing her in all the time they were here. But, no. No, I don't, in fact, believe he had ever made love to any woman, white lady or even black no-good, in all his life. He just didn't give anyone any feeling of that.'

'Madam, thank you,' Ghote brought out at last. 'Madam, my deepest thanks. If ever Mr Robert Dawkins' mind is to become once more calm with that mystery of what was in his wife's head being solved, it would be through you. Madam, thank you.'

He realised then that the brainfever bird had long before ceased its monotonous singing.

CHAPTER ELEVEN

Ghote drove away from the Watsons' jungle bungalow deep in thought. Have I, he asked himself, learnt enough to be able to say I know now why Iris Dawkins, Iris Petersham, Iris Mountford took her own life? Certainly, I am now having a very different picture of her. I am seeing she was not at all just only the quiet English lady Robert Dawkins met when visiting his old friend, Watson sahib. Behind her shy-seeming outside there was a woman who, as a young girl, had had a terrible experience. After, no doubt, some cuddling and kissing with a son of the Rajah of Gopur of much her own age, perhaps as a simple English schoolgirl, hardly knowing what was happening, she had learnt she was going to have a baby. A fearful thing, not to be admitted, not even to be thought about.

And then...then, hardly having given birth to that male child, to find herself shipped away to an England she must scarcely have remembered. There, accustomed all her life to all the fine things a child of the British Resident in Gopur State would be used to, to be made almost into a servant in cold and bitter England. A mind-altering series of shocks.

And Dawkins sahib is not at all knowing anything of it. He cannot have done. If Iris memsahib had brought herself to tell him her sad history – and it is hard to see her doing same – then he himself would have known what might have lain behind her terrible decision. That in some sudden flood of remembrance she had decided not to bring into a world where things such as she had gone through could happen one more child. Her child.

So, now, is all that I have to do to go back to Bombay and ask to see Sir Rustom once more? To tell him what I am finding out and leave him to pass it on, in whatsoever way he is thinking fit, to his friend of old, Mr Robert Dawkins? Then all my troubles would be over. I would be having full credit for carrying out the very, very tricky task I was given. I will be able, on the first day of next month itself, to take up my posting to Crime Branch. To Crime Branch, that mountain top I was fearing always I would never get to see.

And, also, I will be back in Bombay, even if it is for the time being in our cramped flat at the top of the barracks block at Dadar PS. I will be with Protima, my loved wife who is carrying the baby who will be my first-born son. Or daughter, or daughter. To be born soon. When I am there to see.

Yes, that good time, that wonderful time, is just in front of me.

But...

But somehow it is not. I must admit so much, however hard it is to do. I must admit the account I could be giving to Sir Rustom is not complete, not to one hundred per cent. It is as if I would be showing him Iris memsahib, not as she was in her real life, but as she might have been in some film. Or, as she might be in a photograph only. A photograph of a pretty lady, like the photograph Dawkins sahib was thrusting and thrusting into my hands when he was taking it from that drawer in his desk after he could not find its right key.

In his mind's eye he saw now that likeness of Iris memsahib, right down to its painted wooden frame.

But, no, is it not even her proper likeness. It is not. There is, surely, something missing from it. What it is? Easy answer: of course it is not a picture of a woman who has undergone the terrible experience that had happened to little Iris Mountford, that had brought a still shocked and scared Iris Petersham to whatever dak bungalow the Watsons had been living in three years or so ago to meet a man who would propose marriage to her. An end to her nightmare life.

Or not an end to it? Had it finally turned out that Robert Dawkins was not the man to overcome the dark thoughts deep in his wife's mind? And, thinking it over, I am not at all sure Dawkins sahib could be such a man. No.

He brought the Ambassador, still oven-hot, to a halt at the edge of the wide road that would have taken him, had he gone on driving along it, at last to Bombay and Sir Rustom.

No, I must think, he told himself.

No, I do not need to think. I do not need to. What I must do is to drive on to Bombay, but not to Marzban Apartments. Instead to-to the studio of *Too Good Clicks*. Yes, before I am seeing Sir Rustom and telling what I think I have discovered about Dawkins memsahib I must go to that photographer. I must find out just how good Mr Too-Good-Clicks is at his trade. I had thought back at Primrose Cottage that he might not be *too good*, that he had made some mistake in clicking that photo of violet-eyed Iris.

But was I right? True, there was something wrong about the photo, about – yes? – the violet eyes Dawkins sahib was so much praising. But it may be that the photo was not the best one the fellow took. There may be others, and better ones, telling me more.

Yes, there is something more to do. Perhaps one last thing before I can be certain. I must find out if there is a better copy of that framed photograph. And, yes, the proprietor of *Too Good Clicks* may very likely have one. Such people do more than click one only shot. Think how many that fellow in Mahatma Gandhi Road was taking of Protima and myself when we were first married. If Mr Too-Good-Clicks was even half as quick-fire with his camera as our fellow, he will have pictures in plenty of Iris Dawkins. And some, or one only, may be just a little bit better than that framed one shut away in Dawkins sahib's desk drawer.

If it is, if such a photo exists, I may be able somehow to confirm from it what I have thought must be Iris Dawkins' state of mind. The state of mind, long kept under, that at last made her take her own life.

Worth trying. At least worth trying. Alone in Bombay, sent there by her withdrawn husband, sitting and sitting facing the scrutiny of the camera, would she have revealed something of the thoughts she could not keep out of her head?

A heavy truck came roaring past, shaking the little Ambassador right down to its worn tyres. The smell of exhaust lingered in the hot air.

So where to find Mr Too-Good-Clicks? But where, where in entire Bombay, will I be able to find that *Too Good Clicks* studio?

But wait, wait. There was something more printed under that framed photo than just the name of the studio. There was...there was, yes, a telephone number.

He closed his eyes tight, endeavoured to bring to mind again that actual photograph in its painted wooden frame. *The photo thrust into my hands for barely a minute for me to admire. And I was doing that. I was admiring, as much as I could make myself say that I was.*

A second truck came roaring and rattling past.

Damn it, why can't they...

And, suddenly back into Ghote's head came the few words printed at the foot of that frame. *Photo by Too Good Clicks, Bombay.* And then...then, yes, it is there. *Tel: 42-*

No. No, something wrong about that.

Think. Look. Look at what is in my head. Look. See. And...

Yes, 40

Yes, yes. It was beginning 40 and...yes, yes, yes. Ending 28. Yes, Bombay 4028. Definitely.

So, telephone the place. Ask just only Where can I find your studio? And it will be done.

Except in this little box of a car there can be no such thing as telephone. Perhaps, perhaps one day in far future there will be telephones that can go in cars. Perhaps. But not in the India of today. Wirelesses, yes, in some police vehicles. But no telephones.

So, what to do? Again, easy answer. Drive on till I am getting to Pune once more, and then go again to post office. There, while I was asking and asking for address of the dak bungalow off Pune-Mahableshwar road, I was seeing in the big hall, past those slow-slow lines of people waiting to send telegrams, noticeboards listing helpfully *Useful Greetings for all religious and private occasions*. And, yes, underneath those there had been no fewer than four – no, five – public phones.

In Pune an hour or so later he had the pleasure, not altogether expected, of hearing his call to Bombay promptly answered. For once, too, promptly put through and without error.

'*Too Good Clicks*, Mr Chakrabarty, proprietor, speaking'.

Chakrabarty, he had registered. A Bengali name. And doubtless in the usual Bengali way, even in Bengali Protima's way, this fellow will, even from the moment I have got him on the phone, start to talk-talk-talk.

All right, put one stop to that straight away.

'I am phoning all the way from Pune,' he snapped out. 'One thing only I am wanting to know: the address of your establishment.'

He got it. Replaced the receiver.

It was not until early next morning, however, after a night of little sleep in the Pune hotel he had used before, that he was able, sitting in the heat-fuming Ambassador somewhere along the huge sweep of Bombay's Marine Drive, to study the frontage of the *Too Good Clicks* studio, just a little way into a turning, lined with small blocks of flats, called C Road.

Too Good Clicks, he thought, is something of a disappointment. I had long ago fixed in my mind that it ought to be an establishment somewhere in one of the city's main shopping streets. Smart and attractive to passers-by. But, no. Here it is in this out-of-the-way residential area, and by no means looking smart enough to be in some posh location like

Nepean Sea Road or near Malabar Hill itself.

And, as soon as he had fully taken in beneath the garishly painted *Too Good Clicks* name above its window, his doubts began rapidly to harden. Across the back of the window he could see, even from the far side of Marine Drive, there was hanging a large painted canvas, drooping at one corner. Evidently it must once have been used as a back-drop for photographs taken inside. But it showed, not Bombay's landmark Taj Mahal Hotel, but, more or less, the great Taj Mahal itself in far, far away Agra. Scarcely a likely setting for any citizen of Bombay wanting to get themselves immortalised on shiny paper.

And there was, too, he thought now, something else odd about the place.

Why had Robert Dawkins chosen to send his new wife to such a shabby sort of establishment, rather than to, say, the big Army and Navy stores? Or to a studio somewhere altogether more central? Perhaps, of course, he simply had not known anything about photo studios and their standing. He might have just only found this address somewhere, anywhere.

But, on the other hand, might it be that a sahib who had never seen himself as being married, a man despite his ferocious manner fundamentally every bit as shy as the lady who, in a moment almost of madness, he had asked to be his wife, could not bring himself to escort her to a photographer's studio? To stand arm-in-arm with her while the camera clicked away?

Well, perhaps that question will be answered in one minute when I am getting out of the car here, crossing the wide road and entering the studio just into C Road opposite.

Good. Decision is already taken in my head. So, now take same in reality.

He got out of the Ambassador, carefully locked its door behind him, looked both ways along the broad road – few vehicles in sight at this very early hour – crossed, went along to the studio. Pushed at its door, heard a bell above it give a single sharp *ting*.

The door yielded. Good, I have not come altogether too soon. Mr Too-Good-Clicks must be an early riser, wanting to get to his place of work

The studio was not particularly large, just a single open floor covered with a heavily patterned carpet, which, had it been newer, might have spoken of rich luxury. At its dead centre there was standing a throne-like gilded chair, a small table beside it holding a single large and ornate teacup on an ornate saucer. Facing the rather tattered throne were the tall, black-painted legs of a tripod, without any camera topping it.

Now, thrusting aside a bright-coloured glass-bead curtain at the back, a man appeared. Wildly all-over-the-place hair dyed blacker than hair ever could be, with, perched on a large beak of a nose, a pair of horn-rimmed spectacles, one lens rather crooked.

'Mr Chakrabarty?' Ghote asked.

'Yes, yes. That is myself. Sole proprietor *Too Good Clicks*, Bombay's altogether best photographic studio, though I am saying it. Yes, we may not look so posh as some other studios, studios I shall not name. But, believe me, my good sir, my work quite simply excels each and every one of them. Some of those people owning such places are not even true photographers themselves. They are merely employ—'

Ghote broke in.

'Mr Chakrabarty, I am not intending to have my photograph clicked.'

'Not?'

From the Bengali one single syllable. But a deeply shocked one.

Ghote poured his forces into the breach.

'No. I am the person who was telephoning you from Pune last evening. I have driven directly from there – one very early start – to ask you some questions only. I am an Inspector of Police. Ghote, by name.'

'Police? Police? But I have—'

'Never mind what you have or have not done. That is no concern of mine. What I am wanting to know is whether you are remembering taking the photograph, some time ago, of a British lady by the name of Mrs Iris Dawkins.'

He held the wild-haired Bengali firmly in his gaze.

'Yes? Or no?'

'Yes, yes. Yes, I am remembering well. You know, I am not having so many British ladies coming here. I am not able to think why. But perhaps it is because the British are not at all artistic. When they are wanting their photograph clicked they—'

'Mr Chakrabarty, I am not at all interested in whether the British are or are not artistic. Kindly listen to the questions I am asking.'

'Yes, yes, Inspector. But—'

'Number One: Do you have any copy of the photo you took when Mrs Dawkins was here? I have seen original, with the name of your studio printed under, and I wish to examine a better print, if you are having.'

'But, of course, Inspector. Of course, I am having. A

photographer who is knowing his business never fails to click others and to keep copies. It is best practice. Best practice. And you will never find Amit Chakra—'

'I want to see.'

'See? See? What see?'

'The copy prints you are holding of the photo you took of Mrs Iris Dawkins.'

'Yes. Yes, of course. I was only first explaining how—'

'The prints, Mr Chakrabarty.'

The sole proprietor of *Too Good Clicks* gave Ghote one quick frightened look, turned and thrust his way back through the jangling, colourful glass-bead curtain.

Ghote, after a moment, walked quietly up to it and moved its two middle strings gently apart. It would never do to lose sight of such a seemingly dubious character as the *Too Good Clicks* sole proprietor. Or, as Ghote had begun to believe, of the studio's sole occupant, sole photographer, possibly even sole sweeper.

But through the gap he had made in the curtain he saw now that the fellow had at least gone straight to an ancient painted and re-painted chest of drawers. He was tugging open the topmost drawer and peering into it. Patiently Ghote waited, hands either side of the curtain beads.

Certainly, if the *Too Good Clicks* studio did little business among Bombay's British community, it appeared to do well among the less affluent of the many races, from the Burmese to the Chinese, drawn into the ever-hungry metropolis. Photographs after photographs soon were piled on the surface of the chest.

But at last, still watching, he saw Mr Chakrabarty pick out a whole sheaf of photos tied together by a length of twisted pink ribbon – he glimpsed the top one as being in colour – and shuffle the rest of the heap roughly together. Taking care not to set off the least clacking noise from the curtain, Ghote stepped away.

When the tall, stooping Bengali came in, Ghote was sitting quietly in the grimy throne-like chair.

'Yes, yes,' Mr Chakrabarty at once announced. 'I have located the complete file of all the photographs of Mrs Iris Dawkins that I was clicking, despite the passage of time. Yes, despite that. The benefit of a proper and rigorous system of filing. Very necessary, very necessary. There must be seven-eight shots I was taking. It is always best to take more than customer is—'

Ghote thought he had already allowed too much bottled-up verbiage to be released.

But he was not quick enough.

'Yes, yes,' the Bengali raced on. 'And such was especially, I was thinking, worth doing with a British lady, and one who was – it was evident, evident at each and every minute – altogether worried-purried. Can you believe, Inspector, that when she came to collect my photograph she was taking it without giving it so much as a single glance? Inspector, that is something that has never happened to me. Never, neither before nor since.'

But Ghote was not going to hear one syllable of self-praise more, for all that what Chakrabarty had said was yet more contributory evidence for what he was coming to understand.

'Mr Chakrabarty, show me those photographs.'

Glancing at him with a touch of sharp anxiety, the Bengali slid the grimy pink ribbon off the sheaf and handed over the whole small bundle.

Ghote looked first at the photo he had just glimpsed in the Bengali's hands as he turned from the heap on his chest of drawers. A duplicate of the one Dawkins sahib had thrust at him.

Yes, it was exactly the same. Except, he realised as he looked at it more intently, it was not exactly the same. It was plainly the full-face, well-lit shot Mr Chakrabarty had clicked all that time ago, but, thanks perhaps to some extra care in the printing, it showed just slightly more than Dawkins sahib's original had.

It showed, very clearly, those violet eyes that had so imprinted themselves on the British rock's memory. But now Ghote could see that the eyes were not exactly violet. Yes, the right one held that pure colour, though it was rather more a deep blue than true violet. But the left one had in it – it was plain to see – a little triangular shape of what could only be limpid green. In Dawkins sahib's framed copy the spot had appeared to be no more than a tiny blemish. But now it was clear that Mr Chakrabarty was truly a skilled photographer. His camera had singled out that one flick of lucid green in the left eye. There could be no doubt about it.

Yes, Ghote thought, Dawkins sahib, that rock-like man, has somehow been deluding himself in thinking that his wife was a contented, soft violet-eyed creature. Dawkins, despite all his thundering white sahib's assurance, must at heart be a man unsure of himself, willing himself to believe, not what was in front of his eyes, but what he is feeling he ought to be seeing.

But if Dawkins sahib is unsure of himself, does that provide any real confirmation of what I was beginning to think was the reason his new wife, carrying their first child, should suddenly have killed herself?

No – he sighed – No, not any real confirmation. No, I cannot go from this wretched studio up to Malabar Hill and put my case to Sir Rustom. Not yet.

He shuffled through the rest of the photos in the sheaf. Iris memsahib had been taken in half a dozen different poses, none of them showing her to better advantage than the full-face one that Dawkins sahib had paid for. She appeared sitting straight-backed in the shabby throne-chair. She appeared standing behind it, her hands clasping its upholstered back, clamped in irritation perhaps. She appeared standing on her own, rather awkwardly. She appeared sitting holding in her left hand the large teacup now on the table beside the throne-chair. She was evidently making a firm effort to appear to be no more than a tranquil British memsahib in exotic India.

He handed the sheaf back to Mr Chakrabarty who, with immense care, re-wound his length of dirty pink ribbon cross-wise over it.

Watching the infuriatingly slow process, Ghote admitted to himself how little he had learnt starting out from Pune even before sun rise. But, wait, he thought, one other thing I have learnt. I have learnt that Iris Dawkins was altogether a worried-purried lady when she was here having that solemn photograph clicked. And, more, I have learnt also that she did not stop for a moment before she took to her husband at Primrose Cottage the photograph this Bengali talker-pawker had clicked, not even giving it one quick glance.

So, even as far back as that time, was she not the happy woman she should have been? Would a happy woman send, to her friend Pansy Watson in place of the *long letter* she had been asked to write, just only a Christmas card with that one word *Happy* quickly underlined?

Something to think about. Yes.

Out of the corner of his eye he saw that the photographer had at last succeeded in knotting up his grimy pink ribbon.

At any moment, he realised, the fellow will start again.

'Mr Chakrabarty,' he snapped out. 'You have been helpful. Thank you.'

He turned and made for the door. From above him, as he tugged it wide, came the sharp *ting* of its bell.

But he thought as he unlocked the door of the Ambassador, all the while I was driving here to Bombay, underneath I was thinking of Protima. I was asking even if my true purpose in driving all that way was, not to check if *Too Good Clicks* could tell me anything new about Iris Dawkins but to have an excuse to come back here and for some few minutes only to see my wife. To hear if all is well behind that billowing swell of her sari.

Shall I now drive up as far as Dadar? It would not take very much of time.

But it would. Bombay's busy day had in the short time he had been in Mr Chakrabarty's studio come into full hurrying, scurrying, fighting and struggling life. I might have to wait for minute after minute before I can even get to Sir Rustom's Ambassador across on the far side, swirling as the wide road is with vehicles of every sort pushing and jostling on their way to the business heart of the city. Oh God, traffic will be equally appalling all the way up to Dadar. No, it will take, not just only a few minutes to get there, but almost one hour. And even then I would have to be getting back to the road for

Mahableshwar where I must be going once more to Primrose Cottage. There must be some very-very careful questioning there. I must tell Dawkins sahib something about what I have learnt these two last days, and then see what is his reaction.

He stood where he was, stone still, for two minutes more. But at the end of it he knew, as he had done the moment he had become aware of the thundering sound of the reawakened traffic, that he was not going to see Protima.

No, it is my duty, my bounden duty, to get back to Mahableshwar – one six-hour drive – as soon as I possibly can. There is more to be found out there. There must be.

CHAPTER TWELVE

Perhaps encouraged by thinking of duty being done, Ghote made exceptionally good time on his way back to Mahableshwar. So it was not much after one p.m. that he tugged once more at the bell-pull at Primrose Cottage. From inside he heard again the noisily jangling bell. But nothing else. The whole bungalow seemed fast asleep behind its lowered *chiks*, no doubt still well wet from their morning dousing.

But where, he asked himself, is the boy who must earlier have thrown his pails of water over them. Where is Chintu? Not any sign of him from the depths of the cannas bed.

He stood and waited. This must be the first time that *Khansamah* has not appeared even before the ears-splitting bell inside has stopped to ring.

But, no, here he is, resplendent as ever. Perhaps the very thoughts in my head have produced him.

But at once now things ceased to go according to expectations.

One look from beneath the bright-coloured puggaree – golden-yellow today – and—

'Sahib is not to be disturbed,' the towering figure pronounced. 'He is having tiffin.'

'But—'

'You must come back after three o'clock when he has had his *aram*. He may see when he is up.'

After a moment Ghote turned away, without speaking.

Had I known, he said to himself dolefully, that Dawkins sahib likes 'not to be disturbed' while he eats his tiffin and has his rest also, I could easily have found time in Bombay to go up to Dadar and see Protima. I could have found out all about what progress the baby is making. I could have wiped away the stain of that quarrel when Protima was so determined Dr Pramash was wrong in saying it would be five-six weeks before... But then was she saying and declaring he was wrong just only because we were quarrelling? Quarrelling about me having to go so suddenly to Mahableshwar?

No, I will not worry that I was not seeing her this morning. I will not.

In any case perhaps when I am going back to Hotel Restful now I will be finding a letter from her. Or... Or, yes, she could easily have gone to the chai-wallah near to Dadar rail station and paid to use the telephone he has there. Proprietor at the hotel must have noted down any message she was sending.

But what if there is no message nor any green letter-form? Then at once I will write to her. Before I am so much as taking one sip of the lime water I am so much wanting.

And it would be good to get everything yet more clear in my head before I am seeing Dawkins sahib. No, every setback is not a disaster setback. I am needing to think more, much more, about how exactly I can tell that British rock about the terrible life his wife had before the moment he set eyes on her in the Watsons' dak bungalow. More, I must tell him what I was also learning about her behaviour at *Too Good Clicks* studio. If I can decide what I was learning there was exactly meaning.

Oh, and yes. I have not altogether followed up many other things I have been told that could lead me to discover yet more. There is everything little half-pant Chintu was telling me. There was something he said... Something – was it? – about what he told me he had seen when, after he had heard that gunshot, he went eventually from that deodar tree to investigate and peeping in at the french windows saw Iris Dawkins was lying in the pool of her own blood. But what was that *something* I cannot remember. Cannot at all.

Then, too, there is the young man wearing what must have been a blazer Chintu told me he was seeing. The somehow-wrong young man looking over the gate here. If Chintu did describe him to one hundred per cent... But, no, a boy like Chintu, not at all educated, does not know how to describe anybody except just exactly as he has seen them. Should I, though, have asked Chintu more about him?

All right, if I get a chance I will. But now... Now I must take food and then, yes, myself have *aram* on that rest-denying Hotel Restful charpoy.

But, no. No, I must not. Not yet. Chintu must be here somewhere. This is no time to be sitting idle. Somewhere in this big garden Chintu must be at work. So I must go round and round until I have found. And then...then there are questions to put.

* * *

It took Ghote a considerable time to go to every possible place in the big garden, its privacy protected by tall kika-thorn hedges. No little half-pant deep in the shadows of the big deodar. The side-gate Dawkins sahib must use when returning from the Club securely padlocked. No Chintu cowering beside beedi-smoking *Mali*. No Chintu underneath the branches of the cracked and gnarled pipal tree on the other side of the house. No Chintu, it seemed, anywhere.

In the end, though, he did find him. Where he had originally thought he would be found. He had been crouching so far into the deepest shadow of the big deodar's drooping bluish foliage that his half-naked brown body had been altogether invisible.

'Chintu!'

The boy sprang to his feet, his head brushing the tree's lowest swooping branches.

'Inspector, it is you. You only. I was thinking *Mali* had come and I had not smelt the beedi he is always smoking.'

'And you, you were not working itself,' Ghote said sharply. 'If you had been, I would have heard even from your dark corner the chink-chink-chink of your stone hit-hitting those canna seeds. So, unless you are wanting me to tell *Mali* what I am just only seeing, you had better speak truth and nothing less when I am asking you some questions.'

Chintu sat in silence.

'All right, now tell me first. Did you truly see a gun beside Dawkins memsahib when you heard the sound of that shot and went running to look inside bungalow?'

'Yes. Yes, I did. I did.'

And at the moment into Ghote's head came the sight of Primrose Cottage as he had seen it earlier walking up the path beside the cannas bed. The house had looked as if it was fast asleep in the noonday heat, the *chiks* at every window, all rolled right down.

'You are lying,' he told Chintu.

'No. No, Inspector sahib, why would I lie? I saw her body. I saw that gun.'

'You saw it through the *chiks* rolled down at that time of day? You are very-very clever if you were able to do that.'

But, even before he had fully brought out the jibe, he saw it had in no way thrown the boy.

'Inspector, I am not so clever. It is just that on that day it was not hot. *Khansamah* had not told the servants to roll down the *chiks*. *Mali* had not told me to water them.'

Ghote heard this denial with mixed feelings. Had his ruse been successful, it would have made the differing descriptions he had heard of Iris memsahib's body, Chintu's and Bullybhoy's, less of a complication. He could have passed over Chintu's account as nothing more than an invention produced to make himself look important. On the other hand he felt – he scarcely knew why – distinctly pleased that Chintu was turning out to be honest. Amid the daily turmoil back in Dadar he had encountered few people, old or young, who could be relied on invariably to give an honest answer to a police question. So it was a source of warm pleasure to find a wretched, shirtless boy like Chintu saying, at this moment, something with plainly the ring of truth about it.

But he put him to the test once more.

'Very well. But tell me again now: on which side of Memsahib's body did the gun lie?'

'Inspector, on her left.'

'But if *Khansamah* was telling Inspector Barrani it was on the right...?'

'Inspector, on the left.'

Ghote thought for a moment.

All right, Chintu could genuinely have remembered wrongly. He might not even know his right from-

'Raise your right hand.'

Up came the boy's right hand. Unhesitatingly.

'But something more I must ask.'

'Yes, Inspector sahib?'

'You told you had seen a man at the gate here early on the day when later you heard that shot and ran to look.'

'Yes, the man with the many-colours coat.'

'Is that all you were seeing about him? Just that he was different from anyone you had seen before because of the coat he had?'

'No, Inspector. I was telling. He was a bad man. He had bad–bad eyes.'

'Yes, I remember. You said his eyes showed he was a *badmash*. But how? How did they? You were not telling me that.'

'Inspector, I did. I was saying his two dark blue eyes were not just one like the other. One had in it some of green, Inspector.'

'All right. Yes, you did say that. And I fully believe you were seeing that. I am not even going to ask if it was true. But was there anything more about that man?'

Chintu hesitated.

'Inspector, *jee*.'

'Yes? Yes? What *jee*?'

'Inspector, you will not tell *Mali*.'

Ghote could not keep back the smallest of smiles.

'No, I will not tell *Mali*.'

'It is this. When I should have been back here breaking canna seeds I was not. I was not hurrying back to here.'

'All right, you were not doing your duty. But we will let that pass. What did you see more about this *badmash* that you have not told before?'

'Inspector, he was beginning to come into garden. And... And, Inspector, he was shiver-shivering.'

'Shivering? But it was, you were telling, if not a hot day, at least a not so sunny. There had been no need to roll down the *chiks*. So he might have felt a little cold, have somewhat shivered, but no more.'

'But, no, Inspector. I was saying *shiver-shivering*.'

'Very well. But to shiver, even that much, does not make someone a *badmash*. You have shivered, isn't it, when you heard *Mali* coming while you were sitting quietly in the cannas bed, doing nothing at all? What else was there?'

Chintu did not answer.

Was I being altogether too fierce with him? Too much of tiger?

But seemingly not.

'He was,' Chintu added cautiously, 'opening gate.'

'So he was opening that gate. But anybody who had been standing near it might have wanted to do that. It is a very interesting gate, with those twisted old pieces of wood making it. Any idle person might try opening same, just only to see it more.'

'But, Inspector, just anybody would not be able to open that gate. Inspector, it is very-very difficult to lift what is holding it shut.'

Ghote realised then that what Chintu had claimed was altogether right. *I can still, if only a little, feel the place I hurt when I tried to force up that latch.*

'*Thik hai*,' he said. 'You are right. The gate cannot be opened in just one idle moment. And you said also this man—'

'But, no,' Chintu broke in. 'Not man, *Inspectorjee*. He was young-young.'

'But you can be a man even if you are younger than most.'

'He was not,' Chintu stated with firmness. 'He was young-young.'

'All right. Let's see how old exactly. Was he older or younger than myself?'

'Inspector, you are older. You are fully a man.'

Ghote scrabbled in his mind to find a young man, or well-developed boy even, whom Chintu might know and could compare with this mysterious intruder. But no. No, he had no acquaintances in common with little half-pant.

He gave up.

'Then how far in did he come, this too-young man?'

'Inspector, a little way only.'

'All right. Then he could have been a youngster who was just only curious, who wanted perhaps to see gate from other side. You were watching him all the time?'

'No, Inspector. I thought I heard *Khansamah* coming. Sometimes he is coming into garden and then he is having a thick stick he is liking to swing and swing. Inspector, it is to scare me. He is liking to do it.'

'So you ran, quickly as you could, back to here?'

'*Jee*, Inspector. I was quick-quick. When I was hearing shot that church clock had just only began its nine booms and it had not finished when I was getting to bungalow.'

'Very good. Very fast. But, listen. Do not tell anyone what you were doing.'

'Inspector, I must not. There is *Mali's* stick also.'

Yes, Ghote said to himself as wearily he drove back into the town. Yes, I was wrong not to have tried to find this intruder when Chintu was first mentioning same. Here am I, in the householder stage of life, soon even to be a father, and I am just only finding out this about myself. It is true. I do not have as many quick instincts as-as someone like, say, Bullybhoy. I do not have the ability to act at once when my instinct is roused. I always and always have to have one long argument in my head, this way, that way, before I am acting.

I must conquer that.

But now I have at last decided – or have I? – to make my way to Hotel Restful. I have earned some *aram,* if that must be less now than I would like. And I have also a lot to think about.

At the hotel he found that, yes, there had been a telephone call from Protima.

'Yes, yes,' the fat proprietor said, heaving himself up from his second or third afternoon doze. 'Yes, yes, she was telephoning itself, your wife. One very-very nice lady. Very clear voice, yes.'

But it seemed that the message she had left had come long before. Even as long ago as when he himself had been away at the Watsons' hard-to-find dak bungalow. Perhaps, he thought, it might have been at the very moment India-loving Mrs Pansy was telling me the terrible story of Iris Mountford's early life and the boy baby who had disappeared among all India's millions, if he was still alive anywhere.

'So what message was my wife leaving?' he asked dully.

But before the sleep-sodden proprietor had brought himself to answer, overwhelming thoughts of what Protima might have said abruptly rushed in. *I am not at all well, please come back.* Or would it be *I have not forgotten the way you were leaving, I have much to say*?

But-but she must have forgotten that silly argument, and, besides, didn't this mountain heap of a fellow say she was a very-very nice lady? If she was as nice to him as… No, it must be some other message. *Baby is coming*? Yes, yes, it could be that surely, however unlikely as soon as today.

'Her message? What it was?'

'Oh, just only a message.'

'A message? But what did she say? What did she say itself?'

The proprietor sat for a moment or two in sleepy silence.

Is the damn fellow even thinking? Are his eyes beginning to droop?

'Proprietor sahib!'

It was a shout. An absolute shout.

The big fat head on the more than fat shoulders jerked up.

'Yes? Yes, Inspector?'

'What message was my wife leaving me?'

'Oh, Inspector, it was- Must have been just only sending her love. Yes, yes. She was sending you her love. Very good, very nice.'

Ghote resigned himself to never knowing.

Whatever message Protima had left it was plain the sleepy idiot – good God, he was fast off already – had made no note of it and had long forgotten every word.

Nevertheless, giving the wretched fellow a determined

shake, he demanded a new letter-form. Then, before he did anything else, wrote to his wife. At last he let himself take one deep swallow from the tall glass of lime water the proprietor had managed in one bleary shout to summon a bearer to bring. Then, glass put down, he plodded up to the waiting misery of his charpoy at last to settle himself to sleep.

Rested a little, and refreshed not much more, Ghote, calmed by having walked in unhindered quiet to Primrose Cottage, pulled the big bell-knob beside its door. He was not surprised to find the door opened almost at once by the *khansamah*, elaborate puggaree as ever magnificently on his head.

'Sahib will see you now,' the voice beneath the puggaree proclaimed. 'I have informed you are wishing to talk.'

So, not even shown the way by a shout-summoned bearer, Ghote found himself once more in front of Dawkins sahib, sitting, heavy height-adding shoes jutting out, on the same plump flowers-bright sofa.

'Good afternoon, Sahib,' he said. 'I trust you were having pleasant tiffin.'

'Tiffin? Tiffin?' the jutting little British rock exclaimed. 'What's that got to do with you, Inspector-Inspector Whatever-your-name-was?'

'I was inquiring only,' Ghote answered, striving not to sound terse.

'Were you? And have you anything more to the point to *inquire* about now?'

'Sir, it is not so much inquiring as informing. Sir, I have been up to Pune—'

'Poonaaaa, damn you.'

'Up to Poona, sir, where at his dak bungalow I was seeing your friend Mr Watson.'

'Were you indeed, Inspector? And what on earth did Peter Watson find to tell you?'

'Sir, it was not, in the end, Mr Peter Watson who was telling. It was Mrs Pansy Watson.'

'Pansy? Bit of a gabble mouth. Trust she didn't tell you more than you should have heard.'

Ghote swallowed, all but gulped.

More than I should hear, he thought. That was exactly what she did tell. I was having doubts about whether it was right, even as she was telling. And telling is what I also must do now. If what she said to me about the young days of Iris Mountford is to make a difference to what Dawkins sahib is knowing about her, I must tell it all to him.

'Sir, she was telling me- I am not at all knowing whether your-your wife ever told you what Watson memsahib was telling to me. I am thinking not, or you would have written something about it to Sir Rustom, sir.'

'What the hell's all this?'

Ghote braced himself. It could not be put off one second more.

'Sir, I was learning from Mrs Pansy Watson about the early life of your wife, Iris. Sir, were you knowing she was born in India and lived here for her first twelve-thirteen years?'

He had put it as a question, a polite one. But Dawkins sahib's answer came as a surprise, if one that slowly grew.

'Yes, yes. Mrs Dawkins may have occasionally said something about her childhood here in India. But I never took much notice. The sort of India she knew at that age hardly connected with our life here in Mahableshwar. As retired people.'

'Retired, sir?' The question escaped Ghote before he had time to decide it had better not have been asked. 'But Mrs Dawkins was not at all of retiring age?'

'Don't be more of a damn fool than you have to be, Inspector. When a man retires from the Service, naturally his wife goes with him. The question of relative ages does not arise. It does not.'

'Very good, sir. But I am having to inform that the age of your wife is very significant in what I am about to tell you.'

'Is it? Is it? I think I'd better be the judge of that. So, what about her childhood do you think is – what was it? – *significant*?'

'Sir, your wife, who was the only child of Sir Ronald and Lady Mountford was—'

But now Ghote had told Dawkins sahib something that had interested him. More, it looked, than merely interested him.

'Never knew that. Never knew that. Good God, can you imagine it, my dear chap: a woman like Iris never actually once mentioning that her father was Sir Ronald Mountford – he was the Resident in Gopur, you know, the Resident – I can hardly... You're sure of this, Inspector? Perfectly sure?'

'Oh, yes, sir. It came from lips itself of Mrs Pansy Watson who was knowing her all her life. But-but, sir, there is more to be telling.'

'Well, let's hear it then. Let's hear it. But a Mountford, a Mountford. One of the best families in England, you know.'

'Perhaps she was not telling you she came from such a fine family because, when you were meeting her, she was going by the name of Petersham. Sir, the name of the family in UK, sir, who were adopting her.'

'Adopting? I never heard anything about adopting? Not a word. Not a bloody word. How on earth did it come about that the daughter of Sir Ronald Mountford was adopted – somewhere at Home, did you say? – by these people Petersham? What sort of people were they, eh?'

'Sir, they were distant cousins of Sir Mountford but not at all rich. And, sir, so Mrs Pansy was telling me, they were treating your wife, who was a child only when she came to them, very, very badly. Sir, that may be why she never mentioned same to you.'

'Dare say you're right. Yes, dare say you are. Treated her badly, eh? She certainly never said anything about that to me.'

Feeling his task made easier now that Dawkins sahib was speaking to him as if he were almost on the same level, Ghote hurried on with his hardly-to-be-told account.

'Sir, what was happening was this. Sir, one night while Sir Ronald and Lady Mountford were out for shikar… Sir, in camp, sleeping in one and the same tent. In the middle of the night an escaped elephant in musth was trampling them both to death, sir.'

For a moment or two Dawkins sahib sat on his flowers-covered sofa in silence.

'Killed, eh?' he said at last. 'Sir Ronald Mountford killed? You know, I believe I read about that somewhere when it happened. Bound to have been in the *Times of India*. Bound to have been. Sad blow for the whole family. Yes, sad blow.'

He sat on in a silence that looked every inch reverent.

But, standing almost at attention in front of him on his fat little sofa, Ghote knew that the worst, the very worst, had yet to be said.

And how am I to say it? To say to this white sahib who was

taking to wife a lady he was loving for her quiet violet eyes that she, at age of twelve-thirteen only, had given birth to a child? And, far, far worse, to a boy she had been impregnated with by one of sons, equally young, of the Rajah of Gopur. An Indian, though a prince.

But I must do it.

He gritted his teeth to begin. Stopped. Saw suddenly a possibly easier way to launch into that worst of worst.

'Sir, I must tell you...I was saying your future wife was known, not as Miss Mountford, sir, but as Miss Petersham. Sir, she had had to be, sir, packed off to UK, sir, *packed off* were Watson memsahib's words itself—'

But at that moment there came a knock on the door, a discreet but firm knock. One that, it at once appeared, required no *Come in*. It was the *khansamah*.

'Sahib,' he announced opening the door. 'Sahib, Inspector Barrani.'

CHAPTER THIRTEEN

Bullybhoy came striding in, a privileged visitor, without any waiting to know whether his sudden arrival was interrupting any business Dawkins sahib might be engaged with.

And, yes, Ghote thought, I believe now I did hear that jangling bell, only I was so much worrying about what I must say to Dawkins sahib that it was making no impact on me.

'Ah, Darrani,' Dawkins greeted Bullybhoy. 'Just the man. Been hearing some extraordinary things, unbelievable things, from Inspector – er – here. Like to have your opinion. Take a pew. Take a pew.'

Ghote stood, looking at Bullybhoy as he pulled a chair forward, trying hard to stamp down the fury he was feeling. How like the fellow to come bursting in at a moment like this. And how like his carefully nurtured 'friend', the *khansamah*, to bring him into the room in a way no servant should.

In a way, now I think about it, that is very much surprising. But no time for things like that. What will Bullybhoy say, and do, when he is hearing what I was discovering? And, worse, when Dawkins sahib was just only saying that what I had forced myself to tell him, the truth as I was hearing same from Mrs Pansy Watson, was *unbelievable?*

The answer came soon enough.

Dawkins sahib had barely finished giving Bullybhoy his account of what he had just heard – he had told it all more or less accurately – when Bullybhoy delivered his I-am-right verdict.

'Forget it.'

Forget? Ghote had wanted to snap out in amazement.

But, luckily for him, Dawkins sahib had stepped in.

'Forget? I'm not altogether sure what you mean.'

'Simple enough,' Bullybhoy replied sharply, in a way that Ghote thought he himself could never have done. 'Simple enough. Forget it all, forget the whole business of your wife's unfortunate death. It's all been dealt with. I dealt with it. Christian burial carried out *ek dum*. Dare say memorial stone is all but ready, just simple name and dates. All that's needed. Inquest went off – what they are calling *word to wise* – without even one hitch. So, all can be forgotten. It happened in days gone by. No more to be said.'

Not for the first time in Ghote's relations with Bullybhoy, he found himself astonished. How can the fellow say a thing like that, he asked himself. How can he?

'Barrani *bhai*, that will not do,' he said, under the impulse of truth he could not but bring it out. 'You cannot just only bury away all this. Why, that day, did Iris memsahib take the twelve-bore and shoot herself? Dawkins sahib has a right to know, if it can at all be found out. When something like that is happening it is even more than just only his right. The whole world of order and decency has the right to know.'

'Always head-in-sky,' Bullybhoy declared. 'I was with this fellow at Nasik Police Training School, Dawkins sahib. He was always like that, wanting to know till last drop what is lying behind each and every old crime we were examining. Even there I was pointing out that, if you are doing such, you will be having no time to be keeping any sort of law-and-order. It is nonsense only.'

Yes, Bullybhoy, you were pointing that out, Ghote thought. Time, time, time and again. And, damn it, you were persuading each and every person there, from Commandant to lowliest peon waiting to scrub clean the blackboard, that you were right. But you were not. And since I was hearing about the way you were investigating this case itself, the damn too-quick way, I am having an altogether different opinion of you. I would like and like never to set eyes on you again.

But – the thought followed with inescapable logic – Dawkins sahib is one Barrani believer. Or, for him, Darrani believer. He will do what Bullybhoy tells him to.

He set his teeth. Locked himself into silence.

But, damn it all, he thought in a secret place in his head, I am going to find out the whole reason Iris memsahib had for what she did. It is my duty. Sir Rustom Engineer was giving me this task, and I will report my findings to him. But, before that even, I will lay them fully out before this jutting little rock of an Angrezi sahib till he has heard every last word. I will. I will.

And then he had to listen while the rock accepted with full faith Bullybhoy's verdict.

'Yes. Yes, Darrani, I think on better consideration you're right. The thing is to forget the whole business. After all, what's done is done. Only way to look at it. Something terrible happened, but there's nothing to be done about it. So, stiff upper lip, and take it like a man.'

He turned then to Ghote, standing where he had been from the start, his face – he knew – reflecting nothing but a sullen determination not to speak a single word while Bullybhoy was there to hear.

'One thing though, Inspector-Inspector Something. All that stuff you were telling me about... Damn it, about my own wife... Well, now I look at it calmly, her being sent Home and not well treated does mean something. It means, poor woman, she was never, after- Well, after what happened when she was just a child, her parents' terrible death and all that, she was never quite as sensible a person as one would expect an English lady to be. No, not at all. And that shows, if anything does, that she was- What shall I say? Well, pretty much off her rocker when-when she did that.'

Then I have at least put something into his head, Ghote thought. I have told him that his wife was not the quiet English memsahib with violet eyes – that were not exactly violet – he had asked to marry him.

But what has he done with what I told him? He has taken it as an extra reason to put whole business out of his mind. Finished, he has announced. Finished and done with. She is not ever to be thought about again.

And, it came to Ghote then, like a revelation, that from about the time of his own arrival at Primrose Cottage, Dawkins had at least wanted to forget he was ever marrying his Iris. He has wanted to forget he made her a present of a pretty, and expensive, little ladies' bureau. He is wanting to forget he ever arranged for her to visit the *Too Good Clicks* studio so that he could have that photograph in its fine painted wooden frame to hold as a keepsake for ever. He was putting that photograph into one locked drawer.

'Yes, you are right, of course, Dawkins sahib,' he said, low-voiced.

Then he turned to go.

The barbed words he had added in his head to that abject agreement he left unsaid. *If your never-wrong Inspector Darrani was telling you that, it must be so, isn't it? Is it?*

Standing just outside the house door, Ghote allowed more thoughts about the British rock to slide into his mind. Yes, a weak individual at heart. He had found, however, that in India he had the whole weight of the British Raj there behind him, all the way from the Viceroy down. It had bestowed on him the right to give orders and expect total obedience. He had been made a god, if a minor one, a god before whom the mortals below must bow.

All right, yes, I have seen that now.

He set off along the path beside the cannas bed, and found himself thinking once more about what little half-pant Chintu had told him about the young man in the bright-striped blazer. Yes, that fellow was definitely a source of mystery. Why had he hovered so long beside the gate? And then, when he may have seen that Chintu, the weeds-grubber among the tall canna plants, was going off towards the big deodar at the far end of the garden, why had he – if Chintu is to be believed – bent over the gate, lifted up that stiff latch and entered the garden?

And, Chintu is to be believed. I trust Chintu.

So what was the young man doing? After all, it had been on the very day that Iris memsahib had taken that gun and a single cartridge, had put it to her head and... But how had she really contrived that awkward act – pulled the trigger? Because, woman that she was, it was likely that pull it, instead of giving it a smooth squeeze, was what she would have done.

Something more to puzzle about, something more unexplained.

He found himself staring at Bullybhoy's blue police truck parked, with a savage disrespect for the neat grass of the verge, directly opposite.

Yes, that young man's presence, he thought furiously, something more to be explained by Bullybhoy, the great explainer-away of anything that stood in the way of his instantly formed theories. Bullybhoy with his laid-down explanations for everything that had happened inside Primrose Cottage on the day the young man stood here, looking in over the gate and eventually entering. Yes, each of those explanations made to fit neatly into the next until he had the full account put together, an account meaning there would be no more awkward questions, no difficult investigation to be prolonged and prolonged. Oh, yes, Bullybhoy has cleared up everything. To his own satisfaction, and plainly, altogether plainly, to the satisfaction of Dawkins sahib.

But here is one thing he has not cleared up, and will he be able to? Will what little half-pant Chintu has told me be something Bullybhoy will not be able to brush aside to my satisfaction? And not to the satisfaction, if I am any judge, of Sir Rustom Engineer, the man who had one altogether successful career as a detective before he was made the first Indian to command all Bombay police.

But Bullybhoy.

At any moment he may come out of the bungalow, his

massaging and comforting of Dawkins sahib's wounded mind ended, a whisky-soda perhaps swallowed down, jump into his blue-painted truck, swirl it round in a rapidly rising cloud of dust and go, heading off at top speed, back to Mahableshwar PS. And I am not at all willing to see that fiercely Pathan face again.

There was a shady banyan, its curtain of long dangling brown roots down to ground level, only fifty yards or so further along the road. Ghote took to his heels and was inside its shade in barely half a minute.

Standing there happily, he let his breathing settle into calmness. I have nothing to do now, he thought, but wait quietly till Bullybhoy has roared past in the truck. In a moment I can even begin to think once more about this whole business. Very well, Dawkins sahib wrote to his long-ago acquaintance, Sir Rustom, saying his wife's inexplicable suicide was tormenting him beyond endurance, but now he has accepted Bullybhoy's advice to forget all about it. But Sir Rustom has sent me here to find out why she did what she did. And I am not at all thinking he will be as convinced by Bullybhoy's arguments as Dawkins sahib has been. So must I continue with my task? Yes, I must.

There must be more to do, more to find out about what really happened. But what was that? What?

What time it is?

He was about to pull back his shirt cuff to see his watch – the sleeves of the bazaar-bought shirt infuriatingly too long – when from the not-too-distant church there came the solemn time-telling booms of its clock. One, two, three, four.

Bullybhoy in his truck will come past at any moment. How right to have hidden myself away here. If he had spotted me walking ahead in the road, he would, of course, have stopped the truck, got out, hauled me into it and given me one more of his this-is-the-way-to-do-it lectures. At Nasik he was even lecturing the Commandant.

Yes, now that noise must be that truck of his coming.

Coming it was. Only it was not going. Instead Bullybhoy had brought it to a sudden juddering halt, had poked his head out and called across.

'Ghote *bhai*, I can lift you anywhere?'

Ghote stepped out of the banyan's sheltering curtain of dangling roots. There was nothing else to do.

'No. No, Barrani *bhai*,' he called over. 'No, I was...I was just only taking rest in the shade of this banyan. I am not going very far now. So, no thank you, Barrani *bhai*, I am not at all needing lift.'

'If you are saying it...'

And off the truck roared towards the *chauki* over which Barrani ruled.

Then...

'Bullybhoy,' Ghote exclaimed aloud. Oh God, if there has been some unaccountable, conspicuous figure about anywhere in the whole of Mahableshwar – and Chintu's young-young man in that blazer was well out of place – Bullybhoy would have had some notion of his existence. Look at the way damn fellow had pounced on Dawkins sahib and his *khansamah* as soon as he had come to Mahableshwar.

So Bullybhoy must be asked about the youngster in the blazer. He will have to be. I will have to go to the chauki and ask. Oh, yes, I should have taken that lift he was offering. I could even have learnt from him all I am wanting to know just only sitting beside him in that truck.

But now I must once more face the fellow. I must get hold of a tonga if one is passing along the road or I must foot it all the way there to the *chauki* and see him. If he has any idea at all who was that young man hovering outside Primrose Cottage, I must pick his brain.

Grimly, he set out.

But, leaving the *chauki* only a few minutes after getting there, weary and with his bazaar-bought shirt showing large patches of sweat at its armpits, he told himself he need hardly have troubled to come at all. What benefit was it to learn that the youngster Chintu had seen that terrible day had come to Mahableshwar from Bombay somewhere. That is telling me nothing, nothing at all about him. Yes, Bullybhoy said also that the fellow, whose name if he knew it he had not mentioned, is 'educated'. But that is telling me nothing also. I am educated, Bullybhoy is educated, Dawkins sahib – look at it that way – is educated, even if it was not at any Oxford-Cambridge like most of the ruling British. And Chintu is not educated, but he is altogether sharp, and honest also.

And Bullybhoy was careful not to tell me if that blazer-wearing young man is still somewhere about in Mahableshwar. Bullybhoy is not at all wanting any more inquiries being made into Iris memsahib's death. He is stating and claiming that it is all wrapped up. His neat parcel in the post.

But I am not letting myself believe that there is nothing more to find about Iris. No. No, I am damn well not.

Where to go next? What to do? God knows.

Ah, but I do. I am damn hungry. I also, like Dawkins sahib, am wanting some tiffin, even if it may be hours and hours after I am eating same.

And then, by some odd mental process, as he entered the hotel, the word *tiffin* emerged from his head and shone suddenly bright before him.

Yes, there is something else that word has brought, scratching and scraping at a corner of my mind. But what it is? What it is? I am feeling it is somehow important. More, it is something not quite right.

But what? Wha—

And, yes, I have it.

Eased away from where it was concealing itself in my mind, as if it was a tough fragment of the *murgh masala* I have been given here at Hotel Restful – the chicken must have been hatched even before Independence – here it is in light of day. The words *a nasty accident*. Dawkins sahib spoke them as long ago as when I first saw him. Then he had stated that his *khansamah* had told over the telephone when he was at the Club, *There has been a nasty accident*. But I am seeing now those words are not somehow quite the right ones. They were not the right words for a *khansamah* to have used. They were, in fact, the sort of tactful warning which Dawkins sahib would have used himself if it had been he who was telephoning to the Club breaking the news of Iris memsahib's death to-to himself.

CHAPTER FOURTEEN

Of course, Ghote reasoned on, it is possible that Dawkins sahib, in telling me about that terrible day, did not give an exact account. He could have put what would have been his own way of giving a tactful warning into the *khansamah*'s mouth. Possible, yes. But not ringing true. Not to one hundred per cent ringing true for the Dawkins sahib I am knowing.

So why was a message using those words, if they had been used, been telephoned to the Club that morning?

If I go to Club and check on that message as far as I am able, will I get some clue about why those words were used? Yes, I must go there. I must not, like Bullybhoy, seize on whatever half-explanation I can think of and leave it there. I must go myself and ask questions and obtain full answer.

But at once second thoughts arrived. And, the more he pondered them, the more sure he became that this was one of the occasions when not carrying out an instant decision was the right thing to do.

No, do not go rushing over to the Mahableshwar Club at this very moment with tricky questions to be put. It will soon be evening. The place will be busy with members coming for dinner, or to play billiards or just for chatting. And I am not at all certain, even if I am able to get permission to put my questions, that there will be any bearers free to answer. They have their duties.

Better-better to go there at the exact time in the morning that Dawkins sahib was given that somehow wrong *nasty accident* message.

There were, however, more than a few difficulties lying in Ghote's path next day, so many thorny kika branches, before he was able to discover even how many people, members and bearers, were likely to be on the Club premises at the time Dawkins sahib had been telephoned.

Urging on the driver of the tonga he had taken every yard of the way, he had arrived at the gleamingly white Club building exactly at ten. In front of him he saw a flight of shallow steps leading to a wide terrace, the sole sign of life on it being a long rattan reclining chair, empty.

I could just only walk into Club itself through these open glass doors, he thought then. There is seeming to be no one about. Is the place always like this at this hour of the day? But, no. No, wait a little. Wait and see if in some minutes only there is some sign of activity inside.

He had stepped back. He wondered even if he might recline for a few moments, like a true sahib, on the long rattan with its cane-work pockets to either side, one plainly for holding a long drink, the other, deeper, into which a book or newspaper might be let drop as eyelids slowly closed. But at once words from Dr Hans Gross came marching into his head. *The Investigator...should possess abundant energy and initiative.*

He had turned sharply away, thinking that, if only his own blue-bound copy of that great work had been in the deeper pocket of the chair, he could have taken it up, re-read the page laying out what is required of the experienced investigator, checked that he was up to standard.

No, what I must be doing now, he thought, is showing that one quality Dr Gross lays down as vital. *Abundant energy.*

He walked quickly then into the Club's interior. A spacious hall, its neatly patterned wooden floor exuding a pungent resiny odour, and no one about. Not a member, not a single bearer. At the far end, gleaming prominently, he saw a large gong, no doubt for summoning members to luncheon or dinner. Against the walls to either side deep sofas in sombre brown leather, above them green baize noticeboards peppered with lists of every sort, most of them yellowed with long exposure to the light.

Quietly he walked on, past the gong, tempted for a moment to pick up its long stick with its soft white head and give the great brass circle above one resounding thwack. It would bring to life every bearer, every cook, every sweeper in the whole premises, and it would be a hundred per cent enjoyable thing to do. But it would, too, quickly bring, he reflected instantly, some Club Secretary or other, whether British or Indian, and I would be instantly expelled.

So, no. No reverberating gong-stroke.

Quietly, almost on tiptoe, he advanced deeper into the building.

A door bearing a wooden plaque inscribed *Reading Room*. Cautiously he opened it. No one. No one engrossed in reading, or even in one of those armchairs sleeping. Door closed again. On tiptoe still – is it that my shoes are squeaking? – penetrating further. *Smoking Room*. Inside, at once evident, the aroma from many past years of cigars, pipes and cigarettes lingering unmistakably. But, yes, in the far corner a human being. Must be, even if he is holding up the broad pages of the *Times of India*. So the man behind that can be only one person, Dawkins sahib. Absorbed in his daily reading of the paper that he cannot get delivered to Primrose Cottage, or does not want to pay extra for having it delivered.

Door softly closed, Dawkins sahib reading on, unaware. And onwards. *Dining Room*, a small notice beside its heavy door. *By-law 17. Members Are Reminded that Ties Must Be Worn in the Dining Room.*

Ghote looked down at the bare skin under the opened top button of his new blue-checked shirt, as if to compensate for its being so much too long in the arms somewhat too small round the chest. A tie? Where could I find same here? But does By-law 17 apply? Or is someone not a Club member still bound by that rule?

In an instant he decided. Tie or no tie, he turned the door-knob.

Walls panelled in dark wood. Wide windows firmly closed. The smell of food from however far back not yet entirely banished. A dozen tables already laid for lunch in glinting silver and softly glowing white china. But no waiter standing ready for orders. No guests hungrily waiting for – what? – mulligatawny soup to be ladled into their bowls.

Move on.

Oh God. *Hon. Secretary's Office*. And behind its closed door, surely, the Hon. Secretary – a staying-on Briton or taking-over Indian? – sleeping what they are calling *sleep of just*. Go past and hope such sleep will remain undisturbed. But what if, inside there, the Hon. Secretary is busy doing – What? –

whatever it is an Hon. Secretary does when same is awake.

No, cannot risk that. Must find out, if only I am poking my head inside door.

Softly he turned the blank door's knob. Gently pushed. Resistance. Yes, door locked, must be. Hon. Secretary then somewhere safe in his distant home.

So, end of my search? No. No, there must be bedrooms somewhere. Club members will want, from time to time, to provide boarding and lodging for anyone they have invited up to Mahableshwar.

But no. Where did I learn that the Club's sleeping accommodation is further up the hill behind? No matter. I somehow know it. So push on.

A door covered in some thick, sound-smothering green material leading to the back premises. And the moment he pushed it open he saw the khaki-and-green uniform of a bearer. The fellow was perched on a high stool, simply sitting and, eyes closed, dozing.

'Wake up!'

With a start that nearly had the bearer toppling off his stool he came to life. Eyes – or, rather, Ghote registered, one eye – wide open. The other was a blear-covered sightless orb.

'Wha—' the fellow said. 'Who...? Who you are?'

'One police officer wanting answers.'

'*Jee. Jee*, Sahib. If you are asking, I would be telling whatever you are wanting.'

'The truth. The whole plain and simple truth. That is what I am wanting.'

'Sahib, Sahib. I will give it.'

'Very well. Then tell me, why is there nobody to be found anywhere in Club?'

A question that required a moment, some moments, of thought. That was plain enough.

'But, Sahib, yes. Bearers are everywhere. Myself also.'

'Everywhere? I don't think so. It is *Nowhere,* and myself speaking the truth. I have looked and looked, and not one single bearer was I finding.'

'Oh, Sahib, Sahib, you must have not seen.'

'Not seen, is it? Then come with me and show me what I was not finding. And, tell me, is Club altogether empty at this quiet time of the morning also? Are any members here, except only Dawkins sahib reading *Times of India*? And why not plenty-plenty bearers?'

The one-eyed face in front of him hung down in silent defeat.

'So Club is deserted, yes? No members coming this early, except Dawkins sahib. Every bearer, you also, asleep? But what is happening if telephone rings?'

'Oh, Inspector sahib, that is easy. Look. Look and see what is just beside me here on floor only. *Ek telephone.*'

Ghote did look and saw it was so.

'Is this the one only phone in the Club?' he asked, somewhat surprised.

'*Jee*, Inspector. Honsec sahib is saying two would need too much of money. But another he is having in own office. Special number.'

'And is it your duty then to sit by this telephone all day and take messages to any Member who is wanted?'

'Inspector, who else? I am very good at listening to telephone. Perhaps it is because I have one eye only. From birth, Inspector.'

CHAPTER FIFTEEN

A few minutes later Ghote, standing again beside the long rattan chair on the Club's terrace, was thinking carefully over what he had just learnt. Yes, very good. It is plain now that the Club here is almost ceasing to exist at this time of the morning. The whole place is dedicated, it seems, only to Dawkins sahib's peace and quiet while he is reading *Times of India*. Every man and boy in the place is leaving him strictly alone and just only sleeping the time away when there is little to be doing. Dawn-arriving sweepers will have altogether finished their work. The dusting and polishing also will be long over. Nothing to be done until members are arriving for drinks before lunch.

Yes, and thinking of Dawkins sahib here all alone, that is showing, isn't it, one sidelight on the man. He is what they are calling as a loner. He is, and perhaps always was, someone not very happy to be chit-chatting with his fellow men. He was content, until his terrible tragedy, with the company of his violet-eyed wife, though never noticing, it seems, that one of those eyes had in it, as *Too Good Clicks* was revealing, a tiny triangle of green.

Was the one good friend he was ever making in India, I wonder, just only the then Inspector Rustom Engineer? Well, I suppose, Robert Dawkins was knowing also Mr Peter Watson. But how much of a real friend was that man? Not very much, I am thinking. Not after the way my inquiries to him were so quickly cut off. No, the clue here is this: Dawkins sahib did not go to one very good school. He was saying it himself. And almost every other white sahib he knew – I must except anyone in commerce, the box-wallahs as their fellow Englishmen are calling them – had been to, yes, definitely, good schools like Eton and – is it? – Barrow.

No wonder Dawkins had no one else but Sir Rustom to write to when, without explanation, his wife was committing suicide. Yes, things are becoming somewhat more of straight. I am getting a new view of Dawkins sahib. And that, I am thinking, may put me some way further along to discovering...

He found his thoughts somehow dissolving. Instead, he took in at last that he had been staring, unseeingly, at the huge view lying before him, down and down from this high-perched Club terrace to what must be the Arabian Sea, too many miles and miles distant to be seen other than as a lightening of the far sky.

He stood there gazing with an uplifting sense of wonder at the falling-away countryside. Yes, he murmured to himself, yes, this must be one of the far-famed panoramas that everybody talks about when Mahableshwar is mentioned. And, drinking in the sight, he felt a growing sense of being put into place himself in the great scheme of things. Washed away was his preoccupation with following to the final T the rules for the Investigator. Instead he saw himself as a single speck amid the vast sprawl of humanity reaching from little half-pant Chintu all the way up to white sahib Robert Dawkins and, beyond, to peering-eyed Sir Rustom Engineer. From peasant to President also.

But – the thought came softly in – in that huge spread of people each of us has his task. And my own is to do my duty as a police officer, as a newly promoted full Inspector of the Bombay Police Crime Branch, on detachment here in Mahableshwar charged with discovering what must have been in the head of Dawkins memsahib when she took that gun and shot herself.

From somewhere near there had come a sharp hissing sound.

He stopped, puzzled and alerted.

And then from behind the outermost stubby pillar holding up the terrace roof a head poked out.

Chintu's.

'What-what are you doing here? Why are you not in the garden at Primrose Cottage? You are meant to be working-working there. Are there no more canna seeds to break?'

'Inspector sahib, I am sliding out under bottom of locked side-gate and running-running here. There is something I must tell.'

'Come here. Leave that pillar, and come here. If you are having something to tell, tell. And how was it you knew I would be here itself?'

'Inspector, I was seeing, from high in the garden, the worst tonga in Mahableshwar going along the road to Club.'

'All right, that is enough.'

But now half-pant Chintu, although he had brought his almost naked body more fully into view, seemed unwilling to say another word.

Damn it, Ghote thought, was I being too...Too much of tiger once more with the boy? Somehow I am feeling that, if he has come all the way across Golf Course to tell me something, it must be worth hearing. But, impatient as I am, I was shouting at him. Yes, definitely, shouting.

'No, no,' he said more quietly. 'No need to be frightened. I will not eat. So, now tell me what it is that made you come all this way.'

Chintu took two steps forward, hesitated, took another few steps.

He looked all round.

The Club still slumbered, as if the whole building itself was asleep rather than just the people in it.

'Well?' Ghote asked.

'Inspector, I was not telling whole thing.'

'What whole—'

Ghote checked himself.

'You were not telling whole thing,' he said more quietly. 'What whole thing it is?'

'Inspector, the young-young man...'

'Yes, yes?'

No, do not be so hasty. Tact, Dr Gross is saying. And that is applying to this slip of a half-naked boy as much as it is applying to Dawkins sahib or Mrs Pansy Watson down near Pune.

'Yes, Chintu, I am knowing who it is you are talking. And, before-before, you were not telling me all you knew about him, isn't it? I dare say you were having one good reason. But now... Now you are ready to tell, yes?'

'*Jee*, Inspector.'

'So tell.'

'Inspector, I was afraid to tell this. I was thinking you would not believe and would no more listen to me. But-but the young man was doing more than coming in at gate. Inspector, he was going-going right up to side of bungalow.'

'Right up? And in also?'

'No. Yes. No. I am not knowing. I was not able quite to see. I was hearing *Mali* coming. Whee-whee that *lathi* was sounding.'

But I must know, Ghote said to himself. I must know whether that mystery fellow was truly entering the bungalow. If he was, it will alter the whole business. I must know.

'Chintu,' he said, 'listen carefully. You are knowing, well knowing, what you saw with your own eyes, that Dawkins memsahib was shot dead. You were seeing her body there, near those window-doors. You were seeing her blood, the gun also. So it is important-important that you are telling whole truth. When you were down beside bungalow itself did you truly see the young man in the striped coat go inside house? Yes or no?'

'Inspector, it was hard to tell. Inspector, *Mali* was coming. I could hear. So I was not looking-looking at the man I had seen coming in through the gate. But I was seeing him one second before, going near bungalow. But...but – it is truth-truth – I am not knowing if I saw him, or not, going inside.'

'Very well.'

And then, in a flash, Chintu was no longer there. There had been a whirling figure, not a foot away. There had been a dart of movement. And the terrace was bare of any other human being.

Ghote, almost dazed, even went so far as to turn round and glance at that long rattan chair, as if there might somehow be a witness resting on it to tell him that Chintu had been no apparition but a small, solid enough little *mali*'s boy.

And by the time he had turned back it was too late to see where the small figure had run to, which way he had gone.

No, Ghote said to himself, jumping down from the terrace. No, I must not let Chintu disappear like this. No doubt he was in one hell of hurry to get back to that cave-like place at the foot of the deodar. He is scared of the *mali* and that *lathi* of his. But I cannot allow him, much as I like him, just only to come to me here, tell that one thing and then be vanishing.

No, I must get hold of him somewhere where he cannot run off and then question and question him till I have found out down to the last drop everything he is knowing. And the full truth of it.

I wonder, does he have a home of some sort somewhere in Mahableshwar itself, a mother and father there? There must be, if not Bombay-style slums in the town, some quarter where the poors are living. What in old days the white sahibs would have called the Black Town, perhaps they still do.

Right. Decision made.

I must go *ek dum* to Primrose Cottage and, if I am unable to find, then ask. If I am starting now, at once, and hurrying, I would be there only some minutes after Chintu. I could get hold of that *mali* and tell him I must, as a police officer, talk with the boy.

But will I find him? Will *Mali* be able to find? If not, he may still know where the boy can be found in the town. Or will I have to, if he has altogether vanished, seek the help of Inspector Barrani?

No. I cannot. I will not.

* * *

Yet, half an hour later, he was having to admit to himself that it might in the end come down to going, tail between legs, to Bullybhoy. He had, first, contrived to make a quick but thorough search on his own of Primrose Cottage's garden. Then, when he had found no sign of the boy, he had gone to enlist the help of *lathi*-wielding *Mali*.

But he got no satisfactory response.

'That no-good brat, Inspector. He has been trouble-trouble ever since his father was persuading me to give him job. When I am finding, I am telling you, he will be feeling this *lathi* I am having in my hand just now only.'

Ghote ignored the threat.

'*Mali*,' he asked sharply, 'you are knowing his father? He is a friend?'

'Not any more. That fellow – I am knowing him by chance only – was telling me the boy was one hard-worker and would do always what he was told. So what has he been doing? When I could find nothing else for him to do after he had taken out from cannas bed each and every yellow flower that is making Sahib so angry at spoiling colour of same, then I was telling to break more seeds for planting next year. And was he doing it? No. No, no, no.'

'But, yes,' Ghote put in, unable not to defend the boy he had thought of as clever and honest. 'I was seeing, more times than once. He was hammer-hammer-hammering at those hard little seeds. Surely he had broken enough to sow the whole bed again next year?'

'But I had told to do it, and he was not. He was not there under that deodar, doing what I had ordered, whether more seeds were needing to be broken or not.'

'And you are certain Chintu has not been sent by

someone else, perhaps to fetch something from the town itself?'

'No one would dare. Chintu is *Mali*'s boy.'

'But-but if, say, Dawkins sahib himself was sending the boy somewhere?'

'Never. Dawkins sahib is thinking he can give any order he is wanting to and he will be obeyed *ek dum*. But, no, if we are not liking, we are not hearing or not remembering.'

Ghote, eager though he was to get hold of Chintu, gave that reply a moment's thought.

So, the servants Dawkins sahib had surrounded himself with as he stayed on here in India, rather than going to England where – could it be? – there were now few servants, if any, were not always giving him the fine life he had expected. If they disliked one of his barked-out orders, they were somehow failing to hear it. Yes, the weak man is the weak man whoever he is giving his orders to.

'But *Khansamah*?' he asked *Mali*. 'Would he be able to give Chintu some order that would take him out of garden?'

'First he would be asking myself,' *Mali* said with total assurance.

'I see. He rules the servants indoors: you rule Chintu out here.'

'*Jee*, Inspector. Each his own.'

'Then, if Chintu has run off, where would he have gone? To his father, your friend?'

'That man is no more a friend. I was telling you.'

'All right, if he is no friend of yours, then tell me where in the town he is staying and I will go there and perhaps bring you back your boy. Because he is a hard worker, isn't it?'

It needed only for Ghote to snatch away the dangling beedi

from the *mali*'s mouth for an address to be produced. Or rather a series of not very clear directions.

Wriggling off at last the saliva left on his fingers, Ghote strode off, cursing the fact that no convenient tonga happened to be standing anywhere in the road outside.

CHAPTER SIXTEEN

Some luck sometimes must come to me, Ghote reflected as, over-heated from his trudge into Mahableshwar itself and with his head churning as he strove to remember *Mali*'s confused and confusing directions, he had found himself face to face with a man who, in answer to his somewhat doubting shout of '*Chintu's father?*', emerged from a tumbledown hut made from no more than a few pocked sheets of rusted corrugated iron. Barely attached to the blank back wall of a building in the next street it extended crazily almost halfway across the narrow rubbish-strewn *galli* he had at last found.

But, confronting the man's solidly stocky frame, Ghote with a dart of keen pleasure recognised at once through the gaps in his banyan, its cotton almost as much holes as cloth, a familiar torso. Half-pant Chintu's own, magnified.

But will he, Ghote asked himself, be the same as Chintu in character. Will he be as sharp? And, above all, as plainly honest?

More perhaps to the point, is Chintu himself hidden just behind him inside the hut?

He took a moment to think before he spoke.

'So you are the father of that clever boy?' he asked then, comforting himself once again with those words of Hans Gross, *Tact is indispensable, for many awkward situations will be circumvented by its use.* So have I now circumvented?

It seemed he had.

'Yes, Chintu is clever. All are saying it. But what is making me proud is he is honest also. He was born honest and he has stayed honest, even when he is working for that *Shaitan* of a *mali*. You are knowing what is my name?'

'No. How could I?'

'It is Satyamurthi.'

Ghote at once saw the implication. *Satya*, truth. And *murthi*, mouth.

'Yes,' he said, 'that is meaning *truth-speaker*.'

'Then I am telling you. From the first day my father was telling me the meaning of our name I have always and always spoken truth.'

'I am glad to hear it, and I believe you. So... So where is Chintu now? You are knowing?'

'He is inside. He is inside only.'

'So why is he not at this very moment working for Dawkins sahib's *mali*?'

A shrewd look from Chintu's father.

'You are police?'

For one instant Ghote thought of taking advantage of his bazaar-bought shirt and trousers and denying it, of finding some other explanation for his presence. Not many people as poor as Chintu's father would answer questions from a police officer, or not without wrapping their replies in a good thick layer of roof-protecting *kulum* grass. But as quickly he decided to be as much of a truth-speaker as Satyamurthi himself.

'Inspector Ghote, Bombay Police,' he said, careful to keep any hint of the bully out of his voice.

'From Bombay side, and all the same wanting my Chintu?'

'Yes, as it happens I do. But it is only to ask him more about what was taking place some weeks ago at Primrose Cottage.'

'That murder?'

'Murder? Why are you saying *murder*?'

'When a white memsahib, with servants always there to do what she is wanting, not ever needing to lift one hand, is being shot dead, isn't it murder, Inspector?'

Ghote declined to provide an answer. Instead he asked again for Chintu.

And at once the boy's father called for him, and out into the sunless gloom of the *galli* Chintu came. Looking shamefaced.

'Chintu,' Ghote said, 'not like you to be running away when I am asking questions, even if they are hard ones to answer.'

Chintu moved his head from side to side but produced no words.

'Chintu,' his father said, with an edge of sharpness. 'Inspector sahib is wanting answer to questions he is asking. Tell him whatever is truth. Now.'

'*Jee, Pitajee*.'

'Then speak.'

Ghote intervened.

'Yes, Chintu, tell me only why, over at Club, you were running off the way you did. Too fast for me to catch.'

'Inspector...' The word emerged as cautiously as if a lithe, stubby-legged reddish-brown mongoose was putting its nose outside its hole.

'Yes? Go on.'

'Inspector, *Mali* had said I must not talk to you but be doing my work. He was saying I would lose job if I was doing same again.'

Ghote looked down at him.

'But you were talking to me,' he said. 'Even more. You were creeping out of the garden and coming all the way over Golf Course to find me at Club. Why did you do that?'

'Inspector, *Mali* said he would give me *push* from job if I was talking with you.'

Somehow, Ghote thought, that English *push* makes the boy's reason altogether more sensible.

'But it would not be end of world if you were getting *push* from Primrose Cottage.'

'Inspector, *Pitajee* is having no job himself. He is not able to find. And-and I have two-three brothers also, younger-younger than me.'

Ghote, thinking of four boys under the shelter of that apology for a hut, glanced over at Chintu's father for confirmation.

The man who looked so like his small son hung his head.

Ghote wished for a moment, violently even, that he had some influence somewhere in Mahableshwar that would get Chintu's father the job he so obviously needed. But he knew that he had not the least influence anywhere, either in Mahableshwar or even in Bombay itself.

'But, Chintu,' he said, 'if you were getting one job as a *mali*'s boy, you could be getting another before long, isn't it?'

'No, Inspector.'

'No, why not? You are one good worker. You know that.'

'Yes, Inspector, I am. But...'

'But what?'

'Inspector, it is not *Mali* only.'

'Not *Mali*? What do you mean?'

'Inspector, it is *Khansamah* also. And, Inspector, he is saying more than *push*. He is telling if I am ever seen talking with you, I will have my two legs chopped.'

'He was saying that? *Khansamah* was saying he would cut off your legs—'

'No, Inspector. *Khansamah* would never do it.'

'But—'

'Inspector, it would not be *Khansamah* himself. But he is knowing goondas who would do it. Would do that, Inspector, and worse. The very worst.'

'Inspector,' Chintu's father came in, 'I was not at all knowing this. But, Inspector, if Chintu is saying it, it is truth-truth. And there are in Mahableshwar goondas and *badmash* men in plenty to do it.'

'Oh, yes,' Ghote said. 'I am altogether ready to believe you, and Chintu also.'

He paused to think.

'Yes,' he said. 'Let me tell you what to do. Hide Chintu away. Hide him where no one will be knowing. You do that. And I will have some words with that *khansamah*. And after that I promise Chintu will keep those two, fast-running legs of his as well as his truth-speaking mouth. Yes, I am promising that.'

* * *

Murder. *Murder most foul as in the best it is.* As Ghote left the *galli* words from *Hamlet* came once more pouncing into his mind. And they stayed fastened there as if hammered down with steel nails. Murder, the word Chintu's father had spoken in unthinking response to a mention of Dawkins memsahib's death. Murder, the threat to murder that Chintu himself had said might come to him from Dawkins sahib's *khansamah* and the goondas whose services he could buy. That they would cut off his legs, *and worse.*

Can it be so? Yes, of course things like that happen often enough at the hands of goondas. Why should they not happen even in holiday Mahableshwar, even out of holidays time in rains-battered Mahableshwar? But Chintu's father had not only agreed that his son was under threat of death. He had done something else. He had spoken of murder as being the way that Iris memsahib had died.

But she had not. Surely she had not. Sir Rustom tasked me with finding out why, and why only, she had killed herself. Dawkins sahib had written, in despair, to his long-ago friend, or half-friend, begging his help in finding out why his wife had suddenly and inexplicably removed his twelve-bore from its locked almirah, put it to her head and taken her own life, even though she was seven-eight months pregnant.

Pregnant. Ghote, suddenly as if in a darkened midday room at Primrose Cottage a servant outside had swiftly rolled up a *chik*, found his head flooded with thoughts of his wife.

How is Protima? Has she— Can she already have given birth to our child? Is he a boy, the boy I am so much wanting? Or a girl? The girl I will welcome equally? But, no. No. Dr Pramash said it would be five-six weeks even before the birth. But then Protima had said she knew better, that a woman must always know better. And... And, yes, there are births that come well before their full time. But if... If she has been overtaken by such a birth, will she be all right? Will the baby be all right?

Oh, why, why, why did Sir Rustom send me here? But was that my fault? I should, when I had told him my wife was about to have our first child, have accepted his half-meant offer of finding another officer to go to Mahableshwar. But, no, I could not have told Sir Rustom that the birth was to be so soon. I knew nothing about that. All I knew then, before Protima in her rage announced that the baby might come in even a few days, was what Dr Pramash had stated that it would be some weeks before... Before anything happened.

So Sir Rustom was right to send me here, to Primrose Cottage, when I had said no more than I did. And I was sent also simply to find out why Iris memsahib had taken her own life. There was no question of murder. There is no question of murder.

But...but the *khansamah*, that pillar of a man with his splendid puggarees, why should he have threatened little half-pant Chintu with death? Even if he is as viciously ruthless as Chintu has claimed, why did he threaten the boy to that extent? Or—? Was Chintu telling a tale?

At once he knew that it was not so. Chintu was honest. His father had said he himself was 'born honest'. They were, both, speakers of truth. *Satyamurthis*. And that rings true as true. Dealing with the riff-raffs of Dadar has taught me well enough how to know when a boast is a boast and when something said is no more than the plain truth.

So why should the *khansamah* have made that vile threat? It must be because of what Chintu might say to myself.

Possibly he would give away something that fellow has to keep altogether secret. But what would that be? It could not be that business about Dawkins sahib pegging down Chintu as the thief of his watch. Iris memsahib herself had proved that had not been so. No, it would have to be something directly concerning the appalling event that took place that quiet sunny morning, the event a guarded telephone call from the *khansamah* mentioning *a nasty business* had brought Dawkins sahib hurrying back home from his contented perusal of the *Times of India*. To find, not some spoilt tiffin, but his wife's body in that pool of blood.

Yes, it would have to be that. But now I am coming up against one blank wall, a wall as blank, even more blank, than the wall of the house from which Satyamurthi's hut precariously hangs. And I am still knowing nothing about why *Khansamah* should have threatened Chintu. Nothing at all.

Should I go now to Primrose Cottage and question that richly clad pillar of a man? No. To do that would simply tell the fellow that Chintu had defied his threat. Then at once he would set his goondas to find him, and there might not have been time to see he was well enough hidden. Then it might not be a question of cutting off legs only.

So, nothing at all to do?

No. No, by God, there is something. If really Iris memsahib was murdered, it would account for what, almost from start itself, has been puzzling to me. How was it that she contrived to put the muzzle of that twelve-bore, short though it is, to her head and at the same time get a finger round its trigger. Yes, I had told myself it might be just possible, that in the wild state of mind of a woman seeking death, she could perhaps have succeeded in contorting her body enough to have done it. But that was not easy to see, not at all easy.

So, murder it might be. Yes. Might be.

But – a new thought – could it have been murder at the hands of the mysterious young man Chintu had seen, first lingering at Primrose Cottage's twisty little gate, then, certainly, entering its garden, and finally... But this is what Chintu truth-teller could not be totally certain about, finally going into the bungalow itself.

But if the young man had penetrated there why had he done so? And how, then, had he got hold of Dawkins sahib's gun, in its locked almirah with the key to that lock hidden underneath Dawkins sahib's socks in his bedroom? How could any intruder have known where that was?

But there is one easy way to find out. By getting hold of the young-young man, dressed unusually for such a youngster, no summer visitor to Mahableshwar, in a striped blazer. But how to find him now? Without a doubt, if he did shoot Iris memsahib, coming from Bombay as Bullybhoy told me he did, he will have gone back there, top speed, and hidden himself securely away among the city's crowded millions.

So what to do? What to do?

Ghote did eventually find an answer to the almost impossible question he had put to himself. He decided, after goodness knows how many decisions taken, untaken, retaken, dismissed as ridiculous, seen again as not wholly ridiculous. At last, however, he had fastened on to his answer. He would go back to Primrose Cottage and get that dazzlingly puggareed *khansamah* to tell him, not why he had threatened Chintu, but once again what exactly had happened that fatal morning.

Perhaps, perhaps, something may emerge from what he is saying, he told himself. There may be one new detail that is showing that all is not as I have been led to believe. Or, since *Khansamah* – must find out fellow's name – has turned out to be not the hundred per cent respectable figure he was always looking like, there may be something, some little-little thing, he has been keeping back. He may even, in answer to the right clever question I may put, say something that will tell me something I cannot now be knowing.

But what will that be? What can it be? That small-small fact to be found only inside Primrose Cottage. Or perhaps in that garden where there are no primroses.

CHAPTER SEVENTEEN

Ghote decided – it was a decision he arrived at quickly and did not alter – that he would go to Primrose Cottage in uniform, the one he had been wearing when he had marched out of the flat in face of Protima's sky-high wall of denial that Dr Pramash knew anything whatsoever about the processes of childbirth.

Now, he said to himself, when I am needing to overawe to one hundred per cent that villain of a *khansamah*, a proper police uniform it must be, for all that it has sewn on its shoulder-tabs still the stars of an Assistant Inspector. Even wearing what I am at this moment dressing myself in, I may have some troubles cowing down the fellow. Someone who can threaten a little mongoose of a boy like Chintu with having his legs cut off will not be an easy man to break. Nevertheless wearing this uniform – he made a last attempt to smarten it up – I have dealt with Dadar criminals as tough as he is, or tougher, and I was breaking them.

So it was with at least an air of complete confidence that he opened once again the twisted wooden gate of Primrose

Cottage. The right sharp jerk on its stiff latch was, he found, all that was needed. He went then striding up the path beside the cannas bed – three yellow heads had appeared in Chintu's absence – and gave the bell-pull a single vigorous tug.

As he had expected, the jangling sound of the bell inside had hardly ceased when the door was opened. The *khansamah* was there in front of him.

He gave him a long, steady look

Yes, he thought. Yes, the fellow is wearing yet another puggaree. A bright blue one. Must ask- But no side-roads now. Straight ahead without stopping.

'*Khansamah*,' he snapped out. 'I am wanting some words with you. I am preferring in strict privacy. Kindly step outside.'

There was a moment, a fraction of a moment only, when it looked as if the towering, magnificent man was going to refuse. Even to slam the door beside him shut.

But without a word, he stepped out, even if in closing the door he produced a quietly sulky thud.

Ghote took a swift look round.

'Yes,' he said, 'over there. That bench under the pipal tree.'

Taking care to walk a little behind the tall puggaree-topped figure, Ghote steered him to the spot he had chosen, well away from the bungalow itself and the minimal possibility that Dawkins sahib, seeing his precious *khansamah* being marched off, might come out to investigate.

At the bench, which must once long ago have been shaped to follow the curve of the old tree's deeply split and time-tortured trunk, he issued a peremptory 'Sit, sit' and then stationed himself where he could look down at his captive.

'Very well. Now, name?'

Two pale brown eyes stared back at him in astonishment. But not for long.

'Kuldip Mudholkar.'

That, and no more. No *Inspector sahib*. No *Inspector Ghote, sir.*

But it was enough. Positions, top dog and underdog, had been established.

'Now,' Ghote barked out. 'I am wanting to hear your full account of what you saw after you had heard that shot from Dawkins sahib's gun. Not what you were telling Inspector Barrani, but what exactly, minute by minute, you were yourself doing. So, tell.'

A silence.

How long should I let it last?

'Inspector, I was in my quarter, as I have the right to be at any time I have no services to offer Sahib. And all of a sudden I was hearing close by, close by, that gunshot.'

'Time? You are not saying what time that was.'

'Inspector,' Kuldip Mudholkar looked up, with now a glint of impudence in his eyes. 'Inspector, how am I to be knowing this time and that? A *khansamah* is not someone to have on his wrist one gold watch.'

'No gold watch whatsoever,' Ghote snapped. 'No watch of any sort. It would not be fitting.'

A stir of resentment down there on the bench as at each slight puff of breeze the shadows of the pale leaves on the great gnarled tree's dangling branches fluttered and shifted.

'But,' Ghote continued without a break, 'it is all the same important for you to be knowing what time it is. Time for Sahib's *chota hazri* first thing in morning. Time for whatever cup of tea he is taking before he leaves to read *Times of India* at the Club. Time for tiffin. Time for dinner. So I think you are knowing always what time it is, if not to nearest second, well enough.'

But now there came a distinctly rebellious look.

'And shall I,' Ghote jumped in before it could grow, 'tell you how you are knowing same? Very easy. You are hearing at each and every hour and half-hour the sound of the bell in the English church, not so far away. Yes? Yes or no?'

'Yes, Inspector, you are right. I am hearing that sound, but it is coming so often, each hour and each half-hour, I am altogether forgetting I am hearing it.'

'Very well.'

Ghote thought it best to leave the *khansamah* with some vestiges of dignity. He noted though, not without pleasure, that the imposing, puggaree-wearing, polished and primed figure whom he had been so struck by when the door of Primrose Cottage had first been opened to him looked now more like a stuffed dummy. A distant recollection entered his head of the straw-filled shape of the wicked god Ravana, as with the ten-day festival of Dussehra coming to an end, it hung from a high scaffolding about to be touched by the first tongues of devouring flames below.

'So,' he said, 'your full account of what happened after you heard the sound of Sahib's gun. Nothing left out. And, first and foremost, nothing put in.'

Half a minute, not more, for the fellow to gather his thoughts.

'Well?'

'Inspector, it was like this. I was in my quarter, and suddenly-suddenly I was hearing that gunshot. I was knowing at once it was coming from inside. A dacoit, I was thinking.

Has some dacoit come into house? At once, at once, I was going to see. Inspector, Kuldip Mudholkar is no coward.'

A pause, plainly put there for the word of praise to be given.

It took Ghote no time at all to decide to let his defeated witness have what he wanted. The fellow could hardly be encouraged enough to talk and talk.

'One brave move,' he said to him.

'*Jee*, Inspector.'

And a dawning of light in those light brown eyes. A tale to be told spreading in front of him. But, thought Ghote with a glint of grimness, let me detect one only small-small falsehood anywhere, and he will learn it is not so easy to throw dust into my face.

'Go on.'

'Inspector, I was hurrying fast as I could to drawing room, running even.'

'Oh, yes. And you were not at all thinking, is it, that if a dacoit was there with a gun, you would be better to approach with care?'

A moment to think. Which way to go? To tell this inspector-detector I am too brave to be careful? Or to go back and agree with what he has said?

Ghote could almost see the decision being debated this way and that on the man's face.

'Truth, Mudholkar,' he snapped out.

'*Jee*, Inspector. But, yes, I was at first run-running, but then I was thinking. And when I got to closed door of drawing-room I was opening same slowly-slowly.'

'And you were seeing what? Exactly what?'

'Inspector, there was no one there. But, lying by french

windows, there was Dawkins memsahib. Dead. Dead, Inspector.'

'But you were going over to her? To make one hundred per cent certain?'

'No need, Inspector. But, yes. Yes, I was going. It might be better to call a doctor, in case, in case...'

'But you did not go to telephone?'

'No, Inspector. When I was touching body I could see it was altogether too late for doctor. The blood, Inspector, it had gushed out when that shot from the gun had entered the head. And the head itself, Inspector Barrani must have told—'

'Never mind Inspector Barrani. Just only tell what you were seeing with your own eyes. That, and nothing else.'

'Very good, Inspector. I was seeing her head all in pieces. Yes, blown to pieces.'

'But you thought the sound you heard, just only moments before, was from a dacoit's gun. A bullet, yes? Not any pellets from a shotgun.'

Again a flick of a pause.

Then a wide shrug of broad shoulders under the bright red, buttons-gleaming waistcoat.

'Bullet, pellets, not much of difference when they are entering head.'

'All right. Perhaps it was so. Now, what else did you see? Did you see anyone running off?'

The question had to be asked. More than asked, to be repeated with more details.

'You were seeing running off a young man wearing some sort of coloured coat, a blazer, yes?'

But, the moment he had added the question, Ghote cursed himself for his hastiness. Never tell a witness anything without carefully deciding whether you will be given the truthful answer. Fool. Idiot.

At once the reply he now knew he was bound to get came glibly from the lips beneath Mudholkar's curled and oiled black moustache.

'Yes. Yes, Inspector, that was who I was seeing. I had altogether forgotten. I had forgotten even when Barrani sahib was asking me his many, many questions. But, now you have said, I am remembering. Yes, it was a young man and he was wearing – it must have been – one blazer.'

Defeat, Ghote registered. I can hear it in every syllable of that *I am remembering*.

Fellow is laughing in his sleeves.

No going back now, Ghote had soon realised, to the absolute control he had succeeded in establishing over Mudholkar. The straw-stuffed dummy hanging there awaiting the crackle of the flames beneath had been, in one careless moment, changed back into Dawkins sahib's lofty *khansamah*, restored-to-evil Ravana ready again to prowl the world.

He gave Mudholkar a terse 'That will be all'.

But, on his way out of the garden, struggling with the obstinate latch on the little twisty gate, knack momentarily forgotten, a thought surfaced.

What put it there, it immediately occurred to him, is the way I was describing to myself Mudholkar's restored position. *Dawkins sahib's lofty khansamah*. That description, at once translated into a picture, has shown me what really makes the man so *lofty*. It is his puggaree. More – now I am seeing same in my mind's eye – it is that the puggaree he has had on his head has been, almost each time I have seen, of a different colour, down to the bright blue one, fresh and new-looking also, I can see at this moment going away round the side of the house.

Why should a *khansamah*, any *khansamah*, have more than one puggaree to be proud of? Yes, it is the duty of a sahib, who has decided his dignity requires a *khansamah* to open his door, to equip that impressive servant with a fine turban. But it is not a sahib's duty to provide more than one puggaree. He will have provided just one red waistcoat, with plentiful brass buttons, and perhaps just two pairs of fine white trousers and one good solid pair of black leather chappals.

But that is the limit. The man will need nothing more.

Will need nothing more, unless... Unless the puggaree that the *khansamah* has first of all been given had tickled his pride to the point where he is wishing and wishing to have another. One as elaborate but in a new colour. And such a puggaree he could not obtain unless... Unless he has some sort of a hold over the sahib who would have to pay the sum necessary. It might be of course, it just might be, that a master would want to reward years of faithful service by making such a gift. But Dawkins sahib has not been in Mahableshwar all that long. It must have been several years after Independence before he had had all those deodars cut down and named the bungalow as Primrose Cottage.

So Mudholkar must have some hold over Dawkins sahib. But what hold can he have? Why has he been given those new puggarees? And, as puggaree has been added to puggaree, it would seem that hold has grown tighter and tighter. When I first saw a magnificent *khansamah* opening the door I was struck by – how could I not be? – the rich puggaree he was wearing, and I was thinking, I remember, that Dawkins sahib must have a large staff of servants. But he has not. A good number of servants I have seen but not a very large number. So there is some reason, no doubt about it, for Dawkins sahib to favour his *khansamah* far beyond what is his duty.

Now, can I make the deduction that what Mudholkar is knowing is something Dawkins sahib would not, at almost any cost, wish him to have learnt? Yes, the word *puggaree* has, after all, two meanings. One: a turban. But two: a bribe. Now, if I am right about Mudholkar knowing something that makes his sahib give him a good bribe, and I think I can be sure of that, then what can it be that Mudholkar knows?

And all this is depending on that one thing I was observing. Or on four things. Four differently coloured puggarees. So many. But Dr Gross has said it. *Absolute accuracy* in perceiving insignificant facts is one of the most necessary qualities an investigator should have. And – no, I am not deceiving myself – I did observe with absolute accuracy four different puggarees on Mudholkar's head, however insignificant they may have seemed at the time.

But what is following? Nothing but a hundred per cent mystery. What possible hold has Mudholkar got on his sahib? All the questions I was asking, even the questions know-all Bullybhoy was asking, have produced nothing that could be an explanation.

CHAPTER EIGHTEEN

Plodding back to Hotel Restful – what else was there to do? – Ghote found the riddle had not ceased to rocket back and forth in his head. *Can the discovery I have made, such a small thing, somehow be the answer to why Iris Dawkins took her husband's twelve-bore and shot herself that morning? Or are the circumstances I believe I have established not at all what I once thought? Did everything that happened that day happen in…? In, as it were, a wholly different world than the one I am seeing around me at this moment?*

He glanced across to the banyan at the edge of the road where not long ago, behind its curtain of dangling roots, he had hoped to be invisible to Bullybhoy thundering past in his truck. *Yes, that was the world, the duniya of everyday, that was, as it is now, solidly in front of me.*

But must I try to see what could have happened in a different duniya? A duniya where it seems the sahib is not on top. Where, it seems, it is the khansamah who is.

He came to a sudden standstill in the middle of the dusty road.

Shakespeare had spoken again, if in Protima's voice. He saw her now, Prince Hamlet in a sari, leaping up from the *takht* where she had been sitting cross-legged, her battered old college textbook on her knees, darting forward and sharply delivering the rebuke *Seems, madam. Nay, it is. I know not 'seems'.*

And, he thought, what if it is altogether wrong to believe that the seeming *duniya* I have just been seeing, where Iris memsahib did not at all kill herself but was someone else's victim? Did what I was thinking happened there in Primrose Cottage at all happen? What if Prince Hamlet was right and 'seems' is not the way to look at the world? That all that I have just only now thought out is no part of the *duniya* actually existing as I am making my way along this dusty road?

But how can I decide which is the one to trust? This real dusty road *duniya*? Or the *duniya* I had got in my head where the *khansamah* is master, not the white sahib? There is nothing to help me.

No, at least let me test out what I thought that Mudholkar's many puggarees were meaning. Test that against that world I am seeing all round me. Step by step.

Step One. Mudholkar's puggarees. Yes. Yes, those four I was seeing. With my own eyes. No doubt about it. But the conclusion I was drawing from them? Was that, too, in the real world? Think. Yes, how else could Mudholkar have obtained four costly puggarees to wear to his own obvious pleasure except by somehow making his sahib buy them?

Go on then.

Step Two. Mudholkar must really have some hold over Mr Robert Dawkins, that British rock. But already I was suspecting that Dawkins sahib was not such a rock. Already I had begun to believe the world he was putting in front of me was not real. That was so even when, at the first time I was seeing, he was stating he had written to Sir Rustom *in sheer desperation*. Desperation is not a hundred per cent rock-like quality. Not at all. And then there was the way he, altogether in the wrong, rushed to accuse little Chintu of stealing the watch he had carelessly left on the thunder-box in the bathroom. Other things also. Yes, by no means a rock. So, is it possible – likely even – that Mudholkar has some hold over his sahib that is letting him extract from that unrock-like rock first one new top-class puggaree, then another and another and another.

Step Three, now. And this is looking more of difficult. What has Dawkins sahib done to make him yield to Mudholkar's demands? It must be something that has happened as recently as when he obtained that second puggaree. And what in fact – in hard fact – has happened quite recently? Answer: Iris memsahib died from a gunshot. But did she shoot herself with the twelve-bore she knew was locked in her husband's gun-almirah? True, she most probably did know also that the key for the almirah was hidden in her husband's drawer of socks and so could have found it.

But here, I see now, there could be some doubt. Those socks, after the washerwomen in the real *duniya* will have beaten them half to death on rocks at the edge of the big lake where they work, would never have been put into that drawer by the Memsahib herself. That would be a servant's task. So it is by no means certain Iris memsahib did know where was that key.

If she did not, is there a totally different explanation for what happened? Am I right to think that? Worse, am I wrong? Oh, if there could be one single thing to prove to me that I am totally wrong, I would be happy, yes, even though my task goes all the way back to the beginning. Accept that.

But there is nothing to tell me whether I am wrong or right. What to do then?

Perhaps this is a time to decide that I must not decide. Decide to be fully undecided. To see what time will tell me. Yes, indecisiveness may sometimes be good.

Then on to Step Four. Who besides Dawkins sahib himself, far away at the Club reading *Times of India* when that shot was fired, did know where to find the key to the gun-almirah? In theory it could be the servant whose duty it was to put back washed socks into the drawer. Or, let me say, the servants who turn by turn, may have had that duty. Yet why should any one of them go to that drawer and take out the key to the gun-almirah? Why should they want to shoot Iris memsahib? That is ridiculous.

No, wait. Who, sitting over all the servants, would very likely knew also where that key was hidden? The *khansamah*, Kuldip Mudholkar. So could it have been him who took out that twelve-bore? It could, of course. But why, again, should Mudholkar want to shoot Iris memsahib? Can she have found out something about him that would cause her husband to dismiss him? Possible, again. But would Mudholkar shoot her in order to stop her telling Dawkins sahib? No. No, not at all. Mudholkar is the sort of sly quick-wit fellow who would produce a story that in no time at all would explain away everything.

Puzzle. No, the path I have been following, with whatsoever twists and turns there have been in it, is leading now directly into some swamp. All I know for certain is that Mudholkar did telephone the Club, and, as he told Inspector Barrani, he did so to tell his sahib he was needed because 'a nasty accident' had happened.

But that evidence I have about those somewhat curious words *a nasty accident* came per Inspector Barrani, per Bullybhoy. And there is one thing I am knowing: that Bullybhoy will give out any evidences, true or not so true, that will suit his never-bother ways best. He lives in as many different *duniyas* as his I-am-right ways are dictating.

At this moment Ghote simply turned directly round and began to head back, not to Primrose Cottage but to the Mahableshwar Club.

Yes, he said to himself, I must check whether that message was delivered in the real world or if it existed only in some fantasy world Bullybhoy has concocted for one of his tuck-away-the-truth reasons.

At the Club he paused for one moment out on the terrace before going in. Will I discover here, one way or the other, if the alternative story of 'seems' that I have constructed in my head is holding water?

Or will the story I have in my head, in the little brass *lota* I am imagining to be there, will it leak away through some tiny crack in the jug's base?

Sweaty with sudden doubts from the crown of his head to the soles of his feet, he straightened his shoulders and marched then straight inside. Ignoring three Members chatting on one of the leather sofas along the entrance lobby walls, even passing by the big gong at the far end without a thought of giving it a booming tap, he went striding on. Past the Reading Room, past the Smoking Room, past the Dining Room, until in the very back quarters behind the closed baize door he found, perched up on his high stool, the one-eyed bearer he had spoken to before. On the floor at his feet stood the telephone.

Sleeping.

Sleeping on duty. But it took less than two minutes for the single solid fact he had wished for to come into Ghote's hands.

One rough shake saw to it.

'I have something to ask,' he barked almost into the man's face, as his one good eye blinked dazedly back at him.

'It is the inspector who came.'

'Yes, it is. And now: do you remember answering phone when a call came from Primrose Cottage? And taking the message to Dawkins sahib?'

More one-eyed blinking. Then at last words.

'*Jee*, Inspector, I was taking-taking.'

'Very well, and are you remembering what was the message you took?'

'Yes, yes. I must. You are knowing often and often angry Members are coming and saying *Damn fool, you've got it all front to back*.'

'No. No, no, no. You are meaning *back to front*, yes?'

'Front to back, back to front, all the same.'

'Never mind that. Are you, I was asking, remembering the message you took to Dawkins sahib?'

'Yes, yes. I am remembering. It is my duty. *Khansamah* was saying *Tell Dawkins sahib there has been a nasty accident. Say he must come home quickly-quickly. Khansamah speaking.*'

'Those were *Khansamah*'s very words?'

'Sahib, I am always saying just only what I am hearing.'

Ghote thought for a moment, and then put a calculated question to the one-eyed man in front of him.

'Did you have any other message to take that morning?'

A slow spreading silence. For an instant Ghote was tempted to break it with a sharp word, or even with a slap.

But then, looking more closely, he saw that the one-eyed man was doing no more than laboriously thinking.

And at last his head looked upwards.

'*Jee*, Inspector. *Ek* message.'

'Very well. What was it saying?'

'Inspector, I have thought. It was later-later than message for Dawkins sahib.'

'But it came that morning? And what did it say? You can remember?'

'Inspector, I can. I have been think-thinking about same.'

'Very well. Tell me the words. And not front to back, but just as the caller said them.'

And at once they came.

'*Letter from London has arrived after all, from Mazawatee Tea Company. From London. Shall I open it? Or will you come back home? Helen.*'

Ghote needed only a few seconds to come to the conclusion that the bearer had repeated this message truly word for word. He could even understand himself what it was about. The Club member to whom it had been sent must be one of those Angrezi sahibs seeking a job in England now that Independent India had less to offer. And *Helen*? Helen must have been his anxious wife.

So the one-eyed man on the high stool can be relied on to repeat word for word the messages that came to him through the long tube hanging beside the telephone. The words

Mudholkar had said to him had been the very words he had spoken.

And they had included that curious phrase *a nasty accident*. Words that an English sahib might well have said. But not any words that Mudholkar himself would ever have uttered of his own accord. Curious.

Yes, he thought, I was thinking, when I first heard the words *a nasty accident*, that they were not somehow the words *Khansamah* would have used when telling his sahib that his wife had shot herself. They were...what? Yes, as I had thought, they had in them too much of Dr Gross's tact. It is as if they had been spoken by- By, it might be, Dawkins sahib himself. Or as if they were the words of a precisely dictated message being simply, word for careful word, repeated.

Keep it in mind, yes. But one more thing to find out.

'Now,' he said, looking straight into the bearer's one eye, 'tell me what time was it the message for Dawkins sahib was coming.'

'Time, Inspector? You must ask Dawkins sahib what time it was. I am not knowing anything of times.'

And, damn it, Ghote thought, Dawkins sahib is the one person I cannot possibly put that question to.

What to do?

He stood there in blank-struck silence. And then remembered the booming clock in the tower of the English church. Of course...

'No,' he said, 'I am not thinking you would be wearing any watch, and I am not supposing you can see from where you sit any clock on the wall. But I think you must be hearing at each hour, and half-hour also, the sound of the clock at the church not so far away. Boom-boom-boom.'

'*Jee*, Inspector. Boom-boom-boom. Always I am hearing. That is how I am knowing when someone will be bringing me glass of hot-hot tea.'

'Good, good. So once more I am asking: what time was it when that message for Dawkins sahib was coming?'

A smile broke on the one-eyed man's chapped and paan-stained red lips. A wide smile.

'Inspector, it was after the boom-boom clock had sent out nine booms.'

'After? How long after it was?'

The one-eyed bearer looked puzzled. Time meant little to him. Ten minutes or twenty, they must be almost the same in his enclosed world.

But then an answer. A useful one indeed.

'Inspector, yes. Yes, it was just before ten booms.'

Yes. Yes, the fellow has told me now what I am needing to know. That message from Mudholkar came just before ten ack emma.

'You are sure? You are certain?'

Out of that single gummy eye came a look that said clearly *How often must I repeat before you are believing?*

'*Thik hai.* Five minutes before ten o'clock, no more, not so much.'

Head buzzing in a whirl of speculation, Ghote hurried away, leaving, for all he knew, the one-eyed bearer wondering if he had been asleep and dreaming throughout the urgent conversation this inspector had been having with him. It was only when he had descended the shallow steps from the terrace and had in front of him from the Club's famed lookout that wide panorama of countryside spreading down, down, down, a great bowl of calmness, that he was able to stop and make himself think. Then piece by piece he considered what he had just learnt.

Yes, he said to himself, now I can go back to what I was trying to work out as I was leaving Primrose Cottage, not so long ago.

And, yes, at once, now I am thinking about what I have heard, I am seeing one utter contradiction. That old one-eyed bearer was telling me altogether clearly that the call to Dawkins sahib with its *nasty accident* message had come just before ten o'clock. He was in the end hundred per cent clear about the time. But, if the message was to tell Dawkins sahib, however tactfully, that his wife had just shot herself, then it should have come only a few minutes after the sound of the shot, and I am knowing from what half-pant Chintu was telling me about how he heard the shot and ran at once down to the house. Had run down, he had said, while the church clock was beating out its nine chimes.

Could Chintu have got that wrong? Had it been ten booms from the clock he had heard? But, no. No, if he had begun to run just as the first boom came, then a boy as sharp as Chintu would never have got the sum ringing in his ears wrong. I can trust him for that. I can.

So now I am knowing that, for whatever reason, when Mudholkar telephoned the Club it was one full hour after Iris memsahib's death. Why was that? Why would he have waited so long? Can I ask him? No. No, that would be stupid. A fellow as quick-witted as Mudholkar would tell me in a moment any sort of made-up story to account for the hour-long gap.

But when I was on my way just only to Hotel Restful, my head full of William Shakespeare, I had seen what it is likely to be the reason Mudholkar had so many fine puggarees. It is that he has some hold over his sahib. More, that the most likely time for that hold to have gripped was when Iris memsahib had died because there is some mystery about that. I have all along, ever since I was first coming to Primrose Cottage, felt that. Smelt that. If only from what Dawkins sahib was saying, altogether unnecessarily, that Bullybhoy had confirmed he was away at the Club at the time his wife appeared to have shot herself.

And, yes, now I can see better what is that hold Mudholkar has. Can it be that Dawkins sahib must have gone back to Primrose Cottage much earlier than when he had received that *nasty accident* message? And, if so, what might he have found when he arrived after hurrying across the deserted Golf Course? Not that there had been a fire in the kitchen and he would get no tiffin. No. Something else. Was it the sight of his wife in close conversation, or even more than that, with the young man in the striped blazer?

What if that young-young man had already entered Primrose Cottage? What if Dawkins saw the two of them, perhaps, perhaps, perhaps, sitting close together in the sewing room, even on the cot Iris had there for when, in the heat of the day, she wanted to rest.

Of course, the young man may have been no more than– Than what? Think. Yes, perhaps some salesman hoping to persuade the Memsahib to buy something costly for the house. A young man simply doing his job. He would then have gone nowhere near that cot. But, if this was so, would she even have taken him into her sewing room? I am thinking she would not. She would have had no reason to do it. None at all.

So...

A thought came suddenly into his head. It was of the sad and sordid story Pansy Watson had told him as, just inside the jungle there, she had plucked down from the tall Flame of the Forest tree a flowering branch of bougainvillea. The story of what had happened to Iris Mountford when at the age of twelve she had become close friends with the son of the young Rajah of Gopur, a boy of much her own age. How, after the death of both her parents under the thundering charge of that elephant in musth, she had been found to be pregnant by that son of the Rajah and, after the birth of a boy baby, had been hustled off to a cold and unwelcoming England. A boy baby who, if he is still alive, must be only some twelve years younger than herself.

Chintu's description of *a young-young man* slid back then into his mind. A young-young man, wearing a colourful striped blazer. Could it be...? But there is more, surely.

Yes, there is the photograph in the painted frame Dawkins sahib, on the morning I was first coming to Primrose Cottage, thrust at me, with the mixture of pride and the anger at having to tell his story to an Indian police officer. Had thrust out and in seconds only had snatched back. And there is something, something else, dim at the edge of my mind. Something on the day I was coming to Primrose Cottage where no primroses are growing that I feel is part of all this also.

But the photograph. The photograph, when at *Too Good Clicks* I was looking at that better print. I was able to see then, yes, that in Iris Dawkins' left eye there was a tiny triangle of green spoiling the deep colour. The *violet* as her husband had called it, letting a glimpse of his inner feelings show despite his rock-like exterior.

And little half-pant Chintu Satyamurthi, the truth teller, said to me he believed the young man at the gate was a *badmash* because his two eyes were not just the same? Eyes that are not the same are rare. No doubt there are thousands of individuals in the world whose two eyes differ to a noticeable extent, thousands even among India's millions. But sharp-eyed Chintu was able to see at least when that young man at the gate came closer that one of his eyes was not quite the same as the other.

Just like those of Iris Dawkins, Iris Petersham, Iris Mountford.

So... So can I say that the young man who entered the garden at Primrose Cottage on the day Iris Dawkins died was none other than the son she had, at the age of twelve or thirteen, given birth to in St Agnes Convent, Pune? No court-of-law evidence for it. Not at all. But...but a probability, a high probability that this was what did happen. Why otherwise should that individual have for days hovered outside Primrose Cottage? What more likely that this was the reason he had done so?

So now, what actually took place that morning? What could have taken place? Did Dawkins sahib discover Iris in her sewing room at the least holding an unknown young man's hands between her own? Or perhaps even patting him on his cheek. Or perhaps, perhaps, tightly embracing him. And then...

Then did Mudholkar find him there with her dead body? And did the sly fellow then propose an alibi for his sahib? One designed, not simply to conceal the murder he had committed but to provide for himself a hold over his sahib that could get him... New puggarees, yes, but over the years to come more, much more than those?

So did they then think up between them the full details of an alibi? That Dawkins should hurry back to the Club, taking care not to be seen, and there hide himself once more behind *Times of India* and await a telephone call saying he should come back *ek dum* to Primrose Cottage because – and this would be Dawkins' own contribution – because *a nasty accident* had happened?

Certainly, I have word for word evidence such a call was made, and very soon after nine o'clock. Although how my one-eyed bearer, if it should ever come to this, will stand up in the witness-box giving that evidence is another matter. But it is safe to say, surely, that Dawkins sahib came over to Primrose Cottage for some reason or other shortly before nine a.m. that day, almost in fact as soon as he had got to the Club and secured the *Times of India*.

And, yes, yes, yes, I think I can guess why no sooner had he arrived he needed to go back home again. His specs. The glasses he would need to read the paper, the glasses he must have left, as he often did, on top of the thunder-box in the Primrose Cottage bathroom.

All right, a guess. But Dawkins, whatever had brought him back to Primrose Cottage, could well have glimpsed, through the sewing room window, his wife in the arms of an unknown young man. Unknown to him, but not at all unknown to his wife. And not unknown to me. Known to me, almost to a certainty, as the sole remaining male heir of the now aged Rajah of Gopur and, more, as Iris's own son.

So was it...? Could it have been that Robert Dawkins,

overwhelmed with fury under his shakily rock-like exterior, had turned round and pelted along to the french windows, entered the house through them, had then hurried on into his study, hurled himself at the gun-almirah. Had found it, naturally, locked. Had gone then stamping and crashing into the bedroom. Had jerked open that drawer where his many, many socks were kept. Had in an instant dug the gun-almirah key out from under the pile of neatly folded matching pairs. Had raced back to the almirah, opened it, seized the twelve-bore, tugged out a cartridge from its box, pushed it into the gun's breech and then had rushed into his wife's sewing room determined to shoot down the man he saw as her lover?

Who, naturally, hearing all the noise outside the room, would, at his new-found mother's urging, have scrambled out of the window and run off as fast as he could, believing Iris would be able to explain who he was. But, before she had managed to utter a single word, had Dawkins brought up his gun and shot her in the head?

Could that have been?

If so, what then had happened? Answer: think of the telephone call to the Club, the call that had sent him hurrying back home seemingly to be told by Mudholkar that his wife had shot herself with his own twelve-bore. Why had Mudholkar made that call, as I have hard evidence that he did? Answer again: quite simply in order to provide his sahib with that alibi. The alibi swiftly put together by the two of them, Dawkins supplying those words *a nasty accident*, when coming home to look for his once-again lost spectacles, he had seen through the sewing room window as he was hurrying across the garden his wife seemingly in the arms of an unknown man, had seized his gun and killed, not the intruder he had wanted to blast to death but the wife he had thought equally guilty.

It must have been, now I think about it, Kuldip Mudholkar, the ruthless and sharp-witted, who had seen that an alibi could be produced, if his sahib had some luck in getting back to the Club with his short absence there not remarked on. As he would have been able to do at that hour of the morning when all the bearers knew he was accustomed to sit there alone in the Reading Room with the *Times of India*, not to be disturbed.

And it would have been the toweringly strong *khansamah* who... Oh God, once again *Hamlet*. But, yes, Mudholkar must, to have made that alibi doubly likely, have *lugged the guts into the neighbour room*. He must have swiftly carried that body, slight enough though seven-months pregnant, away from the scene of the crime to a more likely place for someone other than Dawkins sahib to have shot her. And there had Mudholkar contrived to smear out more blood for Inspector Barrani to see? All right, he must straight away afterwards have cleaned up, as best he could, the blood spilt, not near the drawing room french windows for all to see but in Iris Dawkins' sewing room.

Can it be that Shakespeare, the all-time great genius, somehow foresaw those events in Primrose Cottage that day, thousands of miles and centuries of time away?

CHAPTER NINETEEN

Ghote stood where he was at the foot of the steps leading down from the Club. But he was no longer seeing the wide-spreading view spanning out over the countryside in front of him. The much talked-of sight might not have been there at all. Nothing was in his head but the possible explanation that had come into his mind for everything that had happened on the day Iris Dawkins had died. But could it all be true? There was, on the one hand, Shakespeare's 'lugging of the guts into the neighbour room'. But on the other hand there was the real unlikeliness of any such lugging having taken place.

The two hammered at his mind like two bare-chested, heavily muscled smiths standing opposite each other over an anvil beating alternately at a piece of softening red-hot metal.

Which is right? Which?

I must try to decide.

Somehow I still want what I have at last thought out as being the truth of the matter to be that truth. It was all seeming so right, so much of logical. I can see myself now listening to Protima, sitting cross-legged on the *takht* in the flat reading from *Hamlet*, and jumping up, imaginary sword in hand, to plunge it through- What is that curtain thing called? Yes, the harass- No, the arras. Yes, through the – is it after all harras? – no, the arras where old Polonius had placed himself in hiding and into... Into his guts. But Shakespeare did not at all mention any blood. Perhaps he was forgetting it should have been there, leaking out from beneath that- that arras-harras?

But is that vision I was having of a murder in Primrose Cottage after all altogether wrong? Even if it was seemingly sent to me across the ages and the oceans by Shakespeare himself? Is what really happened that day just only what I was told did happen?

Told by Inspector Barrani, coming to Primrose Cottage as investigating officer. Told by none other than my old enemy from Nasik days. But Bullybhoy... Have I not found out since I have seen him at work here in Mahableshwar that he is the world's Number *Ek* champion maker-up of whatever it suits him to say? Didn't I always at very back of my mind suspect as much at Nasik? But I was not ever liking to say it when everybody, from Commandant down, had come to believe Bullybhoy was the best student who had ever been there.

Yet, as I am seeing it, there must be doubts about whatever he was giving out concerning his investigation here. And... And, yes, actually that investigation was not even conducted directly by Bullybhoy. It was conducted at second-hand out of what Bullybhoy was told by Dawkins sahib's *khansamah*. By none other than Kuldip Mudholkar.

Oh, why, why, why was I myself not that Investigating Officer coming over from Mahableshwar PS when that death occurred at Primrose Cottage? Why was I not sitting there in the seat that Bullybhoy is now occupying? Why was that fellow, yet once again, pipping me to post? If he, somehow, had not got his seat in Mahableshwar it might have been myself who would have gone over to Primrose Cottage that day. And the first thing I would have done would be to examine the body, what bloody Bullybhoy was liking to call as the *corpus delicti*.

And what would I, as Investigating Officer, have seen? Yes, I would have seen, after Mudholkar had lugged those 'guts' into the neighbour room, Iris Dawkins' body lying just inside those french windows where she might have shot herself with her husband's twelve-bore, difficult though that would have been to do. But that spot would not have been in fact where she had been shot. So would I have seen her body lying in a whole pool of blood, as Bullybhoy himself described to me?

I would not have. Not if Iris was shot in her own sewing room. The blood, and there would be plenty of it, would then have been there in that room. If there had been any by the french windows, it would be just only what Mudholkar, that ruthless individual intent on getting his sahib deeper into his debt, had managed to smear on the floor after he had carried Iris's body from the sewing room. And in the sewing room – I would, as Investigating Officer, have conducted a thorough search of whole premises – I would certainly have at least found traces of water on the floor, left where most of Iris's blood had been spilt.

But when, weeks afterwards, I saw that spot in the drawing room there were no evidences there whatsoever. So how can I now possibly decide which of those two accounts of what happened is correct? Shakespeare's, the one I would like it to be because it would mean my reconstruction has got it right?

Or the one that everybody has always been believing, even Sir
Rustom?

Mine would have accounted for the one thing that has
worried me ever since I was coming here. Why had Iris, if she
had for some unknown reason wanted to end her life, taken
the appallingly difficult step of putting the muzzle of that
twelve-bore up near her head and at the same time tugging at
its trigger?

But, think. Now I am reconstructing that unlikely scene in
my head once more, there is something else. The gun itself.

As Bullybhoy described the scene to me, it was lying at
Iris's right hand. But – and this is the evidence of my own
eyes – I know from one of the photos of Iris I was shown by
that too good photographer, Mr Chakrabarty, sole
proprietor, that one of the times he clicked her after taking
that portrait photo, she was sitting in that throne-like chair
with a very large teacup and saucer held in her left hand. Her
left hand gripping a saucer too heavy not to be held where it
was quite safe. So she must be left-handed. She must be. It
would be the natural way she would hold anything at all
weighty. And, if she was left-handed, the gun, had she really
managed to tug at its trigger, would then have fallen to her
left-hand side.

But Mudholkar said it was by her right hand, and
Bullybhoy repeated that, and Dawkins sahib had stated it
also. But could he possibly, in all the time he had lived with
Iris, have never noticed she was left-handed? Yes. Yes, that is
possible, strange as it seems. Possible, when you realise,
Dawkins sahib never dared see his wife as a real woman but
only as the person he wanted to believe was a possible mate
for himself. All of them saw her as, like themselves, right-

handed. It is only little Chintu, who sees just only what he is seeing, who told me what must be the truth.

Yes, what I have discovered, however much it is differing from what Sir Rustom wanted me to investigate, is the truth. Shakespeare was right. Chintu also was right in what he saw. Iris Dawkins was murdered.

But...but what am I saying? What am I thinking? I am thinking that, far from having been sent by Sir Rustom Engineer, ex-Commissioner, to find out, if I could, just only why Dawkins memsahib committed suicide, I have found out – if I have – that she was murdered.

And the murderer is Sir Rustom's old friend. Or at least Sir Rustom's one-time acquaintance. The man he was sending myself to help him in his seemingly deep trouble.

And I will have to go now to Sir Rustom, there in his flat at the top of Marzban Apartments on the cool height of Malabar Hill, and tell him that the man he once went on shikar with is a murderer. I will have to tell him that the Dawkins sahib I was at first seeing as one British rock was inside himself just only one mixed heap of miserable feelings. Of altogether unBritish doubts and fears about who he really was.

With leaden, leaden steps he set off back to Hotel Restful where Sir Rustom's ancient Ambassador was waiting for him. The car, he found himself thinking, that will have to take me to Bombay and, there, at the end of a dark corridor hung with framed photographs of Parsi worthies in their tall, black-lacquered hats, I must at last find myself standing in front of the tall authoritative ex-Commissioner to recount to him what he will not at all want to be told.

* * *

But as, yet more depressed and weary, Ghote came in sight of Hotel Restful he was astonished to find its sleep-heavy proprietor had deserted his reposeful reception desk. He was coming, at a waddling run, towards him.

'Ghote sahib, Ghote sahib,' the richly ghee-filled fatty even managed to call out now at the top of his wheezy voice.

Ghote came to a halt, not quite able to believe he was seeing what he was. But, as the proprietor came nearer, heaving and swaying, he acknowledged that it was in fact none other than himself who was being so urgently, if hoarsely, hailed.

'Yes? Yes?' he shouted. 'What it is you are wanting?'

The huge wobbling bulk arrived at last within a yard or two.

'Ghote—' Exhausted puff. 'Sahib.'

Unable to produce another word the corpulent exhausted long-distance runner, hands clasping bent knees, sweat shining on every inch of bared flesh, groaned and snorted.

'Proprietor sahib,' Ghote said, 'be taking your time. There is altogether too much of sun to be running out in open like that.'

'Yes.' Slow straightening of back. 'You...right, Ghote sahib.'

A few more harshly indrawn breaths.

'But you are having something to tell myself?'

'Yes, yes. Telegram.'

From the back pocket of his by no means clean bulging white trousers the hotel's proprietor pulled out a creased and folded sheet.

'Take, please.'

Ghote stepped nearer and grasped the narrow slip.

A telegram? For myself? What on earth—?

Then he thought of the only person who might have reason to send him a telegram. Protima.

With fingers suddenly as sweat-wettened as the proprietor's own he straightened out the whitish slip and read its pasted-on grey strips dotted with capital letters.

INSPECTOR GANESH GHOTE AT HOTEL RESTFUL MAHABLESHWAR. Then below the actual message. BIRTH EXPECTED IKMINENTLY.

For a long moment that final *Ikminently* sent waves of utter incomprehension through his mind. *Ikminently, ikminently.* What on earth did that...? Some medical term? What was an *ikminent* birth. What could it be?

Then he took in the signature PRAMASH MD. This is from Dr Pramash. Dr Pramash whose patient Protima has been ever since she was sure she was going to have a baby.

Protima, he all but exclaimed aloud. My own wife. The baby. Yes, this must mean she was right. The baby is coming sooner-sooner than Dr Pramash was expecting. He is saying it is coming IKMINENTLY. No, IMMINENTLY. And myself. Where am I? Yes, Krishna is not there beside his Radha among the upspringing plants and flowers of the month of Chaitra.

A new thought then, a terrible one.

If the baby is coming much, much too early, is any birth this early dangerously premature? Dangerous to the baby. Dangerous, dangerous, dangerous to my Protima.

The proprietor, breath back now, was saying something.

'Inspector, when I was reading, at once I thought you must be getting this news. But where you were? Impossible to know. I was thinking-thinking. But no answer. Then- Then I was seeing one slow walking man coming down hill into

Bazaar, and I was saying to myself *If only he is my good friend from Bombay itself, Inspector Ghote*. Then in one-two seconds I was recognising, and I am coming run-run-running.'

Through the swirling mists of his thoughts and fears Ghote managed to take all this in.

'Thank you, thank you, proprietor sahib,' he shot out. 'But now... Now I must be going fast as I can back to Bombay.'

CHAPTER TWENTY

Sweeping the Ambassador – much, much faster than was safe – round the S-bends of the road down from Mahableshwar, Ghote told himself he now had a good reason, the best but also the worst of all possible reasons, to be heading towards Bombay. He truly now had to get to Dadar PS and the little flat at the top of its barracks block. His wife might be, at this very moment, in danger there of death. Or, would it be... Can it possibly be in the delight of having, despite every hazard, happily given birth to a child alive?

Slewed across the road ahead he saw a broken-down truck. He came to a rapid halt. Waiting till the truck had been pulled back to safety from the precipice it had lurched towards, he began to think again.

Yes, as soon as I have found out whether the baby has come, whether Protima is safe, where she is even, how she is, I will have to see Sir Rustom. I will have to tell him then what I am thinking really happened at Primrose Cottage.

But...but what if after all I am wrong about what happened? All right, Dawkins sahib wrote his letter to Sir

Rustom begging for his help. And would he have dared do that if he feared anyone who in answer came to Primrose Cottage might, just might, find out the real truth? That it was he himself who had shot his own wife?

Butting and butting his head like an obstinate goat at this renewed unsettling thought, in the end he did contrive to do some damage to it.

Yes, of course. Of course, this is it. It is altogether possible that Dawkins, terrified that, despite his Inspector Darrani having assured him Iris's death had been a case of suicide, the murder he had committed would come to light, had eventually hit on the idea of writing to his acquaintance of old, almost forgotten Rustom Engineer, and telling him Iris had inexplicably killed herself. Doing so would only add a convincing postscript, he must have thought, to the alibi he had already set up.

Yes. Yes, that must be it.

He managed at last to manoeuvre the Ambassador past the hauled back obstacle – thank goodness, no scrape on the paintwork – and allowed his thoughts to move onwards.

Primrose Cottage where there are no primroses, whatever such flowers may look like. All I am knowing about them is that, according to poet Wordsworth, they grow by some river's brim. And I know that much only if what Dawkins sahib was quoting was correct. But all the same I somehow think primroses, whatever they are, tell me something, something about Dawkins sahib himself. The way he was choosing a new name for the too-Indian *The Deodars*, yes. It is showing how, despite his decision to stay on after the British were leaving, he is all the time disliking and despising us Indians. But more. More, he is ready, isn't it, to deceive even himself with those primroses that are just only something he would like to have but cannot obtain. He is living all the time in a world that is not existing.

And when did reality burst through? If I am right, it was at the moment when, glancing through the window of his wife's sewing room and seeing her – what? – embracing a young stranger.

Yes, at that moment the rock-like outer casing of the man must have fallen inwards to leave nothing but a swirling of absolute rage. Suddenly Dawkins must have seen his sweet and violet-eyed wife in the very act of betraying him. The new wife for whom he had bought that prettily feminine bureau and had had re-covered in bright flowery chintz that plump sofa. He had seen, though he had long believed he did not dare take to himself a mate, the lady he had at last brought himself to marry proved through and through a woman such as he had feared all women were. Unsafe. Ready, as soon as they had seen what the manly man they had married was truly like, to cast him away like the weakling he knew himself to be. As I, too, know him to be after all I have discovered since I saw, standing in front of me, the unexpectedly short man with his stomach stretched by that starched white shirt with the striped tie dangling down it.

But how...how can I tell Sir Rustom Engineer, ex-Commissioner, that it was Shakespeare who, across all the ages, told me what must have happened that morning at Primrose Cottage? All right, Sir Rustom managed to see the film of *Hamlet* in the one week it was showing at Eros. But that will hardly be enough to make him sympathise with a detective claiming to have solved a case with the help – it is ridiculous only – of the great long-ago Bard.

* * *

At last and at last, up, up, up the interminable flights of legs-aching concrete stairs of the Dadar PS barracks block Ghote went, thighs soon quivering uncontrollably from the effort he was having to make, groaning breaths increasingly hard at each step to haul in.

Must...must find... What-what if-if Protima dead. Baby also. Both.

For a moment he halted, unable to contemplate the vision that had come to him.

Then common sense returned. It-it may be she was just only rushed to hospital, ambulance bell clanging? But which hospital? Which would it have been?

Go on up. Up, up and up.

The door of the flat.

Key. My key. Where it is?

Sweat-sticky hands shoved into trouser pockets. Nothing.

God, did I leave them at Hotel Restful? Take them out when I was arriving... Not needed in Mahableshwar. And what? What did I—?

Body utterly exhausted, from effort, from dread, he could not stop himself falling forward against the door.

Which swung open.

Nothing to stop it. If lock is not...

But then...

'Husbandjee, it is you?'

Protima's voice. Singing out from deeper inside.

Sounding happy.

Happy. So...so she is well? But-but she cannot just have given birth when she is sounding so, what they are calling, full with beans.

And, as she came out from the bedroom, it was at once

evident that she had not given birth. Not at all. Out had come that full-sailing belly, speeding faster than ever to the harbour awaiting the precious cargo.

'But—' Ghote said.

Protima gave a wide, wide smile. A grin even.

'I was thinking, you see,' she said, 'that only a telegram would bring my husband back to where he must be, beside his wife who will soon-soon be the mother of his son.'

'Or his daughter,' Ghote answered automatically with the words he had so often spoken over the last months.

Then the implications of what she had said came, all in one block, into his mind.

'But birth is not due yet? Not for days, weeks even? It is not at all *ikminent*? Why did Dr Pramash...? No. No, he was not at all sending that telegram. I see it all now. You. It was you only sending same.'

'Of course, of course. I was just saying it. Nothing but a telegram, signed also PRAMASH MD, would bring my husband back from that terrible hill-station where, just because he was sent there by that big pot, Sir Rustom-fussdom, he was trying to find out why some Angrezi sahib's wife had committed suicide.'

Fury splattered into Ghote's mind. Never, never in all the time of their marriage had Protima, independent and brick-obstinate though she could be, done anything as contrary as this to everything he stood for. Never before had she peeped into his police life. Peeped in and, with clawing sharp-nailed fingers, sought to change it. To her own specifications.

What must I do now? he jetted out in internal rage. Must I strike her? No, no. To beat a woman who is soon-soon to be the mother of your son – or daughter, daughter – that, beyond doubt, is impossible. But to go? To leave her straight away, at this exact moment? Could I do it? I could. I could. And she is deserving it. Totally disloyal. Totally disloyal to her husband to whom she has sworn loyalty, walking three times round the fire at the marriage ceremony. Attached to myself with the scarf. Yes, attached.

But...

But can I really do it? Howeversomuch she is deserving. And...and though, yes, in a way she is deserving that punishment, she is deserving of something else also. A pregnant woman is deserving, not just of respect but of care, utmost care. Her mind is not always and always in her perfect control.

So what am I to do? Which answer to take? Into which pan of the scales must I put the weight? Oh God, I cannot make up my mind. Why is everything so hard to decide? There I was only this morning, away in Mahableshwar, trying to decide between what I thought was the truth of Iris Dawkins' seeming suicide and what everyone else was saying and stating, that she had not been shot by anybody other than herself. And I was thinking that was a hard enough decision to have to come to. But now...

Now, yes, I have a ten thousand times worse decision to make. What to do about Protima, my wife, the wife I love, Protima carrying the child we are going to have, our first, the first of the family that is about to come into existence? And, yes. Yes, that is a heavier weight for the scales. But in which pan to put it?

He saw himself then suddenly as, of all the unlikely persons who might stand for himself, a *sabjeewallah*, cross-legged on some pavement beside his heaps of carrots, potatoes, brinjals and whatever else he had on their gunny sack in front of him. Held high in his right hand the short length of brass chain leading down to the two identical pans of his scales, ready to weigh the carrots his customer had carefully counted out. Ready, too, with an adroit thumb to make his weights-pan sink just a little deeper and bring in just a few *pice* more of profit.

In my right hand...the cheating thumb. The vision wavered. Faded now into nothingness, into a semblance of reality. If, there in Primrose Cottage that day, Iris Dawkins had ever used that twelve-bore she would not, not, not have had a finger of her right hand at its trigger. She was left-handed, left-handed however little her self-concerned husband had realised it. But I saw in that photo at the *Too Good Clicks* studio that she was definitely not right-handed. So she must, she must, have been shot by someone else. And that someone surely must be none other than Robert Dawkins himself.

That I have decided. Decided and decided and decided. Now I can go to Sir Rustom—

Sir Rustom-fussdom, how dare Protima say that. How dare she set herself up to judge the man who had been the first Indian to hold the post of Commissioner of the Bombay Police, and who also was calling me as the sort of officer who could understand a white sahib like Robert Dawkins.

So shall I, now, at this moment, say not a word to her, but turn on my heels and go down, down, down the concrete stairs? Go outside to—

To what?

The thought of the bleak world he would have to enter, the world without Protima, and, almost as bad, a world where he would be no more than a distant figure to that daughter, that son, he would be father to. In just only three-four weeks more, perhaps even two-three.

No, there are some decisions that take themselves.

'Chicken,' he said.

It was the term of endearment, however far removed from the outward truth, that he had occasionally used to his wife.

He glimpsed what, at first, he thought was a small smile of triumph parting her lips. But then he saw her eyes and the sudden line running from nose to chin that had appeared on her face. And he realised that the twitch of her lips was the first tiny sign of the relief she was feeling. The hoped-for but blankly unexpected relief.

Yes, she knew she had been wrong, very wrong, to have done what she had. No doubt she was acknowledging now, if without a single word of regret, that she had in the depths of depression sent that telegram. She had, she was admitting, done something she ought never, for a single moment, to have contemplated. And now she knew she had been freed from all the consequences, whatever they might have been.

'Chicken, listen. I must not stay for more than one hour. One hour of just only sixty minutes, and no more. Because, now I am in Bombay, I must go to Sir—'

No.

No, I see in a flash now it is too soon to go to Sir Rustom with whatsoever account I may have. I was wrong to think it was the time for that. What did Dr Gross say in condemning 'the Expeditious Investigator'? I remember the exact words. *The smallest piece of forgetfulness or the most pardonable carelessness may have the gravest and worst consequences.* And have I forgotten some small thing? Or been somewhere pardonably careless? I may have been. I cannot swear that I was not. So what I must do, in place of going to Sir Rustom, after one hour here only, is to go all the way back to Mahableshwar. There I must check and recheck everything that has come into my mind about what truly was happening there. That is my duty. To be sure. To be a hundred per cent certain.

'So I am forgiven for the terrible-terrible thing I was doing?' Protima's voice came to his ears.

Easy to answer.

'It was not so very much of terrible. It was wicked, yes. Very wicked. But you were very-very worried, feeling the baby might come earlier than you thought, and so that telegram – Poor Dr Pramash made into forgery victim – was the natural thing to send. Or at least natural for someone like yourself, think and decide all in one sentence. And not even a spoken sentence.'

'Oh,' she exclaimed, eyes shining, 'my husband, who is not really a man who cannot make up his mind.'

She gave a little chuckle.

'Only one who is slow to do it.'

CHAPTER TWENTY-ONE

Yes, Ghote thought, as at dawn next day he brought the decidedly travel-battered Ambassador to a halt outside Hotel Restful once more, it is in fact one damn good thing that Protima sent me her PRAMASH MD telegram. If I had not gone to Bombay because of it, I would almost certainly have been about to decide to go tomorrow. To go, not to find out how *ikminently* Protima was going to give birth, but to tell Sir Rustom that Dawkins memsahib's death was not suicide but murder. As I was sure it was. As I am, even now, almost sure. But, no, I must be giving Sir Rustom one water-tight case. Nothing forgotten, nothing done with even pardonable carelessness.

I see that now. I see I need proof of every bit of what happened as I can possibly get. And, yes, if I am to act as an Investigator Dr Gross would approve, there is more than a little I ought to be able to find out still. So, first, what?

No, first one good sleep, if proprietor sahib over there has not given my room to someone else. If he has not, it is – daylight now or no daylight – one good long sleep for me.

Brain must be in altogether top condition.

And then...then tomorrow it will be to check, check, check, even after so much of time has passed since that gunshot rang out at Primrose Cottage. Even after the time also before Dawkins sahib, for whatever reason, wrote his letter to his old acquaintance, Sir Rustom. Who sent none other than myself to investigate. To check everything still possible to check.

Yes, first of all now to find out if any other one of the servants was hearing that shot. And perhaps to discover with double definiteness at just what time it came.

It seemed nevertheless to be somehow wrong to be going to tug once more at the bell of Primrose Cottage – two or three hours lying flat on the torture charpoy had done their work – when only the day before he had thought of himself as leaving Mahableshwar perhaps for good, with that telegram BIRTH EXPECTED IKMINENTLY burning in his pocket.

No little thing about Primrose Cottage seemed to have changed from the time he had first seen it. The latch on the twisty little garden gate needed as always the right quick jerk to get it open. The red cannas in the long bed beside the path to the door were just as tall and as red as they always were, except for one single yellow bloom at the far back of the bed. But no half-pant Chintu was there to deal with the spoiler of the pattern. Away at the edge of the garden the ancient, crack-seamed pipal tree stood where it always had been, the stirrings of breeze making its pale slivers of leaves tremble shimmeringly.

So give that tug to the bell-pull.

And, once again, there almost at once was Mudholkar in

his magnificent uniform with, yes, puggaree surely yet another colour, this one sun-brilliant yellow.

'Dawkins sahib is at home?' he asked. 'I am wishing to see for some moments only.'

'Bearer!'

And, once more, in less than a minute came the patter of naked feet and a bearer arrived.

'Take Inspector sahib to Sahib,' he said. 'Tell that it is myself who is sending him.'

As Ghote followed the slap-slap-slap of the bearer's bare feet, he noted a new fact. Mudholkar had spoken firmly as if his word was a law always to be obeyed. But, when I was first coming here, the fellow had not been so sure that Dawkins sahib would accept my arrival without being given time to decide whether or not to see me. The *khansamah*'s hold over the master is clearly gripping yet harder.

And, yes, I have now been shown in when Dawkins sahib is having his tea, the large cup in his right hand wispily steaming. A plate of biscuits at his elbow, half consumed.

'Inspector? You? Well, what can I do for you?'

Noticeably different in manner now from the tubby little British rock addressing *some damn native* I was encountering when I was standing in front of him for the first time.

Rapidly, so as not to leave time for much consideration, Ghote put his request to be allowed to go round the bungalow 'putting to bearers et cetera some extra questions I have thought of.'

'Very well, very well, I suppose so. If you think it's necessary.'

Leaving with unobtrusive quickness, Ghote then began his

round, putting to each bearer and each maid that he came across his single question. *You are remembering day when Dawkins memsahib was shot?*

And each one of them in turn echoed the answer the first bearer had given, the one who had led him to the drawing-room where his sahib was having his tea, who also had lingered just outside the door with the object, of course, of hearing as much as he could of what was being said inside.

'You are remembering the day when Dawkins memsahib was shot?'

'*Jee haan*, Inspector. Who could forget?'

'You are remembering, even, just where you were when that sound came of a gun being fired?'

'I was here itself, Inspector. At this spot only. I had not taken away breakfast dishes till then.'

All right, more or less at the right time. Dawkins sahib, hurrying, would probably have reached the Club. The *Times of India* would have been waiting for him.

It was eventually, as the church clock boomed out the half-hour after five, that for the last time he asked of a rough-handed girl from the kitchen his unvarying question. The answer he got, exactly the same as all the others, confirmed, he felt, the first piece of the extra proof he had set out to check on. The shot that had killed Iris Dawkins had been fired shortly after nine a.m.

One other thing to be done, however. To make sure there was not yet another servant to question. No piece of carelessness left for Dr Hans Gross's voice to warn him of.

Standing just outside the bungalow, reassured at last, Ghote asked himself whether this in itself was all the proof he needed so as to be able to tell Sir Rustom, without fear of any logical gap appearing, that Robert Dawkins had killed his own pregnant wife.

But, no, he decided in less than half a minute. No, to be absolutely *Gross sure* I must go on to do more. I must walk exactly the same path Dawkins sahib must have taken from the moment that, through the window of his wife's sewing room he saw her in close proximity – I will say no more than that – to a stranger dressed in a dazzling blazer. To the young man who was, in fact, her own son.

Yes, I must trace out that path inch by inch even. But how to do it? How to do it when Dawkins sahib himself is inside the bungalow?

His dilemma was instantly solved. The door behind him opened and Robert Dawkins came out.

'Ah. It's you, Inspector. Still here?'

'Yes, sir. Yes, I am just only taking a little time to think whether I have done everything I ought to have done.'

'Very good, very good. Nothing I can tell you, I suppose. Just off to the Club. Like nowadays to give myself a drink at the bar about this time.'

'Yes, sir. No, sir. No, there is nothing I would be needing from you.'

So now... Now Dawkins sahib, all unknowing of what I am thinking about him, has gone to the Mahableshwar Club in what must be his usual way since the death of his wife, so now to work. Will the movements, back and forth, that Dawkins must have made that day, from the moment he saw what he had until the moment he squeezed the trigger of his twelve-bore, take more of time than would fit the outline I have in my head?

Quickly Ghote walked, almost ran, round the outside of

the bungalow, past the french windows, their *chiks* rolled up today, and on to the small window of the sewing room. There he stood peering in, trying to imagine what Robert Dawkins' thoughts would have been had he seen inside his wife with an unknown man. Would the two of them have been, as I once thought of them, clasped in each other's arms, son and mother with only twelve years separating them? As I believe very possibly they were. It will be, yes, the first time either of them has seen the other since that moment Iris had realised the baby she had only just brought into the world was no longer there. A moment, surely, she could never have forgotten.

What had the nuns at St Agnes Convent in Pune said to her? Ghote wavered between thinking of them as evil unyielding moralists and seeing them as, perhaps, kindly souls unable to stand up against the rigid opinions of the ladies who had become aware that twelve-year-old Iris had given birth to a child.

But, more urgently, what would Iris Dawkins, Iris Petersham as she had once been called, Iris Mountford as she herself had been named when Lady Mountford had given birth to her, have felt if she had been convinced, after all the years that had gone by, that the young man who had presented himself to her was truly her own son? From what he had learnt about her from Pansy Watson he had little doubt that she would have seized the chance of putting right the iron decision that had separated them all those years ago.

Yes, it is surely altogether likely that such a mother would have clasped her new-found child, however little of a child he now is, hard to her bosom. And, if so, it is almost as likely that the sight Robert Dawkins saw through this very window will have sent whatsoever emotions he is capable of feeling racing and raging through his head.

So? So what would he have done? What would I do if I saw my Protima embracing so fiercely some unknown man? I would burst out into rage. A rage one lakh times, one crore times, more strong than the rage I felt, for one moment only, when I discovered it was Protima who had sent that BIRTH EXPECTED IKMINENTLY telegram.

So then what? No, I myself would not go and find some gun and seek to shoot the intruder with same. Or would I? Would I? Yes, I must answer. Yes, in a rage such as that I might, perhaps only just might, have seized a gun, if a gun was there, and... And killed my own wife. So I see it as possible, possible at the very least, that Robert Dawkins, the man who for most of his life had not dared to find himself a bride, would be utterly shocked at the falling-away of all that he had come to believe his pregnant wife was. He would then, surely, surely, surely have thought of the gun locked away in an almirah in the room just next to the one he was staring into.

So, yes, I must...

He took a swift glance at his watch to check the exact time. Why do I not have one posh one with a dial for seconds also?

Then four sharp paces brought him back from the sewing room window to the french doors.

Would they be open now, or at least not locked? Assume they are. So, then, five seconds more and see myself, as Robert Dawkins, standing in front of the gun-almirah. So imagine myself there. Yes. I would reach out for the knob on the almirah door and-and a check. *Damn thing locked*, I can hear Dawkins sahib say it, or perhaps just only muttering the words.

Then he would remember where the almirah's key is kept.

But, yes, now I must enter the house myself and go from the almirah to the Dawkins' bedroom, where I once searched through all those clothes Iris memsahib was possessing. There I must look in the big rosewood wardrobe I was not needing to search before, Dawkins sahib's wardrobe.

Luckily it turned out Dawkins had left the bungalow's front door just half an inch open so Ghote was able to get into the study, unseen by anyone, and stand, once more imagining himself as the British rock, in front of the the tall polished almirah.

Yet I must be careful, he said to himself. I do not at all want that damn fellow Mudholkar to see me, not at any price. However, for the moment I must be safe.

Another glance at his watch to see how much time he should add to the estimated seconds it would have taken Dawkins to go from the sewing room window in at the french windows and on to his study and the gun-cupboard.

Then I must, imagining Dawkins remembering where its key should be kept, go at a rush over to the door here. And I must do what he did. Open this door a crack. Peer out. No one in sight. Quickly across to the bedroom.

But what if, as I do this in reality, I find a servant is busy sweeping? No, no problem. I can turn him or her out with one quick *Go*. And, inside, it will be across to the tall rosewood wardrobe.

It went like a dream. In a few seconds, not forgetting another glance at his watch, he was tugging at the wardrobe's left-hand brass handle. Right, it is unlocked, if ever it is locked. Swing both dark rosewood doors wide. And, yes, it is the top drawer below the shelf where the socks are most likely to be.

A jerk to open it, and here they are.

However many pairs of socks does a white sahib think he has to have? Never mind. Dip in. And, ah ha, at once the touch of something metallic. A key, a small brass one just right for an old almirah.

Seize it. Turn round – I am Robert Dawkins in a towering, blotting-out rage – and out of the bedroom in three-four seconds only. Into the study again and over to the almirah. Key into keyhole. Would his hands have been shaking? Allow a moment for that. Turn key, tug door open by it. And, in a neat wooden holder made to fit a gun-barrel, here it is, the weapon. The twelve-bore. The very gun that killed Iris, the weapon which that know-all slacker Bullybhoy should have retained.

Take it out? Why not? Tell-tale prints on it long ago wiped away. By a servant? By the man who had used it to shoot his wife? By ever-helpful Mudholkar? No matter.

One more glance at my watch. Some quick calculation, simple addition sum, with some subtractions for when I was stopping to think. And I must be off-

No. No, no, no. Forgotten to load the weapon.

But, yes, that little drawer on the almirah's other side should be the one. It is. Open it. And, still there, a small, thick cardboard box. Take off lid. And, still in place as if Sahib was soon to set off for shikar, two neat rows of red-coloured cartridges. With a gap where one has been taken out. A single one. The cartridge – it must be – that sent its load of heavy little pellets into Iris Dawkins' head.

But who sent them hurtling towards her? She herself? No. No, I cannot now believe that. So, if I am altogether wrong, who else?

No time for thinking now. Shove cartridge into gun's breech. Have I been as quick as- As Dawkins would have been?

Yes, though I have never loaded a gun like this, I have been quick. Not many seconds to add to my sum. Total must come now to some minutes.

Achcha, fast back to the room's door, throw it wide, along the passage to-to the sewing room.

But, no. What if I am seen? Some servant may come. So, no. This must be all imagined.

Timetable abandoned now, Ghote removed the cartridge from the breech of the twelve-bore, restored it to its box, replaced the gun in its wooden grip in the almirah.

A virtual twelve-bore held, strictly in imagination, in both hands, he went at a loping run along the passage and up to the sewing room door. There he paused for a second, trying to work out what Robert Dawkins, armed like himself – except that in reality I am not – would have had to do to open the door in front of him.

Answer, surely, just let the gun hang down from his right hand holding the butt, even with a finger through the trigger guard ready to fire the shot his high-fuelled anger would still be the focus of his every action.

All right, imitate that.

Imaginary gun swung downwards from his imaginary gripping right hand. With his left he grasped the sturdy round knob of the door. He could, almost, summon up the impetuous fury that must have driven Robert Dawkins.

The knob did not turn.

He gripped it harder, just wondering if it was somehow jammed in too tightly. Or is it that my hand has become sweaty?

Turn it. No more success.

What-what the hell must I do? If the knob equally resisted Dawkins, what would he have done?

What he would have to do is to put the gun down so as to get a good right-handed grip on the obstinate knob. Ah, yes, like this.

He stooped, laid the imagined twelve-bore carefully on the bare polished wood of the passage floor. Yes, Dawkins would have wanted to make not the least noise to disturb the guilty pair. But, wait. He would have already, surely, made more than a little noise, if he had come rushing at full speed along the passage, the heavy heels of the brogues he wears clumping out.

Never mind, I am here now. In my imagination with the gun, the very weapon that was used to kill Iris Dawkins.

So, turn that stiff, stiff knob with my full force, fling the door wide and go crashing into the empty room on the far side.

And the knob, held firmly in his right hand, already hastily wiped on his trouser leg, did turn. But the door stayed shut.

He pushed at it and pushed, thinking he had not needed to do all that arithmetic if it had been rendered unnecessary by this unexpected obstacle. But what was keeping the door closed? There was no keyhole beside the knob, so there must be a bolt of some sort on the far side, though it was difficult to see why Iris Dawkins should ever need to keep the door shut, unless sometimes she took her *aram* on the cot there.

So why can I not get in now? There must be, must be, someone in there, someone to have closed the bolt when they shut the door behind them. But who? And why?

He raised his fist to deliver a sharp blow on the smooth

surface defying him. Then stopped himself. Can it be Dawkins
sahib himself inside there? Did he, instead of trotting off to
have his drink at the bar of the Club, change his mind, come
back and locked himself for some reason into his wife's sewing
room? Yes, the room where – if Shakespeare's vision of the
guts being lugged holds true – he had actually fired the shot
that had killed her. Could he... Could he, say, overcome with
remorse in some way have gone in here? To wish it all had
never happened? He would have had time to get round to
here, I think, without my having seen him when I was busy
with the almirah.

So what to do?

For what seemed like long minutes he stood there, the
imagined twelve-bore on the floor at his feet, and tried to
come to a decision. Knock on the door and call out *Who's
there?* Or even bang on it with the butt of this imaginary gun
in the way I would do leading a raid on some... Say, on some
matka gambling den, ready to seize evidence of the Cotton
Market price numbers they are making use of always? But my
gun is truly imaginary. So, in a hundred per cent polite way,
must I just only call out *Dawkins sahib, you are inside?*

But what if he answers, *Yes, yes, damn you, what do you
want with me?* What if Shakespeare was altogether wrong
and no murder took place in this room on the far side of the
door? What if there had never been a young intruder clasping
in his arms Iris Dawkins? Then I would be falsely accusing an
innocent man of murder, And-and not just an innocent man
but an innocent white sahib. And white sahibs still, after the
time that has passed since they were rulers in India, are people
of influence, people who must not be offended by a simple
police officer. My career in ruins. Ruins. And at the very

moment when I am putting one foot on lowest rung of the Crime Branch ladder, the ladder I have hoped and hoped I would one day climb up high.

But I am not able to stand here beside this locked door for minute after minute, if I have been that long. Whoever is inside may come out. Or even if, as I am almost believing, Iris's son on that fateful day hearing all the noise outside was able to scramble through the window and run, run, run for his life, then whoever is inside may do same now. And there is the chance also that some servant may appear at the far end of the passage and be asking what it is I am doing. Or, even if he or she is asking no more than can they help me, it will still be difficult, very difficult, to say what I am doing here, even if there is no real gun lying at my feet.

Why, oh why, is it so hard so often to decide what to do?

But, for once, a dilemma was solved without the need to wrestle the way to an answer. Yet it came in a way he found not at all to his liking.

From inside, suddenly he heard the click of a bolt being snapped back. The door was in a moment opened wide.

And Kuldip Mudholkar stood there in the full authority of his magnificent *khansamah*'s uniform from glitteringly polished black chappals to sun-yellow puggaree.

'It is Inspector Ghote,' he said, with surely a hint of mockery.

CHAPTER TWENTY-TWO

This is the man, Ghote thought, I am seeing as some kind of accomplice in the murder of Iris Dawkins. And, more, he is a man – I have the evidence of truth-telling Chintu, Chintu Satyamurthi, for this – who has goondas ready for a small-small price to hack off a boy's legs, or... Or ready, if paid enough, to kill an off-duty, unarmed police officer who is finding out more than he was expected to?

He began even to stoop down in order to snatch up the non-existent twelve-bore with the non-existent cartridge in its breech.

Then in the same breath he realised what he must do. Take the initiative.

'What were you doing in there, Mudholkar?' he barked out. 'What were you doing that was so secret you must be bolting the door?'

Mudholkar's tall frame seemed in one moment to shrink to something like a normal height, although Ghote registered that there had been no actual movement beyond a slight droop of his head, all but almost invisible save for the nodding of the sun-yellow puggaree.

'Well? I was asking what you were doing inside there, door bolted.'

'Nothing, Inspector. Nothing.'

It was feeble as could be.

'Nothing, is it? Then tell, please, what exactly was that nothing?'

Mudholkar's eyes shifted from side to side.

'Inspector,' he said, almost wheedlingly, 'I was suddenly remembering that no servant had been in the room since...'

'Since when? Since, I am thinking, Iris memsahib was shot in there?'

'But, yes, Inspector, after that had happ—'

He came to an abrupt stop. Looked now from side to side with an altogether different urgency as if seeking from somewhere, from nowhere, from the air around some possible reason why he had let himself agree that the sewing room itself was the scene of Iris's murder.

'But why now were you inside?' Ghote went on, seeing a broad path opening in front of him knowing as he did now, that Iris Dawkins had indeed been shot by her enraged husband in the room outside which Mudholkar was standing now, magnificent uniform looking somehow all at once as bedraggled as if he had been caught in one of Mahableshwar's monsoon downpours.

No answer.

'Are you forgetting I am a police officer authorised to question?' Ghote said. 'I have put one question to you. I require one answer. Why were you in that room there with the door bolted also?'

'Inspector...'

He came to a baffled halt.

'Answer.'

'Inspector, I— Yes, I was looking. Looking for something.'

'Something, is it? Just only something? What? A rupee coin you had dropped? Or perhaps a one-*paisa* only? Do better than that, Mudholkar, while you still have the chance.'

'Inspector, I was thinking when that young man who was in there, hearing some noises, was getting out of window and running off he was leaving behind part of a letter. A letter I have seen.'

'Ah, running off. He was running off, is it, on the day Iris memsahib was shot dead?'

'Inspector, when I was- When I was in here before...'

He jerked his head back towards the sewing room behind him. And failed to go on.

'Yes? When you were in there washing blood from floor after you had told your sahib he should go back again to the Club while you took Iris memsahib's body to where Inspector Barrani would see when he was coming, what then?'

It was plain that Mudholkar had given up now any attempt to hide the truth about what had happened that distant day. He stood there simply accepting what was said to him.

'Then? Then, Inspector,' he answered at last, 'then it was when I was just seeing on the floor one scrap paper.'

'And...? What were you doing with same?'

'Inspector, I was going to put it in my pail of water with the blood also to throw it out. But I was dropping, and hurry-hurrying I could not wait to find. Then I was altogether forgetting. Till just only now, Inspector.'

'So you had come back in here when you were suddenly remembering that scrap of paper. Because you thought, if this police-wallah from Bombay might find that paper scrap, and learn from same what whole letter was saying.'

'*Jee haan*, Sahib.'

'Yes, so tell me now what did it say? Do not try to make me believe you were not reading same.'

'Inspector, I was not able to read. That fellow who was in here must have snatched just as he went out of window, leaving only top itself torn off. But top itself I was seeing when I was washing floor. It was letter from Rajah of Gopur, Inspector. One line I saw in own handwriting, telling something to Mrs Iris Dawkins.'

'Dawkins memsahib? I am not understanding why the Rajah would write to her.'

'No, no, Inspector. It was not written to her. It was written for her.'

'What do you mean? *To* and *for*? I am not at all understanding.'

'Inspector, I am telling you whole truth. Inspector, please remember. Kuldip Mudholkar is telling you full facts.'

'Now?' Ghote said, with a bite of contempt. 'Now you are telling whole truth. At last. But go on, man. I will at least remember you came to the truth in the end.'

'Inspector, that one scrap paper had on it address *Gopur Palace* and Rajah's name also. And... And it was beginning something like *Dear Mrs Dawkins, This is to say that my grandson, Ram, last of all the Gopur line, is—* And then, Inspector, the sheet was torn. That son, Ram, was snatching same before he was run-running off.'

'But you are sure of this? Sure that the words – in English, was it? – you were seeing were exactly as you told?'

'*Jee haan*, Inspector. And I am able to tell you why.'

'Tell then.'

'Inspector, Rajah of Gopur has now sent his Dewan to Mahableshwar. He is staying at Regal Hotel itself, and he is asking and asking questions about—'

Ghote knew then, without any more telling, what had caused the Rajah to send his appointed prime minister to Mahableshwar.

'About his grandson,' he finished Mudholkar's sentence for him. 'And how are you knowing this?'

'Inspector Barrani.'

The two words were all the explanation Ghote needed.

He guessed what must have happened. Bullybhoy, who made it his business to know everything that happened in Mahableshwar, had found the young watcher at Primrose Cottage. He had questioned him and learnt he was the lost grandson of the wealthy Rajah of Gopur.

Of course, he thought then, when Bullybhoy told me the mysterious young man had gone back to Bombay and lost himself among the five million people struggling for existence there that was simply not true. He was being kept safely somewhere in Mahableshwar. And now, for some reason, the Rajah of Gopur, an old man by now, must have wanted to be reunited with this last of his line—

Wait, no. Watson sahib was telling me there in his dak bungalow that the Rajah's *brat had died* – he was saying – *and good riddance*. But who must be still alive and heir also to the *gaddi*? None other than the child of the boy who, long ago at the age of twelve, seduced the daughter of Sir Ronald Mountford, then the Resident in Gopur State. And, of course, the Rajah must want now to find this last grandson of his, however much of British blood was in his veins, so that the line of rulers of Gopur can go on down the years.

Yes, he added to himself in a swift aside, my guess was right. The young man at the gate was the child Iris had years ago. But, no, it was not a guess. It is one reasonable deduction to make after I was hearing from half-pant Chintu he thought the intruder must be a *badmash* because his eyes were of slightly different colours. Then later I was having glimpse of truth when I was seeing that clear photo at *Too Good Clicks* studio. It was showing Iris memsahib's left eye had in it that small green triangle spoiling its deep-blue colour. A glimpse I had, but not until now did I realise all that it was meaning.

But Mudholkar hearing from Inspector Barrani, from Bullybhoy himself, about the Dewan being at the posh-posh Regal Hotel, is something I would have preferred not to have happened. It means I will have to go and talk with Bullybhoy once more. Bullybhoy who told me, laughing in his sleeve, that the boy in the blazer had gone back to Bombay to be lost among its many millions. I hoped I had seen the last of Bullybhoy, but now...

But has that young man, the elderly Rajah's only remaining heir, been here in Mahableshwar, in hiding, ever since Iris Dawkins was shot within a minute or two of him escaping from her sewing room? It is altogether likely. But now the Rajah's Dewan has visited the *chauki* asking for help in finding the missing heir, and Bullybhoy, in his seat there, must be all eagerness to provide the wealthy Rajah with that help.

Has he already taken the Dewan to where his men, trained to tell him everything happening in Mahableshwar, had kept him informed that they had hidden the young man? Hidden, perhaps like old Polonius behind some harass. No. No, not harass. Arras.

The train of reasoning, long though it seemed, had taken Ghote barely half a minute to work his way through.

'And Inspector Barrani,' he asked Mudholkar now, 'has he been able to tell the Dewan where that young man is hidden?'

'Inspector, I am thinking he has not.'

Oh yes, Bullybhoy will want to make the Dewan go on searching so that the reward when at last the missing heir is produced will be all the greater. Altogether Bullybhoy style.

Ghote stood in silence for some moments, trying to make up his mind as to what his best course now must be.

Achcha, I have had that confession from Mudholkar that he was fully aware how Dawkins sahib in rage did in fact murder his wife. Mudholkar himself went to great trouble to conceal what had actually happened. By lugging guts into neighbour room. So, yes, I could arrest the fellow, here and now.

But, no, I am not at all sure that I am in fact able to do that. What am I at this moment? Am I still Assistant Inspector Ghote, Dadar PS? If I am, I do not have any powers out here in Mahableshwar. Or am I a full member of Bombay Crime Branch, with Inspector rank? But, even if I am, I am not at all sure I can effect an arrest so far away from Bombay as Mahableshwar. What to do?

All he could come up with was to go to Bullybhoy and say *Inspector Barrani, I am bringing you evidence that Dawkins sahib's khansamah, Kuldip Mudholkar, has admitted to me that Dawkins memsahib was shot by her own husband, and that he himself rearranged scene of the crime so that it had the appearance of having taken place elsewhere. It is your duty to go now to Primrose Cottage, put to Mudholkar the facts I am able to give you and, when he has confirmed, arrest him?*

But...but Bullybhoy has explained with full reasons that Dawkins sahib could not have fired that fatal shot. So what will he do when I am saying to him he did? I do not know exactly. But of one thing I am sure. He will not want to do as I ask.

Oh God, I wish I could make up my—

No. No, I have.

'Very good, Mudholkar,' he said, looking the tall *khansamah* full in the face, 'I am going now to telephone Inspector Barrani. I will ask him to come here and question you about what you were telling me. I then fully expect him to arrest you on a charge of-of abetment under Indian Penal Code Section 108, being *a person who abets the commission of an act which would be an offence, if committed by a person capable by law of committing an offence with the same intention as that of the abettor.*'

CHAPTER TWENTY-THREE

Bullybhoy did not like it. Not at all. But when Ghote, crouching low over the telephone in the Primrose Cottage drawing room, put it to him inflexibly that he had no alternative he capitulated.

'Oh, if you are insisting, then, of course, I will come, for whatever reason you are having.'

Faced with Ghote's firm decision to go, were he not obeyed, to put in front of the former Commissioner of Bombay Police, still a man of influence in every state in the nation, the facts he knew about how disgracefully Iris Dawkins' death had been investigated there was nothing else for Bullybhoy to do.

So barely ten minutes later there had come the familiar roar of his blue truck and the man himself stepped out of it, pushed open the little rustic gate of the garden. No trouble to him to flip up the obstinate latch. Leaving the gate wide, he marched up to the door and rang furiously at the bell, sending its clatter jangling through the whole bungalow.

Ghote nodded to Mudholkar to perform his *khansamah*

duties, thinking it would be the last time, tall-turbaned, that he performed them. And then, abruptly, wondering whether in fact it would be.

Yes, I have made Bullybhoy come here. And, yes, I have held over him a threat he has had to respect. But...but he is not just only Inspector Barrani, known still to Dawkins sahib no doubt as Inspector Darrani. He was once also top student of our year at Nasik PTS, where without any sort of difficulties, it seemed, he ran the place almost as much as did the Commandant.

A man not to be underestimated.

'Inspector Barrani,' he said. 'You have made very-very good time.'

'When I see a thing needs to be done,' Bullybhoy replied, 'I am not sitting on my bottom and thinking about it, like some people I could name. I am jumping up and doing it.'

'Good,' Ghote answered, as if the rule of instant unthinking action was one he altogether shared. 'Then shall we get down to matters straight away?'

He led Bullybhoy, not into the drawing room where, just days ago, he had followed a bearer, under *khansamah*-barked orders, to stand facing Dawkins sahib, immovable British rock, plump on his plump flowers-covered sofa. Instead he took him into the sewing room, where long weeks ago Dawkins sahib, overwhelmed with rage at seeing in a stranger's arms the woman he had chosen to be his wife after all his wifeless years, had come stumbling in, twelve-bore at the ready. And had then shot her.

'Mudholkar,' he said in a voice defying disobedience, 'go and stand in that corner there, facing us at this table.'

With one swift tug he pulled Iris Dawkins' deep-drawers

work-table out into the middle of the room and swung a chair to it for Bullybhoy to sit on.

'I'll get you some paper, Barrani *bhai*,' he said then. 'You will need to make good notes.'

'Never made a note in my life,' Bullybhoy snapped out, his confidence creeping back like an incoming irresistible tide. 'Only get-nowhere, paper-bound officers make notes.'

'Nevertheless, Inspector, since this is a matter involving something yet more serious than the Section 108 offence Mudholkar here will shortly be facing. I think you had better make notes, and in full.'

He took a handful of the never-used rose-pink writing paper from Iris Dawkins' pretty little feminine bureau and put it in front of his fellow inspector.

'You are having a pen or some pencil?'

'I'm not a damn coolie, am I?'

Bullybhoy tugged from the top pocket of his uniform a blue ballpoint.

For a moment, as much to give himself encouragement as anything, Ghote indulged in a hope that its ink would be on the point of running out. But he said nothing.

He looked across now at Mudholkar, almost surprised to find him still resplendent under his elaborate puggaree, however despondent the face behind the long curled black moustache.

'I am going now to tell Inspector Barrani here what answers you were giving to the questions I asked you just outside this door,' he said. 'If you are thinking I have added a single word to those answers, or that I have got anything whatsoever wrong, do not hesitate to say so. But I must warn you, also, any tricks in what you say will bring you more trouble than you are liking.'

Then point by point he began going through the curious interview that had taken place just the other side of the sewing room door where he had stood, Dawkins sahib's imagined twelve-bore on the floor beside him. One by one he repeated the answers he had screwed out of the tall *khansamah* as, with wriggling reluctance, he had produced his account of what had happened on the day Iris Dawkins died.

'I was following up,' he said to Bullybhoy, by way of introduction, 'some thoughts I had been having about what might have happened that day when – I think you may not have known this, Inspector – when Dawkins sahib over at the Mahableshwar Club, about to read in his usual manner *Times of India*, found he had left behind here his specs.'

A quick glance across from where he was standing at Bullybhoy's shoulder over to Mudholkar, back braced hard into his corner. Good, no attempt to challenge any of that.

And Bullybhoy? All he could manage by way of asserting himself was abruptly to look up and snarl, 'How can you all sit in this fusty little room with not one breath of fresh air?'

What an appalling fellow, Ghote thought.

But nevertheless he went across and opened wide the room's one window.

'Better?' he asked, controlling as best he could the sarcastic touch he had put into the question.

Bullybhoy made no answer.

Ghote went back to what he had been saying.

'The second one of those calls had brought Dawkins sahib to a point outside the window I was just opening, and what he was seeing there made him, I believe, go rushing for the gun he kept in the almirah in his study. Finding it locked, he had then gone to where the key was kept, somewhat of hidden,

under the many socks he had in one of the drawers of his
wardrobe.'

He looked down now at Bullybhoy. He was sitting still,
fiddling with the uncapped blue biro, waiting to write down
Mudholkar's actual answers to the questions he had been
asked earlier.

All right.

'So I in my turn was following out the path Dawkins sahib
must have taken. From outside the sewing room window into
the drawing room via the french windows—'

Again he paused. It had been Bullybhoy who had
needlessly instructed him what french windows were. Point
out now he had not needed to be told? No. Keep to business
in hand.

'In through those windows, on into Dawkins sahib's study
and over to the almirah there, finding it locked, as Dawkins
sahib had done, I was going to the bedroom, like himself, and
locating the key still under his many pairs of socks. Returning
to the almirah, I opened it and took from it what I was
finding, surprised that a murder weapon had not been kept as
evidence but had just only been returned to its accustomed
place.'

And, yes, the capped blue ballpoint now suddenly ground
down on the pile of rose-pink writing paper.

Good.

'Then...then I was going, hurrying with some amount of
noise, along to sewing room. But there I was finding its door
tight shut. In fact, bolted. But I was able finally to make the
person who had locked himself in there come out. It was this
man here, Kuldip Mudholkar.'

He glanced now from Bullybhoy, who was holding himself

still as a carved statue, to the *khansamah*, looking – no other word – daggers.

'So now, Barrani *bhai*,' he said, 'if you will take cap off your ballpoint, it will be time for those notes you said you would make.'

Ballpoint's cap tugged off, with unnecessary violence.

'First question I was asking. What else could I ask? *What were you doing inside there, with door bolted also?* Perhaps not my exact words. But gist I am giving. And the reply was *Nothing.* A little more of hard-nose needed, and I was learning he was in there for purposes of – he was trying to make me believe – clearing up because no servant had entered in all the time since the murder. But here it was that you were making your mistake, isn't it, Mudholkar?'

Silence in the corner. Furious silence.

'Yes, because you were replying then, and now I am using exact words, well recalling same. You were replying, after you had said you were suddenly remembering that there was something left in the room there *after that had happ—* Yes, Mudholkar, before you had finished saying the word *happened,* it had come into your mind that no one was supposed to know that anything whatsoever had happened in there. Certainly not that Iris memsahib had been shot. It was then that I knew it all.'

Bullybhoy who, he had seen, had been carefully writing down Mudholkar's answers, stopped now and turned his face up towards him.

But it is hard to make out whether the look he is giving me is one of admiration – Bullybhoy admitting, if only to himself, that I have been quicker than he was? – or one of pure speculation. But he may well have been speculating about how he could present what Mudholkar said, what Dawkins sahib did, in some altogether different light.

In any case, go on. There is more that came out.

'Next,' he said, 'I was asking, not once but more than once, why you, Mudholkar, were now in that room at all? And at last you were answering. You were, you said, *looking for something*. And, no, we agreed it was not just only one rupee coin you had lost, not even one *paisa*. It was a piece from a letter. You have made your note, Inspector?'

Bullybhoy looked up.

'A letter. What letter, for God's sake? Who cares about some letter?'

'Oh,' Ghote replied, 'wait till you have made some more notes about it. Listen to one more answer I was getting. This: *Inspector, that one scrap paper had on it address Gopur Palace and Rajah's name also.*'

'I am not needing to make any note of that,' Bullybhoy said. 'I am well knowing Rajah's Dewan is here in Mahableshwar, and what he is doing also.'

'Yes, that I had thought,' Ghote said. 'But are you seeing what is meaning that the Dewan is searching for the last remaining heir of the Rajah?'

'The last?'

Now he had surprised Bullybhoy.

'Yes,' he said, 'the Dewan searching for that young man is meaning that the person you have been knowing about for so long, Barrani *bhai*, knowing about and not at all telling myself, is the son who was born to the twelve-year-old girl who was becoming, long after, the wife of Dawkins sahib.'

Bullybhoy had let his ballpoint drop on the dark surface of Iris Dawkins' sturdy work-table.

Ghote looked at him. A new thought had entered his head. Cautiously he produced it, on tenterhooks to see if Bullybhoy would snap up the half-concealed bait it had occurred to him to offer.

'And this young man,' he said, 'being the son of Iris, and not at all her lover, is something that may, if Dawkins sahib in court is having one clever pleader, produce a verdict that is coming, not under Section 302 but under Section 304. Just only *culpable homicide not amounting to murder*.'

'Then...' Bullybhoy said.

Yes. Yes, slowly he is working out what that might mean, not just for Dawkins but for himself as well.

He urged him onwards.

'Then, you will be seeing, Barrani *bhai*, that no one will be too much worrying if the investigation was not carried out to high standard. About that I will be consulting Sir Rustom Engineer, when in some hours only, I will be seeing him in Bombay. Perhaps all I will need to be mentioning about yourself is that it has been you who arrested this fellow here.'

'Yes,' Bullybhoy said.

It was a word that seemed to Ghote sweet as the sweetest alphonso mango.

But it would have to be, he reflected, an alphonso carefully tucked away to be savoured to the utmost at some convenient time. Now I must make sure Bullybhoy does what I have said he would have to do. Arrest Mudholkar on that charge of abetment under Section 108.

For a moment or two he left him to digest the bitter pill he had just been made to swallow. Then he said, 'I am thinking you can take him away now, Inspector. Of course, fully under arrest.'

'Kindly do not try to be teaching an officer senior to yourself what is his business,' Bullybhoy snapped back, recovering his usual manner quickly as a deflated balloon puffed back to full-size.

He looked up at Ghote as if expecting some sort of an apology. Ghote looked back down at him.

A moment's silent battle.

Then Bullybhoy stood up, faced Mudholkar in all his now battered glory and bounced out the words of the charge.

'Inspector,' he then said to Ghote, 'have the kindness to come with me to my vehicle. I am not one of those officers who is always having a pair of handcuffs dangling from his belt, and I am not wanting this fellow to make one break for it. Even at PTS I was always saying: it is not enough to arrest a *badmash*, you have to put him altogether behind the bars.'

'Yes, I am remembering,' Ghote replied, thinking *alphonso mango, alphonso mango*. 'Excellent advice.'

So they went in a small procession out of the sewing room, down back along the passage where, not all that long before, Ghote had crept holding in his two hands a purely imaginary twelve-bore shotgun. Out into the hall.

Ghote himself nipped forward and opened the front door of the cottage without the aid of any servant. Bullybhoy's truck was standing directly in front of the garden gate. A few quick paces along the red-coloured path and then Ghote opened the twisty gate's stiff latch with one flick of the fingers of his right hand. He thrust the gate wide.

A couple of minutes later he stood there at the side of the road watching Bullybhoy drive away, sending up behind him a tremendous cloud of dust. Mudholkar was now safely fastened to a pair of handcuffs hanging from one of the bars installed on the truck's sides. A sullen, if colourfully dressed, mass.

Eventually Ghote turned and slowly made his way back into the bungalow, as much to give himself time to think about everything that had happened than with any particular purpose.

He gave a glance at his watch. All but six o'clock.

What a lot, what a hell of a lot, has happened this afternoon.

As if to set a seal on his thought, the clock in the church boomed out its six reverberating strokes.

Inside, he just stood where he was a foot or two from the closed door looking back on it all. He moved off at last, and realised in a moment that his aimless feet had brought him into Dawkins sahib's study, standing looking sightlessly at the well-polished doors of the gun-almirah.

There it is, the gun, he thought, just only behind these doors. The doors that, not so long ago, I was actually finding the key for – in, yes, that socks drawer – and unlocking as I was tracing out what I deduced must be Dawkins' steps if he had, in truth, shot his wife. As I now know that he did, even if I was in the end not actually taking out the twelve-bore and going with it, held between my two hands, towards the sewing room. But it was there, behind the bolted door, that I found Mudholkar and learnt exactly what had happened on the day Iris Dawkins died.

But Dawkins, where is he? Over at the Club still, I suppose. Having that blotting-out drink he is needing more and more often before he sets off for home, his bath, his 'dressing for dinner' and the dinner itself, all unknowing that his crime has now been found out. Should I... Should I, in fact, hurry over there and arrest him before he learns Mudholkar is in custody and that the whole story of how his wife was murdered has come out?

But no. No, once more I have no power here to effect any arrest. It must once again be Bullybhoy's task, though I will damn well see he is carrying out same.

But telephone the chauki at once. Mudholkar will be safely behind the bars now and Bullybhoy can go to the Club and do what has to be done.

So will Dawkins sahib be coming here before much longer, under arrest, alcohol-filled head perhaps resounding once more of the solemn words of a *Times of India* editorial read this morning, or checking if the weather-wallahs got right its *Partly cloudy skies forecast*?

Then, while his thoughts still lingered over that picture, there came – a violent unexpected shock – the sharp bark of a gun. Loud almost as if it was beside him in the hall itself.

CHAPTER TWENTY-FOUR

For an instant Ghote stood, frozen in shock. Then, in as short a time, he realised where the sound of the gunshot had come from. From Iris Dawkins' sewing room, the scene of her death.

In less than quarter of a minute he was there, confronting once again the blankly shut door. But now it was not bolted against him. A twist at the knob, a thrust. And, as somehow he had known it would be from the moment the sound of that shot had come to his ears, there lay the body of Robert Dawkins, the man who had, in this very place, killed the wife he had believed was being unfaithful to him.

Yes, of course, Dawkins came back from the Club earlier than I thought he would. Had he, once more, left his spectacles on top of the bathroom thunder-box? Had come back and seen Mudholkar at the garden gate being led off and handcuffed to the bar in Bullybhoy's truck. In an instant he must have realised that his own crime was known to-to the intrusive police inspector from Bombay. And then – he would have had time – he had got the same gun with which he had killed his wife and had shot himself in the place she had died. Had done, at last, what a white sahib was expected to do, *the decent thing*.

The scene was, it came to him almost at once, an appalling parody of the one Kuldip Mudholkar had cunningly altered on the day he, too, had heard from inside the house the altogether unexpected sound of a gun being fired. The body lay flat on its back, as if, like the *guts* Mudholkar had *lugged into the neighbour room,* it had been knocked over by the weight of the concentrated cloud of heavy shot propelled into it from just a few inches away. Only this time the muzzle of the twelve-bore had, in truth, been held just under the head while a finger had groped below for the trigger.

Dawkins' face was a pulpy distorted bloody mass, horribly like his wife's must have been when he had shot her at close range. Those too-pale blue eyes which had put into his mind the notion of a man who, for all his bluster and bullying, was soft as ice-cream, still just visible among the pulp.

Rising smoothly up in the softly gleaming steel-walled lift on its way to Marzban Apartments Flats 20 and 21, Inspector Ghote, the silent and attentive liftman at his side, felt the muscles of his stomach tightening and tightening.

What if I am unable to convince Sir Rustom that what I have discovered in Mahableshwar is the truth? It is so much different from what I was asked to find out, just only what had made Mrs Iris Dawkins take her own life. But now I am having to say that she did not at all take her life. I am having to tell that it was her husband, Sir Rustom's former friend, who had shot her with the gun which everybody believed she had taken from its locked cupboard, put to her head and somehow tugged at its trigger.

What if Sir Rustom barks at me *Impossible*, tells me that his friend, Robert Dawkins, must have killed himself because he could not endure thinking that his beloved wife had done the same thing? What if he says he is knowing Robert Dawkins and that he is a man who would not hurt a woman for any reason whatso—

The lift came to a halt, quietly as a bird alighting on a tree branch.

'This is floor for Flat 20, Sahib. Flat 21 also.'

'Yes, yes. Yes, I will get out.'

He saw the lift doors part in front of him. He took a hasty step forward. Another. Then another.

Behind him the liftman impassively touched the doors button and they closed as smoothly and swiftly as they had opened.

Ghote stood there on the landing, stranded.

Then he pulled himself more upright, squared his bony shoulders.

No, he instructed himself. No, Robert Dawkins was never one good friend of the days-of-old Inspector Engineer. Robert Dawkins had gone for shikar, to hunt the fat chital deer in the jungle not far from Nasik, with the Parsi police officer he had happened to meet because he had seen him as a man who, when Independence came, was bound to rise fast in the Police Service, someone a Briton 'staying on' as he intended to do might one day find useful. And Inspector Engineer had, of course, risen and risen until he had become the first Indian to hold the post of Commissioner of the Bombay Police.

No, Sir Rustom would know that Robert Dawkins, for all the sharply commanding manner he had borrowed from the best of his fellow British sahibs, was, inside, nothing like them. He would have been not a little surprised, when all these years later, to get that letter from Robert Dawkins imploring his help in unravelling the mystery of what could have made his new wife, pregnant with his first child...

Oh God, Protima. Should I have gone to find her before I was at all coming here to sky-high, towering Marzban Apartments? Protima is just as advanced in her pregnancy as Iris Dawkins was. No, more advanced, more. Oh, yes, that telegram I was getting BIRTH EXPECTED IKMINENTLY, was just only a rather wicked thing Protima was doing because she was so much needing to see me. But she may truly now be quite near, perhaps only two-three weeks away, from the moment she will bring into world my son-

No, my daughter. Or my daughter or my son.

But I am a police officer on duty... Under the orders of ex-Commissioner Sir Rustom Engineer. It is to him I must be reporting. *Ek dum.*

And it is a murder that I must report to him. Yes, a murder. I know that is so. I have found it out. I have found it out following the advices of the great Dr Hans Gross, foremost writer on subject of *Criminal Investigation*, that first-class book I was so lucky one day to be spotting among a pavement vendor's mixed-up and muddled stock. What was next to it even? I can see it in mind's eye now. *Tiger Tim's Annual 1952.*

The bright-red cover of that New Year's book from so long ago shining in front of him, Ghote took two long strides to where, beside the heavy teak door with the number 20 brightly shining in polished brass on it, there was the bell with its fat button.

He gulped.

And put a firm finger on that button. From inside came a discreet buzz. And, almost as if that sound itself had operated some mechanical device, the door swung open.

And it was Sir Rustom's servant, just as implanted in his memory as was *Tiger Tim's Annual 1952*, who was standing there.

'To see Sir Rustom. Inspector Ghote.'

And, not for the first time, he hugged that title to himself.

Yes, I am Inspector Ghote, and I have been chosen to join Crime Branch, the topmost unit in the whole of the Bombay Police charged with major investigations, charged with investigating crimes that are affecting the most influential of all Bombay's millions of citizens.

'You were coming once before,' the servant said. 'I will see if Sir Rustom is available. Kindly step inside.'

For a moment, as he entered, Ghote experienced a gale-strong wish that Sir Rustom would not after all be *available*.

Then…then I could go, fast as I can, over to Dadar. To the police station, to the barracks block, to climb and climb to its very top. And there I could find out just how long it might be before… Before the birth.

The servant, a green-checked towel across his left shoulder today, walked unhurriedly away along the corridor Ghote so vividly remembered, its Parsi dignitaries of old, each in his tall black-lacquered traditional hat, looking down at him with time-dulled unseeing eyes. Unseeing, but not unjudging. And the gale of wishing in his head suddenly hushed.

No, I have something to tell Sir Rustom. I must hope then he is actually available. I have to report to him that a murder has been committed. I have to tell him that I have found out who committed that murder. Robert Dawkins, his long-ago British friend.

Standing there, he looked round the small entrance hall, which he remembered not at all from his earlier visit. There were, he saw, two small chairs against one of the walls, delicate affairs in gold-painted wood with neat green plush seats.

Should I sit on one of them, he asked himself. When Sir Rustom's servant is returning will he expect to find me doing so, in the way a proper visitor to the flat here at the top of high-rising Marzban Apartments would do? Or – an even less pleasant thought – will he express, with some cold glare, his master's unseeing disapproval of me? Am I not at all the sort of visitor, a lowly inspector of police, who should happily sit there?

He looked from one chair to the other. And he stayed standing.

His dilemma was, a moment later, solved for him. The servant, feet noiseless on the carpeted corridor, had reappeared.

'Sir Rustom will see you now itself,' he said.

Sir Rustom was looking almost as he had done when, at ten a.m. precisely, just two days after Ghote had learnt he was soon to join high-as-the-sky Crime Branch, he had last admitted him to his presence. Grey-suited, large spectacles on his long nose, hands, age-marked and long-fingered, gripping the arm-rests of his tall ornately carved chair.

'Ah, Ghote. Come in, come in. Take a chair – pull up that one there, you'll find it comfortable – and tell me what you've discovered about that unfortunate business in Mahableshwar.'

Ghote hesitated over taking up the offer of that comfortable, equally finely carved chair. When he is hearing what I must tell him will he want instead to have me standing at attention in front of him? As if I was appearing on a charge of insubordination itself?

But, no. No, Sir Rustom has asked me to sit on this chair, he will expect me to do so.

He pulled the chair an inch or two forward, seated himself, crossed his legs, hastily uncrossed them.

Sir Rustom gave him another encouraging smile.

'Now, tell me all about it,' he said.

'Sir... Sir, what it is I have to tell is not- Sir, it may not be what you are wanting to hear.'

'Very well. I've spent a lifetime hearing things I didn't want to. So, one more, if it's as you say, will do me no harm.'

'Yes, sir. I mean *No, sir*. Sir, I will tell you.'

One gulp, concealed as much as possible.

'Sir, I have to inform that Mrs Iris Dawkins was not at all committing suicide. Sir, in the end there was no question of ascertaining whatsoever reason for that she might have had. Sir, Mrs Dawkins was murdered.'

Sir Rustom sat a tiny bit more upright.

'Well, Inspector,' he said. 'You will have to go some way in justifying that. Who was it who murdered the lady? You know?'

'Sir, I do. Sir, it was Mr Robert Dawkins himself.'

Now Sir Rustom sat in silence.

Thought after thought went racing through Ghote's head.

Now I have said it. Now will he get up from his chair, look down at me and say that word that I was thinking he would? *Impossible*. But it is not at all impossible. It was happening. I found it out: Robert Dawkins, white sahib, blind with rage, seized his twelve-bore gun and shot the wife who, he believed, had totally betrayed the iron-rigid trust he had placed in her. Had shot her in the face, to blot her out for ever. But can I say this to Dawkins' friend from the past, Sir Rustom Engineer himself?

Then, in a flash of decision, the answer came to him.

Can I tell him? I can. I must. I must say, not just that Dawkins sahib shot his wife, but I must tell him what was in his mind when he did that. What I have realised must have been in his mind. It is the truth.

'Sir Rustom,' he burst out. 'Sir Rustom, please be thinking. You must be knowing what truly like was Robert Dawkins. That, howsoever much he was behaving like a white sahib, he was not such a man. He was, sir, a man who would tell lies to make himself seem something of bigger. Sir, remember his lies about how many chital he was bagging as against how few you were. And, sir, at his Primrose Cottage bungalow, before I had even seen himself, I was seeing his *khansamah*. Sir, a man to be found at the residence of a rajah, a maharajah even, so fine was the uniform Mr Dawkins had given him. Sir, Dawkins sahib was not a man born to rule, whether in India or in UK itself. Sir, I was thinking of him, when I came first face to face with, as one British rock. But, sir, soon I was beginning to see he was not at all such. Sir, in course of investigations at Mahableshwar, I visited a dak bungalow near Pune where I was meeting a certain Mr and Mrs Watson – Sir, he is a Forest Department officer – and, sir, his wife, a very-very nice lady, was telling me how it was at their dak bungalow, or another one in same area, Mr Robert Dawkins was seeing for first time Miss Iris Petersham, as she was then, and was at once falling in love with. Sir, with what he was seeing as her violet eyes—'

'Steady on, Inspector. I'm afraid you're beginning to lose me. What's this about violet eyes?'

Ghote saw he had been given a chance that he needed.

Violet eyes were one of the things that sent into my mind one beam of light all through the world of Robert Dawkins, British rock with one soft interior. Because Iris Petersham's eyes were not pure violet. They were, as I saw in the photograph shown me by that shifty Bengali, Mr Chakrabarty, just only a dark blue, though not without beauty. But they were spoilt also by that tiny triangle of green in the left one, the very same mark she had passed down to the son she, at the age of twelve, had given birth to.

He took a deep breath and managed to repeat the gist of those thoughts to, now stern-faced, Sir Rustom.

'Very good, Inspector. I see you are gifted with deeper insights into the people that come before you than many of your fellow officers. But go on.'

Ghote, who in his urgency had brought himself to the very edge of his chair, moved, with something of a jerk, back to safety.

'Sir Rustom,' he said, contriving to relax a little, 'at the dak bungalow near Pune I was learning from Mrs Pansy Watson what had been the life of Iris Petersham. Sir, something Robert Dawkins was never knowing. Iris Petersham was, in fact, the only daughter of Sir Ronald and Lady Mountford – Sir, he was Resident in Gopur State but was killed with his wife also by an elephant in musth – but I was learning from Mrs Pansy Watson as well something altogether miserable. Sir, Iris, shortly after her parents' deaths, was, at age twelve or thirteen, giving birth to a son. A son, sir, by the Rajah of Gopur's own son, just only a schoolboy, aged twelve also. She was, as soon as her child – a boy – had been born, sent away to UK, sir. And she had only just returned to India when Dawkins sahib met her, and… And married her *ek dum*.'

He paused, actually out of breath.

'I begin to see how you came to this decision of yours, Ghote,' Sir Rustom said. 'Dawkins, a man filled to the brim with ideas about the woman he married which were, if you like, so many castles in the sky. He could have wanted to kill her, if…'

He sat for a moment or two, thoughts plainly jostling through his head.

'But do you know…?' he said at last. 'Did you find out what must have unloosed that rage in Dawkins? And did you, or did some officer in Mahableshwar with proper powers, arrest him?'

'No, sir. It was not necessary to arrest Robert Dawkins. Sir he was administering to himself the death penalty. Sir, with the same gun that he had shot his wife. In the same place that her death took place, he was putting that gun to his head and pressing trigger.'

'Yes, poor fellow. Poor fellow, not up to anything he had undertaken. And he knew, did he, that what he had done had been brought to light?'

'Yes. Yes, sir. He was seeing – nobody was knowing he was there – his accomplice, the *khansamah*, being taken away in handcuffs. I am supposing this was what made him take up that twelve-bore of his. Yes, sir.'

'Good, good. A fine piece of investigation, Inspector. Very good work.'

Ghote felt a rosily warm glow spread all through him.

At once to be checked. It is not true that I should have full credit for finding out how Iris memsahib died. There was someone else also.

'Well, sir,' he said, 'I must admit I did also have some most useful assistance.'

'From some more junior officer at the Mahableshwar station?'

Ghote, seeing for an instant Bullybhoy sitting at his desk, almost grinned.

'No, sir, not any police officer. It was, as a matter of fact, the very sharp-eyed little *mali*'s boy at Primrose Cottage itself. One Chintu by name. He had noticed, one day, that a young stranger he had seen at the garden gate was shivering despite the sun being shining. But the young man was shivering, sir, with excitement. Because-because he was just about to meet the mother he had never before met.'

'The disinherited grandson of the Rajah of Gopur, the sole remaining male of the Gopur line,' Sir Rustom pounced.

'Yes, sir, yes. You have seen it.'

'Good. And that sharp young fellow has been suitably rewarded, I hope.'

'He can be, sir. With your assistance.'

'He shall have it. He shall have it. My duty at the very least. And, wait. Wait, yes. Yes, I believe I may have the very thing for him. A *mali*'s boy, you said? Does he take any interest in the work?'

'Oh, yes, sir. He is altogether most diligent. And he knows about things. It was he who was telling me that canna seeds are so hard they must be broken before they are planted. Something I did not at all know.'

'And neither did I. Neither did I. So an intelligent young fellow.'

'Yes, sir, yes.'

'And, you know, as it so happens a cousin of mine, very distant but a cousin nevertheless, is, I was told the other day, setting up a strawberry-jam factory just outside Mahableshwar. Bit of a jump from the garden at Primrose Cottage to those strawberry fields, of course. But it seems to me that to have a bright lad like your Chintu there at my cousin's elbow – he's not altogether bright himself – might be rather a good idea.'

'It would be a most wonderful thing, sir,' Ghote murmured.

And then he came to a total halt.

In a moment afterwards he found himself blabbering out something impossibly irrelevant. Like a suddenly arriving on-rushing rain-heavy monsoon cloud, into his mind there had come, a new, and somehow overpowering thought.

'Sir,' he burst out, 'there are no primroses in the Primrose Cottage garden, as Dawkins sahib was naming the bungalow formerly known as The Deodars. Dawkins sahib was telling—'

'No primroses at Primrose Cottage, by Jove,' Sir Rustom interrupted. 'A good point. Yes, a very good point. Part of the protective curtain, you might say, which Dawkins was always holding up to the world.'

'Yes, sir, one harras,' Ghote put in before he could stop, though at once cursing himself for once again letting the sight of Protima lunging forward with her imaginary rapier get in the way of finishing his account.

'Arras actually,' Sir Rustom smilingly corrected him. 'Yes,

I think Dawkins' mental curtain could be called his arras, though as it happens, I have the word *arras* pretty well to the fore in my mind just now. I believe I told you, in fact, when you were last here that I had just been to the excessively drawn-out film of *Hamlet*, longer even than the play. Did you, too, see it by any chance?'

For less than an instant Ghote hesitated.

'No, sir, no,' he said then. 'We were wanting to go, my wife, who is a graduate in English Literature, is very much liking. But I had to—'

'Your wife,' Sir Rustom suddenly shot out. 'But... Inspector, excuse me one minute. There is a very urgent telephone call I must make, in my study next door.'

He pushed himself up from his carved chair and began, with not very vigorous old-man's strides, to make for the door behind Ghote.

As he reached it, grasping the doorknob, he turned back.

'But first,' he said, 'my dear fellow, I must say I now completely agree with you. Dawkins, as you have described him, could certainly have murdered his poor, innocent wife. Not a doubt about it.'

'Yes, sir,' Ghote said. '*Foul deeds will rise, though all...though all* something does-does something to prevent same.'

But the ex-Commissioner had vanished from his sight.

Although in fact, Ghote thought, when Protima is using those *Hamlet* words it is most often to point out to me some 'foul deed' she is thinking I have committed. That boiling dekchi she had left me to watch when suddenly morning sickness... The one that somehow got burnt.

* * *

Sir Rustom's urgent phone call did not last long. He came back to Ghote in less than five minutes. On his face, inexplicably, there was an absolutely beaming smile.

'My dear fellow,' he said, 'I have some good news for you. Very good. You see, it was only after you had left for Mahableshwar, on my instructions, and indeed in my wretched old Ambassador itself, that I recalled something you had mentioned. That your wife was with child. And I wondered then whether, after all, I shouldn't have relieved you of the, as I thought, minor task I had given you. But too late, of course. So... So, my dear fellow, I then took the liberty of making some inquiries, and... Well, of arranging, when I had found out how soon your wife's confinement was likely to take place that, if necessary, it should be at the Parsi Lying-in Hospital, where I happen to sit on the board.'

Ghote felt as if he had suddenly been translocated like a long-matured yogi, into another part of the world. Protima, and Sir Rustom knowing about her state. The Parsi Lying-in Hospital. But why had that Parsi place taken in Bengali Protima? And...*some good news*... Can it be? Is it? Do I believe...? Am I...? Am I a father?

'Sir Rustom,' he burst out. 'Sir Rustom, what good news it is?'

'Oh, forgive me. Should have told you right away. Right away. Inspector Ghote, you are the father of a fine healthy boy, born at the Lying-in Hospital no more than half an hour ago.'

In a bright cocoon of haloing light, Ghote in an instant saw himself, somewhere in the unknown regions of the Parsi Lying-in Hospital, plucking from Protima's arms a baby, glowing with health. A baby boy. His son. *My son, my son, my first-born*. Plucking him up, giving him at once a father's welcome-to-the-world kiss. Restoring him to Protima's held-open arms. Kneeling then at the bedside and greeting her, the new mother, his wife, his wife, with another kiss, long and loving.

'But-but—' All he could find to say to still-smiling Sir Rustom was, 'But Protima was not due to give birth *ikminently.*'